DEATH DELIVERS

Doug Wells left his wife inside and went to investigate the strange Ford pickup. He took about two steps into the driveway when he saw something out of the corner of his eye. Crouched down by the side of the house was the figure of a man. "Who's there?" he blurted.

"Wayne from Conlin's Furniture," the man announced himself. "I saw something out here. If you have a flashlight, you better get it."

Doug didn't stop to think how strange it was that Wayne, the furniture delivery man, was standing in his front yard at midnight. He was just entering his living room when he felt a blow to the back of his head. Wayne Nance stepped over Doug's body, removing the knotted clothesline from his pocket as he made his way to the bedroom where Doug's wife, Kris, lay sleeping . . .

TO KILL
AND
KILL AGAIN

TO KILL
AND
KILL AGAIN

John Coston

AN ONYX BOOK

ONYX
Published by the Penguin Group
Penguin Books USA Inc., 375 Hudson Street,
New York, New York 10014, U.S.A.
Penguin Books Ltd, 27 Wrights Lane,
London W8 5TZ, England
Penguin Books Australia Ltd, Ringwood,
Victoria, Australia
Penguin Books Canada Ltd, 10 Alcorn Avenue,
Toronto, Ontario, Canada M4V 3B2
Penguin Books (N.Z.) Ltd, 182–190 Wairau Road,
Auckland 10, New Zealand

Penguin Books Ltd, Registered Offices:
Harmondsworth, Middlesex, England

First published by Onyx, an imprint of New American Library, a division
of Penguin Books USA Inc.

First Printing, August, 1992
10 9 8 7 6 5 4 3 2 1

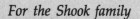

For the Shook family

Acknowledgments

I first crossed paths with a serial killer twenty years ago.

I was sitting idle at my desk in the city room of the *Watertown* (N.Y.) *Daily Times* one sunny afternoon in May 1972 when a small group of children suddenly appeared in front of me. They had a story to tell. It was about a man named Arthur Shawcross. Shawcross, they said in unison, had taken Jack Blake, a playmate of theirs. They had witnessed it. In fact, the ten-year-old boy was missing. But local authorities did not leap at this new lead. Instead, all summer long they steadfastly refused to believe the children's version of events. It wasn't until September, when Shawcross was arrested for the murder of a second child, an eight-year-old girl whose strangled and raped body was found under a downtown bridge, that the children were finally heard.

Karen Ann Hill would be twenty-eight years old today if local authorities had been willing to believe the children's story. Shawcross, who at the time was an Attica parolee, was convicted of manslaughter in the girl's death. He went back to prison, where he served fifteen years of a twenty-five-year sentence before he was paroled in 1987—to kill again. In the first week of 1990, as a pilot of a New York state police helicopter hovered over a park west of Rochester, searching for a missing woman, a presumed victim of that city's serial murderer, he spotted a car below. Arthur Shawcross was behind the wheel. Almost immediately, the parolee was linked to more than ten murders. Years before, he had confessed to killing Jack Blake. Now, again he would confess. A deputy police chief would admit that it was only by chance that the pilot even noticed the car. "The hand of God was also at the controls," he said.

We cannot always rely on an earnest child to step forward, or wait for divine intervention to show the way, to inform us that a murderous sociopath is in our midst. Our eyes and ears are capable of seeing and hearing, but as the story of Wayne Nance shows, the mind isn't always ready to believe.

This book is not about Arthur Shawcross, but it was my experience with this specimen of that most elusive breed, the serial murderer, that drove me to write this story. I am grateful to many people who shared their close encounters, who despite what they saw and heard were unable to interpret the hidden, diabolical meaning. Principal among these witnesses are: Douglas and Kristen Wells, Sheila Claxton, Julie Slocum, Joni DelComte, Cindy Bertsch, Joyce Halverson, Vern Willen, Dory Modey and Ruth Ann Rancourt. I especially also thank Ronald MacDonald, William K. Van Canagan, Greg and Mary Lakes, Robert and Georgia Shook, Rick and Laura Davis, Harry Northey, Martin Spring, Darlene Smith, Don Harbaugh, Marge Frame, Hal Woods and the Ruana Knife Works, Inc., and Kim Briggeman and Michael Moore, both of the *Missoulian*. I also express gratitude to the friendly people of Missoula, Montana, who helped me with this project.

I am deeply indebted to Missoula County Undersheriff Larry Weatherman, County Attorney William L. "Dusty" Deschamps, Sheriff's Deputy Stanley Fullerton and to Dale Dye of Hamilton. I owe a debt of gratitude to Professor Robert W. Balch at the University of Montana, and to Robert R. Hazelwood, a supervisory special agent at the FBI's Behavioral Science Unit.

I am grateful to my agent, Jane Dystel, who channeled my inspiration. I especially thank my editor, Michaela Hamilton, for showing me the way. I also thank Stephen Michaud, a friend and fellow journalist, for his invaluable expertise.

And above all, I thank my wife, Bridget, the careful reader who has supported me one hundred percent.

Author's Note

The names of three victims in this book have been changed to preserve their anonymity. They appear in the story as Howard Brein, Denise Tate and Janet Wicker. All other names are factual.

"People begin to see that something more goes to the composition of a fine murder than two blockheads to kill and be killed, a knife, a purse and a dark lane."

—Thomas DeQuincey
On Murder, Considered One of the Fine Arts, a lecture (1827)

Prologue

All kinds of people like to live in nice places like Missoula, Montana. The streets are clean. The air is exhilarating. The people are friendly. And there's plenty of hometown pride to go around. The same kids who go to grammar school together graduate from high school together. The University of Montana, right in town, is the next step for many who stay on in Missoula, staking out a career and raising family in this palm-sized metropolis with all the feel of small-town America.

The verdant, high ridges of the surrounding Rocky Mountain ranges—interconnecting as the Ruby, the Garnet, the Sapphire, the Mission, the Bitterroot—rise as if they had been fashioned on purpose as massive, protective shoulders, embracing the valley below in a crucible where man can build his shelter in peace.

This far northwestern corner of Montana that lies west of the Continental Divide, where the milder climate finds its inspiration in a Pacific orientation, has always been an oasis for man. Some ten thousand years ago, Asian peoples migrated here via the Alaskan peninsula, discovering a bounty of bison and mammoth. Nearly two centuries ago, when Meriwether Lewis and William Clark searched for the Northwest Passage, an imagined water route to the Pacific, they became the pathfinders instead for successive waves of fur trappers and mountain men, who were followed in turn by miners and timberjacks and cattlemen. Lewis and Clark had traveled on foot, by horseback, and by boat for more than two thousand miles in Montana alone, charting what would become America's fourth-largest state. To the east stretched the prairie, a vast, sometimes baking-hot place that, despite its rugged appearance, was also an elusively subtle rainbow of greens and browns under an endless blue sky. To the west, the northern Rockies, the lion's share of which lie within Montana's borders, arched as the backbone, articulating some of the most beautiful intermountain valleys to be found in the United States.

Now, as they have been for millennia, the mountains are still heavily forested, covered with tawny grass and speckled with huckleberry and scrub. In the fall, the cottonwood trees in the valley still turn red and then orange with the first frost. The evergreen needles of the larch, higher on the hill next to the Douglas fir, still turn yellow and then fall to the ground, appearing dead through the winter but prepared to sprout again in the spring, always repeating the cycle.

But for more than a decade, beginning in the dead of winter in 1974 and ending in the early fall of 1986, the business-as-usual serenity of this ideal Western habitat was shattered. For the span of those twelve years, the community's wide green valley was transformed into a landscape of fear and loathing: Someone—or some *thing*—was preying on their open, trusting natures, culling the young and the beautiful, the pride of the community. The first victim was a child, a girl of five who was brutally raped, stabbed, and murdered.

Then, only a matter of weeks later, in the late afternoon of a Maundy Thursday, the lawmen would be called to the scene of a second murder so diabolical that words could not be found to categorize it. It was the sadistic sexual torture murder of a minister's wife, the work of a true homicidal deviate. As word of this second murder spread, fed by rumor and exaggeration that further embellished the facts, Missoulians young and old were soon locked in a new, alien state of paranoia.

While the sheriff's department didn't explicitly link the two killings, the talk of the town did. The townspeople were already swept up in rumors about devil worship in neighboring Idaho, where only months before, in November, a young newlywed couple from Rathdrum, in northeast Idaho, mysteriously disappeared. Word had spread that the couple had been abducted and sacrificed by a satanic cult, that Rathdrum was the center of a devil-worshipping cult. In the minds of Missoulians then and now, Rathdrum, though two hundred miles away, is considered to be just over the hill. And it was no big stretch of the open-minded imaginations of many Missoulians to believe the tales that linked satanism with news reports of cattle mutilations reported in the Plains states to the east, beginning in the fall of 1973, and in eastern Montana in 1974. The animals were found with their lips, udders, and genitals removed, cut off with what was alleged to have been "surgical precision."

An unusual spate of recent unsolved murders and disappearances under investigation elsewhere in Montana, some of which had the imaginable mark of a mad satanist, also stirred the public soup.

So it was not surprising that the word in Missoula was that the little girl, and now the minister's wife, were the latest victims of a killing cult, or that this latest ghastly murder had become the talk of the luncheonette counters, the subject around the dinner table, and the reason why women were no longer going out of the house alone at night. It hung in the airless corridors of the county courthouse like a gas with invisible but suffocating power over the sheriff's department. Even by the wildest standard of murder in Montana, this one didn't register. There was no way to rank it among the legendary barroom brawls or domestic savageries that ended in someone's death. It was, in a word, preposterous.

But it was to be only the beginning, one young deputy would learn in due course, as his entire law-enforcement career would become notched again and again with the indelible signature of one killer. Larry Weatherman, who was a rookie when the killing started, would collect the corpses, found dumped by the roadside or half-buried in the woods just east of town, left there by Missoula's own serial killer, a native son, who killed and killed again with immunity. He was a local boy who attended local schools. He was a remarkable worker and a talented artist. He was incredibly sweet to the women who knew him, more attentive to their emotional needs than even their boyfriends. He was always there with a gift or flowers or just a card. He never forgot birthdays. He was someone who could be counted on if a favor was needed, who would go out of his way to help anyone. All one had to do was ask. He was the veritable boy next door—and in the case of the minister's wife, he *was* the boy next door, a friend of the family.

With each new grisly discovery, Larry Weatherman, who would become captain of detectives, would also become the principal caretaker of yet another unsolved murder. First there were two. Then four. Then six. Seven. And it wasn't over yet.

Neither Weatherman nor anyone else could see that the boy next door, who had in fact been a prime murder suspect when all the killing began, harbored a split personality that plotted one sadistic, torturing murder after another while also managing to impress almost everyone with doting favor upon favor. Neither Weatherman nor anyone else would see that the unseen menace, who held an entire community in suspense, was someone with a name and a face they knew well. Captain Weatherman was not geared to detect the sometimes-changing M.O. or the escalating scale of risk associated with each successive crime, both of which served as the killer's grant of immunity. The victims were not prepared for the dialectic of a haunted mind that would prey so easily on their trust. Everyone who knew the killer was blind to the deep, dark pageantry of his emotional side, where ordinary human feelings had been supplanted by something else—a hidden reservoir of treacherous, fickle, and violent fantasy.

Whether the girl named Chryssie Crystal Creek saw it coming will never be known. What is known is that sometime in the early part of 1984, someone had taken his fresh kill up into the mountains east of town. He would have navigated the steep, rough logging road in a four-wheel drive pickup, then carried the naked corpse the rest of the way up a slope that overlooks a rocky gulch. The creek bed below would have been drying up to nothing more than a furrow of polished stone. Once at the top, at the almost imperceptible headwater of tiny Crystal Creek, he would be rid of her. There he would dump the body, shot twice in the head—once in the back and again in the temple—for animals to pick over.

In time, the waters would return. The skeleton would be buffeted on the rocks, smashed into pieces to be carried along with the drainage of Crystal Creek, downhill to the Clark Fork River, westward past the small outlying towns of Bonner and Milltown, on through Missoula, where it would flow westward still.

By the time she was found, more than a year later, all that Captain Weatherman would be able to determine from the fragmentary bone evidence was that he had another young, white female murder victim, which he would name, as he had the others before, with a practical nod to the local geography. He would call her Chryssie Crystal Creek. The date was September 9, 1985. He was beginning to get a sinking feeling.

PART I

Chapter 1

A Girl Named Robin

The big truck's chassis heaved under its own weight, coming to rest. The driver jettisoned the remaining air in the brakes, punctuating the silence of the parking lot with the chisel-like sound of escaping air. In the next automatic move, he swiveled to face the girl who sat across from him, pointing to the door handle, signaling for her to get out.

At first she hesitated. Then he raised his voice, motioning again toward the door.

There was no point in delay. The girl collected herself and began angling her way out. She didn't bother to say good-bye, or even to thank him for the ride. She just slid off the seat, out the door, and down the long step to the pavement, listening to the monster engine rev, watching as the rig inched back onto the highway, shifting sequentially into higher gears, crawling away into the night.

It was late summer in the Rockies. She tugged at the collar of her beaten raincoat, shielding her throat against the cold, studying her next move in the same moment that she was dismissing the significance of having lost her ride. It was over some stupid argument. But there was always another ride, another cup of coffee, another cheeseburger with fries. Down the road. Wherever that would be.

After the truck was gone, she saw that she had been dumped on a football-field sized asphalt parking lot. It was a truck stop, and the sign high overhead told her it was Taber's. Through a milky, vaporous light, she could make out the inside of the restaurant. It was deserted. A car sped past, followed by a loud pickup truck. Then, in an interval of silence, her attention focused across the highway, where an inviting hubbub beckoned.

To her left, the spotlighted sign of the Reno Inn promised fine food and drink, although it didn't appear to be any kind of sure bet. Without enough money even for a beer, she scanned further. Directly across from Taber's she could see the dark outline of a more promising target. The sign outside said it was the Cabin, and it was obvious from the comings and goings of its customers that it was a cowboy bar with a much grainier edge than Reno's. It would do just fine. And she wasted no time in crossing the road.

Her name was Robin.

It was late August of 1984. The place was the strip in East Missoula, a truck town just east of Missoula, Montana, and a place where trouble is always waiting to happen. As she neared the entrance to the Cabin, her eyes targeted the bouncer at the door. He wore a big smile and she couldn't help noticing his handsome physique, evident under a tight, Star Wars T-shirt worn with the sleeves cut off.

His name was Wayne. He recognized right away that this girl was from out of town. She told him that she had just been kicked off a truck after she had gotten into an argument with the trucker. She didn't have any money. That was not surprising, either, given the slept-in appearance of her trench coat. He also could see that she had beautiful, pearly white, perfect teeth. She said her name was Robin. About five-foot-four, she had auburn hair, which she had recently dyed and—maybe partly because she was heavy set, probably weighing close to 140 pounds—very large breasts, which he couldn't help but notice.

Wayne poured on the charm and in no time had escorted Robin inside, bought her a beer, and was getting to know more about this new arrival. When the obvious question arose—where would she be staying?—Wayne offered the solution. He invited her back to his house, which was no more than three blocks away.

Wayne was not the only person who noticed Robin on this night. Julie Slocum, a barmaid who had harbored a crush on Wayne for four years, was at first curious about the ragamuffin that Wayne towed into the Cabin. When it became clear Wayne planned to take Robin home after work, Julie was more than curious. She was outraged. Her jealousy flared as she studied the short, dark-haired, heavy-set stranger. To her, it was not surprising that this new girl found Wayne attractive. He was the super guy who would go outside after work and scrape the ice from everybody's windshield and brush the snow off their cars, who would show up at her doorstep with flowers behind his back, and remember her birthday with a card and a present, and not forget her on Valentine's Day, either. When Julie's sister had a baby, Wayne gave Julie a stuffed animal to pass on to the new mother he didn't even know. He was like a sweet brother to her.

And Julie had always figured that Wayne's disinterest in any romance with her was pegged to the fact that she was heavy set. Julie knew Wayne well enough to know that he always seemed to end up with "fat broads," as he would call them, but she knew he didn't like it. So why was he in pursuit of this one? What did he see in this no-name drifter? Wayne never asked anyone to go home with him. Julie had been invited into Wayne's home, had been in his room, a private sanctuary that she knew only a few had ever entered. What was going on? Wayne never took anyone home. Ever.

But he did that night. And when Wayne and Robin left together at closing time, Julie planned to check things out the next day. She would stop at Wayne's house in the afternoon and try to figure out what Wayne saw in this girl, who, it seemed, was so much like herself, even in age.

Home for Wayne was a one-story ranch-style house on Minnesota Avenue, a straightaway dotted with stop signs; trailer homes, some of them haphazardly built up as disguised frame structures; and the odd, plain, one-story house, like his own, where he lived with his father. The number of parked vehicles—cars, pickups, semis, motor homes, and even flatbed trailers— typified a struggle for affluence among working-class poor who spent little or no time tending to a front lawn.

On the night he invited Robin to crash at 715 Minnesota Avenue, his father, George, a long-haul trucker, wasn't home. He was out on the road. Julie knew that Wayne might have hesitated bringing a girl home with him if his father were there because George, it seemed to her, had Wayne on a pretty tight leash. It been this way for years, especially when Wayne's mother was alive.

But now, even though Wayne was a grown man who was twenty-nine years old, had been in the Navy, and held a full-time day job in addition to his part-time bouncing at the Cabin, he was always ready to jump through hoops for his father. He would suddenly leave a party to get home because he said his father wanted him home early. Or he would leap for the phone at work whenever his father called. It was unnatural, Julie thought. But, then, who was she to judge? She liked George. Just as much as she liked Wayne's mother, Charlene, whom she had worked with at the Cabin until her death in 1980. And she liked Bill, Wayne's brother, who also had been a bouncer at the Cabin and who had gotten Wayne the part-time night job.

Wayne's day job was at Conlin's Furniture, a giant warehouse store in Missoula, where he made local deliveries and worked as a warehouseman. Julie knew the particulars of Wayne's life well enough to know that he would be around in the afternoon when she stopped to check things out, because it would be his day off from Conlin's.

* * *

Julie fidgeted as she sat there, lounging in George's favorite armchair, listening to Wayne and watching with precision as his glances darted frequently at Robin. The conversation was circuitous and nervous. Neither Wayne nor Julie, who up to this time, she thought, were two kindred spirits, brought up the subject: Where was this girl from? How long was she going to stay? What would George have to say about it?

"So what are you guys up to today?" Julie asked without much real interest.

"We haven't figured it out, yet," Wayne answered, throwing a smile at Robin.

That was the kind of friendly chatter the three of them shared. They were visiting, presumably getting to know one another, but actually they were not. As the conversation rolled along, Wayne and Julie offered bits and pieces of their personal histories, all of which Julie already knew. She and Wayne had spent hours together. On more than one occasion, they had stayed out all night to watch the sunrise from the promontory at the top of Deer Creek. They spent many evenings together, sometimes getting a little drunk or a little high, looking across the Clark Fork River at the modest glimmer of light emanating from the little town of Bonner. They were drinking pals who took off for the riverbank on hot summer days to slug Charlie Birches, Wayne's favorite mixture of vodka and root beer, or Booze Milk, a concoction of vodka and milk. They went to the movies, even the drive-in, together, and they spent a lot of their free time just driving around in the woods, high on pot, having a good time.

As a matter of pride, Julie didn't want to appear to be digging for information about Robin. So she didn't pry until Wayne left the room.

"Where're you from?"

Robin was a friendly type. She of course told Julie where home was, but Julie was still preoccupied with knowing more about the relationship of these two newfound lovers. She would only recall later that she thought Robin said she was from Texas, or that she had been in Texas for a while. One thing was certain. Robin didn't have an accent of any noticeable type.

The conversation drifted to more serious topics: men, marriage, and children. Julie felt right at home talking to Robin about these things. And Robin helped cement a ready bond by volunteering the information that she had almost had a child. But she didn't. Robin told Julie that she had recently had an abortion. All Julie would later recall about that private moment of what she describes as "girl talk" with Robin is that Robin had no immediate plans, had just been booted off a long-haul truck by the driver, with whom she had some kind of argument, and that she probably would be hanging around with Wayne for awhile.

A day and a half later, Julie stopped in again. In fact, for the first couple of weeks after Robin's arrival, Julie made it a practice to drop in every other day. The visits didn't shed much light on the relationship. She could see that George had welcomed the girl into the house. Because Robin had no clothes except what she had on her back, he offered to buy her some jeans and shoes, in trade for doing some of the housework.

"Christ, this was Wayne's home," George would recall later. "I can't say 'You can't bring nobody home.' He had his own room. She was broke. She didn't have no clothes."

In every other way, Wayne's life seemed to change little. He worked at Conlin's by day and showed up as usual at the Cabin.

What struck Julie as different, though, was Wayne's bragging about his sex life with Robin. Julie always had the impression that girls who liked a lot of sex weren't Wayne's bag, but he bragged to her about Robin, saying she wore him out, that she gave him blisters. And because Julie was Wayne's presumed confidant, he would also tell her that he was getting disgusted by it.

To the guys who worked with Wayne at Conlin's warehouse, it was a different story. He didn't hold back in describing his relationship with the voluptuous Robin.

"We have a great sexual relationship," he bragged to Rick Mace, his boss, who had some reason to doubt the claim. Rick had always known Wayne to be shy around women.

But aside from the infrequent bragging moment, Wayne kept Robin in a low profile. He showed pictures of her to one of the saleswomen at Conlin's, but he never brought Robin into the store. Rick Mace was the only employee at Conlin's to ever meet her, and that meeting wasn't prolonged enough to be memorable. Rick had said hello to her one day as she sat in Wayne's truck.

Wayne had good reason to keep Robin in the

wings. For most of the summer, he had been dating another, much younger girl. Her name was Joni Delcomte. She was a heavy-set brunette, the daughter of Jan Del, a country-and-western singer of some local renown. And Joni didn't know anything about Robin.

Joni was eighteen years old, fresh out of Missoula's new Big Sky High School, when she started dating the twenty-nine-year-old Wayne Nance, and he seemed like the nicest guy she had ever met. He was the kind of man she dreamed about marrying someday.

She first saw him at a rodeo when Rick Mace and Wayne came over to sit with Joni and her girlfriends. Wayne was charming, and he seemed so sweet. When he asked her to go out, she jumped at the invitation. They went to the movies and took long picnics together, but they spent most of their dating time that summer at bars and nightclubs, including the Cabin, listening to Joni's mother perform.

What made her believe that Wayne was the best boyfriend a girl could ever hope for was his incredibly attentive manner. Every time he came over to her house, he brought flowers. He always arrived when he said he was going to come. He painted pictures for her. He carved her name in a small rock. He was quiet and considerate, and even though Wayne was more than ten years her senior, to Joni they were just two young people in love. Wayne took her up a dirt road off Deer Creek, where they would wade barefoot in the clear mountain water. They lolled on the warm grassy stream bank, picnicking and petting, drinking Miller Lite. Joni had no way of knowing that Robin was back

at the house doing the housework for Wayne and
his dad, waiting for Wayne to return.

One night, when they were alone in Joni's
house, the necking and petting got more serious. It was the first time they had ever made
love. But to Joni, it seemed it was over just as
it had begun. Wayne acted strangely. Just as
soon as Wayne had made love to her, he was
getting up and getting dressed. He wouldn't
look her in the eye. He seemed embarrassed.

"Good-night," was all he said. Then he left.

Joni didn't read much into the fact that he
had made such a quick exit. Maybe, she thought,
he really was embarrassed about letting things
progress so far.

That night, after Wayne had left, she was
able to dismiss his abnormal behavior the same
way she dismissed his never taking her to his
house. She knew Bill, Wayne's brother, and
George. She had met them at the Cabin. One
day, she was sure, he would take her home.
For now, she was joyously happy. She told her
friends that she was going to marry Wayne. He
was the kind of guy who was so incredibly
aware of what women want to feel. He was the
most affectionate person in the world. This was
the guy.

But their one-time lovemaking session would
lead nowhere. And Wayne would not, it turned
out, ever invite her to his house. A couple of
weeks later, after they had spent a few more
nights out together, Wayne had an announcement to make. It was in early September. As
he and Joni sat alone in the backyard of her
mother's house, Wayne started to cry.

"I'm getting too serious about you," he told

her, pausing to find the words. "I don't like how I feel when you aren't with me."

Joni knew it was coming. The breakup. But she didn't show it. She listened.

"I'm not the type to have a family and I don't like being so serious about somebody. We have to break up."

Wayne was sobbing through his words. Joni wasn't. She didn't say much, and though there were no tears, it wasn't because she wasn't hurt. She didn't want to make it any harder for Wayne. She played it cool.

As Wayne poured out his heart, blubbering away, he began to see that Joni didn't seem to be upset at all. It angered him then, but he didn't show it. Joni learned later that Wayne was angry and hurt that she didn't at least cry a little. Wayne had told her sister's boyfriend about how unaffected Joni seemed by their breakup. But Wayne and Joni remained friends, and on the few times they crossed paths afterward, it was as if there never had been a romance. Behind an opaque exterior, Wayne was playing it cool now, too.

The last time anyone saw the girl named Robin was on the night of September 28, 1984, when Wayne brought her to a party. The occasion was Julie's birthday, but it was a festive time of year anyway. Summer was over. The seasonal change that was always under way was inspiring. The days were still warm and bright. The nights were cool and clear, and the air was full of snap. With the whole town rejuvenated by the return of thousands of University of Montana students and the start of the

Grizzlies' football calendar, Missoulians were characteristically upbeat.

But not Wayne. His summer flings were over.

Joni was out of the picture. Robin was suddenly gone. And Wayne's friends began to notice a new dour mood. He didn't exactly announce the fact that Robin was no longer in his life. The news was elicited first by a Conlin's coworker, Keith Merseal, who was also an incorrigible joker. Everyone noticed that Wayne was in an unusually sullen state. When he got this way, there was always a forbidding undertone to his dealings with others, and most of the time it was best to just steer clear. But not Keith. He was right there, ready to test Wayne's temper.

"What's the matter?" Keith inquired, pacing his questioning while making sure the other guys heard his punch line. "Didn't you get any last night?"

Wayne wasn't amused. He didn't break his concentration.

"She's gone."

That's all he said. Keith and Rick Mace and the others let it ride. Later, when he was ready to talk about it, he told them that she had left with a trucker. Then, later still, he said he had taken her to the bus station and put her on a bus. There was no clarification from Wayne about the first version of the story, and nobody bothered to ask.

Julie also noticed a change in Wayne. Soon after her birthday party, Julie saw Wayne again at the Cabin. This time he was alone and he seemed distracted.

"Where's Robin?"

"She's gone," was all he said.

"Gone? What d'ya mean gone? Where did she go?"

Wayne didn't answer right away. He was stacking coolers and definitely avoiding eye contact.

"Wayne," she pressed him, with the legitimate curiosity that a good friend is allowed to indulge, "why did she leave town?"

"I put her on a bus," he said. He still wasn't looking at her.

Julie didn't find it hard to believe that Robin had left town on a bus. But she was troubled by the fact that Wayne seemed to be dodging her. Julie's romantic ideas about Wayne aside, weren't they supposed to be best friends? After all, wasn't she one of the privileged few who had ever been allowed into Wayne's room? She had been impressed by that, as much as she was by the Navy corners on his bedspread. There wasn't a wrinkle on it. To her, the organized clutter seemed neat. It was sort of a museum of Wayne's life. Mementos of his mother, mementos of his Navy days, plus all the handmade knife and dagger paraphernalia that verified to her that Wayne really was an accomplished artisan.

"Everything has a place and a place for everything," he said to her. And he knew, too, if something had been touched.

"What about all these bird feet, Wayne? All these claws? Are these real?"

His answer was yes. They were real. He collected birds' feet and claws of all kinds. To the smitten Julie, it was the perfect answer from this man she adored, eccentricities and all. He even collected real birds' feet.

The only dominant theme reflected in his exhausting array of stuff was an obvious interest in medieval weaponry. Knives were lined up in rows on tabletops and in drawers. Swords hung from the walls along with Wayne's own handmade weapons, like the wooden club accented with nails. There were brass knuckles resting next to a horde of vitamins. It also seemed he never threw anything away. Felt-tip markers lay next to his toothpaste. There was a plastic bust of a black woman, a U.S. Navy telescope, body-building weights. *Playboy* and *Penthouse* magazines—some opened, many still preserved in their plastic-wrap seals—were stacked in heaps. The bookshelves seemed to contain every fragment of Wayne's life from childhood on. There was an implied order within these four walls, and Julie didn't understand it, but she was fascinated just the same, even by its unholy aspects.

Wayne had arranged small tabletop shrines. The bookshelves were stuffed with paperbacks on the occult, mythology, satanism, and Viking literature and history. The only window was covered by a sheet of black plastic for added emphasis.

Wayne collected an assortment of fake detective badges. And he collected, drew, and kept maps of Missoula and surrounding towns, as well as handmade maps of local trailer parks, maps of a nearby apartment complex, and diagrammatic layouts that he himself had drawn of the homes of some of his friends. He had clipped a newspaper ad showing a group of woman hairdressers at a local beauty parlor, and taped it to his dresser after drawing circles around some of the faces of women in the picture.

There were posters of Conan the Barbarian and sage-like quotations from Leonard Nimoy. Along the walls and across the ceiling he had strung string after string of soda and beer can pop-tops. Wayne's vast collection of cassette tapes nearly filled an entire wall.

Beneath the trim Navy-cornered bedspread, Wayne slept on a green rubber sheet. Julie didn't know about that oddity. And she didn't know that Wayne occasionally looped the bed-posts with short rope ties. He would tie the white clothesline ropes in such a way that who-ever was restrained by the ligatures could easily escape if need be. If Wayne had shared this sacral enhancement with her, she might have been more than just fascinated by Wayne's bi-zarre bedroom. But he didn't, and all that mat-tered to her was that Wayne was a friend who took better care of her emotional well-being than any boyfriend ever had, and it saddened her that Wayne avoided her for weeks after she grilled him about Robin's disappearance.

Maybe, she thought, Robin did blow out of town on the same restless inspiration that had brought her to Missoula in the first place. But that was not the case. The truth was that Robin hadn't left. She was no more than three miles from Wayne's home on Minnesota Avenue, buried face up and nude in a two-foot–deep grave in the woods just above Bonner Dam. She had been shot once in the back of the head and twice in the temple.

Chapter 2

A Christmas Grave

It was a windless, overcast afternoon, and very cold. The frozen Clark Fork River appeared below as a giant white serpent, ice-packed, its undulations stilled to the eye, but its waters flowing endlessly westward beneath the ice pack, draining the high-elevation ridges of the Sapphire Mountains, a north–south range of the Rockies some ten miles southeast of Missoula. The river angles through Bonner and Milltown, through Hellgate Canyon, into Missoula, and beyond to Idaho, eventually to join the tributary system of the mightier Columbia River.

The man who plugged his way above this vista of winter's majesty on a Monday afternoon was a wildlife photographer. He was stalking photo opportunities, pausing frequently to check light readings, glancing upward to the trees for birds, and keeping a keen reconnaisance behind his steps. He was on the slight rise known as Bonner Dam, and he was quite alone, because it was the afternoon of Christmas Eve 1984. Everybody else was downtown in the stores, getting off work early or huddled inside against the arctic temperature.

As he scanned the lower trees of this wooded place, his eye caught something. He couldn't make it out at first, so he walked closer. It was something sticking out of the ground, and it was black. Approaching, he could see that it didn't resemble the typical downed tree limb, or dead, snapped pine trunk. When he got right up to it, he recognized it, and then he reeled back in horror. It was a blackened human leg, protruding from the rock-hard ground at a forty-five–degree angle. There was the knee. There the ankle. The foot.

Blood raced to his head. In a reflex, he anxiously looked back along the vague trail that he had just descended. It was still dead quiet. There was no one there. He made rapid mental notes about exactly where the grave could be found as he clambered back down the ridge and across a field to his car, sheltering his camera against the cold inside his coat, very eager to call the sheriff's department. He would tell them the protruding leg marked the grave. It was under a large spruce, about 100 yards from the top of the dam. It was along a little-used dirt lane.

Captain Larry Weatherman knew the spot well, but only by its reputation. The rocky knoll and the grassy, flat spot underneath had been a popular place for teenagers for years. In the Seventies, along with the changing times, it was *the* place to throw a keg party, or to rendezvous with friends and enjoy some hallucinogens.

Flanked by his deputies, Captain Weatherman tromped his way up to the spot. It was easy to find. But it was not going to be easy to get this body out of the ground. The earth wouldn't break against the digging gear they had brought. Weatherman radioed for someone to bring up a tent and a portable heater. Maybe a few hours of heat would soften things up. It was getting late by the time the tent and the heater were put in place over the grave. Then Weatherman had to decide whether he was going to get his deputies up here tomorrow, on Christmas Day, to dig a corpse out of the ground. He decided to wait until Wednesday. Maybe the earth would have softened up enough by then to enable them to make a forensically correct exhumation of this body. Though he had his doubts that it would be easy even then.

So for two nights, on Christmas Eve and on Christmas Day, the grave of the girl named Robin was enshrined in a tent, eerily pitched in the black wilderness. The only sound was the periodic blast of hot air from the thermostatically controlled propane heater.

And on Wednesday, when the deputies returned to Bonner Dam, they discovered that Weatherman had been right about how hard the ground was. The deputies had to use chisels. It was as if the body were encased in granite.

It was easy to make a sex determination. The dead woman's large breasts were still present and intact. The skull, Weatherman could see, was fractured from the impact of bullet wounds. As the first bullet entered, it would have precipitated a rapid expansion of the gases within the cranium, exploding the bone apart. After the site was excavated with the same kind of care given to an archeological dig, Weatherman was disappointed that no bullets were recovered. That told him that it was most likely that the young woman had been killed elsewhere and then dumped here. He dreaded to think what it meant, now that he had two unidentified bodies—both young females—who had been killed and dumped on the eastern edge of town.

The first was the body of a younger girl who had been found along Interstate 90. She had been stabbed in the chest and tossed down an embankment. By the time anyone noticed that she was there, her corpse had become almost completely desiccated. Weatherman's attempts to identify this girl, whom he dubbed the Beavertail Hill Girl in reference to the slight topographic rise of Beavertail Hill along the highway near the site of her fragmented remains, had so far been futile. It had been years since the crew of a slow-moving Burlington Northern freight train spotted the girl's bones laying up against a chain-link fence that ran along the track line. That was late January of 1980. Weatherman theorized then that whoever had killed this girl had thrown her off on the roadside, and that her body had then rolled down the bank coming to rest against the fence. In the year and a half that the body rested there, it became nothing more than a sun-parched skeleton, reduced to a hubble of almost indistinct artifact. It was as if it had lain in repose, *sub rosa* in the landscape, alongside Montana's main artery—a kind of existential eye on the comings and goings on the interstate.

The girl's hair had completely separated from the skull. It looked more like a strawberry blonde's hairpiece that now, having fallen off, lay up against the fence, snagged in place. Her dress was gathered in a tight wrap around the neck. There were no shoes at the site, and no underpants. Police recovered a pair of earrings and some other inexpensive jewelry. An incisive wound to a rib indicated that the cause of death was a stab wound to the chest. It was estimated that she had been approximately fifteen years old.

That case was now nearly four years old and going nowhere. Captain Weatherman had no reason to suspect that those two murder scenes, except for their relative proximity to each other and the fact that the girls had been dumped after being killed elsewhere, were in any way related. Weatherman was certain by now that the Beavertail Hill victim wasn't a local girl. Perhaps as soon as the end of the week he would know the identity of this latest victim. In the meantime, he decided to call her Debbie Deer Creek, after the creek that flows down off the mountain to join with the Clark Fork.

An autopsy performed by Dr. Ronald Rivers produced two distinct, forensic identifiers, which gave Weatherman hope. The dead girl had perfect, pearl-white teeth. There were no fillings or restorations, and Dr. Rivers also recorded that one of the victim's lateral incisors had rotated outward. This would be invaluable in the search for the girl's identity, because it would be unique in the dental-chart catalogue of missing persons. The second key to identifying the girl was her hair. Debbie Deer Creek's dark-auburn hair had been dyed. While hair samples are not usually considered a final arbiter in forensic matchmaking, the series of color-changing dyes in this case showed up like layers of paint on a car. Her natural light brown had been first dyed a deeper brown, and then a dark auburn.

Dr. Rivers estimated that the body had been in the ground for approximately three months. In that time, no one who fit the girl's description had been reported missing in Missoula County, which led Captain Weatherman to think that she was from out of state. And no one called the sheriff's department after the *Missoulian* ran a brief news item about the discovery of a body on Bonner Dam. The newspaper's story about the photographer's find was limited to a few paragraphs on an inside page under the headline "Body Found East of Town."

On Thursday, the day after the body had been carved from the frozen earth, Captain Weatherman broadcast a nationwide description of Debbie Deer Creek's body to other law-enforcement agencies. He had run a description of the Beavertail Hill skeleton through national police computer networks every six months, and he was still waiting for a response. And just as he had commissioned an anthropological reconstruction of the Beavertail Hill Girl, he commissioned one for Debbie Deer Creek. It would be done by Dr. Michael Charney, a forensic physical anthropologist at Colorado State University in Fort Collins. He would place the new plastic likeness on the top shelf of the bookcase in his cramped, windowless office, right next to the now-aging bust of the Beavertail Hill Girl.

Captain Weatherman isn't a man to give up easily on a homicide. He would sift the evidence, rethink the motives. He would wait, if that's what was called for, for as long as it would take. He was not going to give up. It wasn't just professional pride. There was the sense of duty to the families of these murdered girls who would have no way of knowing what had become of their children.

The tall, bespectacled captain, who chooses his words slowly and carefully, displays an inordinate degree of humility for someone in charge. Like many others who have chosen a career in law enforcement, it was his lifelong goal. Born and raised in Anaconda, Montana's copper town, his father and his uncle worked in the smelters. But Larry Weatherman had bigger dreams. After graduation from high school and a Navy tour in Vietnam, where he was in the first battalion raids at Danang, he returned to Montana to marry his high school sweetheart. He was graduated from the University of Montana with a degree in sociology and went immediately to work for the Missoula County sheriff's department. Now, as chief of detectives, he represents a new breed of Western lawman.

The respect he is accorded by his detectives is evident as they pass him in the narrow corridors at the sheriff's department, nodding to the man in charge who walks with a deliberate, slightly gangly gait, and seems to be always engrossed in thought.

When Weatherman joined the department, in the early years of the Seventies, Missoula was so quiet after dark that some nights of the week the only deputy sheriff on duty in all of Missoula County was the jailer. Nobody was on patrol. Things were different then. As in 1950s and 1960s, the Missoula of the 1970s saw very few violent crimes against persons that didn't involve families. They were easy cases. The killer always seemed to leave a trail a mile wide right to his front door. By the time Weatherman joined the department, the tide was going out on those simpler days. There used to be one or two homicides a year, at most. Some years there were none. The murder rate in the busiest years would peak at four or five a year. Still, they were cases that got solved. But now, with the addition of Debbie Deer Creek, Weatherman would add yet another case to his growing number of unsolved murders, all of which dated back to the early winter of 1974. There were a total of five. Debbie Deer Creek would make six. Five of the victims were women, and the cases either appeared to be or definitely were sexual homicides.

For Weatherman, it all seemed to date back to one cataclysmic crime. It occurred on April 11, 1974. The rookie Weatherman was summoned to a murder scene that would redefine the meaning of homicide for him and everyone else in this quiet Western university town. It was a brutal sex murder. The victim was a minister's wife.

PART II

PART II

Chapter 3

The Minister's Wife

The origin of the name Missoula has always been in dispute. One popular legend ties it to the Indian word Issoul, meaning horrible, an undoubted reference to the canyon east of town through which the Flatheads had to travel on their way to big buffalo hunts on the plains. The Flatheads were peaceful, but the murderous Blackfeet would lay ready to ambush all comers at the narrow opening of the canyon. What is more certain is that the name of the canyon, Hellgate, is handed down from early French-Canadian trappers, who called it *Port de l'Enfer* for the same reason.

It doubtless did not cross Donna Pounds's mind as she rode eastward through Hellgate Canyon on a snowy day in April that an ambush lay ahead. It was Maundy Thursday, the day before Good Friday. She had been along for the ride with a friend, an Avon lady, who was making drop-offs to customers. Now they were headed back to West Riverside, a small settlement, not even a town, about six miles east of the city. Her husband, Harvey, was still at work downtown, most likely eating a late

lunch at the store. Harvey was an itinerant
preacher of fundamentalist bent who yearned
for his own flock. He supported the family by
selling men's clothes in one of the better shops
in town, Yandt's Men's Store. His specialty was
shoes, and he was known to be a fine shoe
salesman when he didn't have his mind on
church affairs.

Both Harvey and Donna were equally devout
Christians. Together they had attended the
Prairie Bible Institute in Calgary, Alberta. A
mother and a housewife, Donna also worked
part time in the Christian Book Store downtown and was a volunteer at St. Patrick's Hospital. But it was Harvey who had really taken
to the cloth. So much so that his own brothers
often tired of his moralizing, which could be
triggered by the mere sighting of a beer in the
refrigerator. It rubbed them the wrong way,
too, when they learned that Harvey had bought
another set of encyclopedias to help him with
his ministry work. He already had four sets.
Or to see him add another harmonica to his
collection. He had nearly fifty already. Or when
he acquired another swell piece of fishing gear,
because Harvey and Donna, who unlike her
husband was as unselfish and giving as they
come, didn't have the kind of money to lavish
on selfish hobbies, especially when it was plain
to see that the children could use some better
clothes.

Harvey was forty-four. He had grown up
stone poor, a child of the Depression, and
maybe that explained his need to have some of
the things he didn't have as a boy. Then, too,
there was the overhanging threat that his life

could be snatched from him at any moment. Harvey suffered a congenital heart condition that already had claimed two of his four brothers. One brother, Mike, died at age twenty-three. Sam, another, died before reaching age thirty. His youngest brother, John, who lived in Tacoma, Washington, also suffered from the condition. His oldest brother, Jack, who lived in Reno, Nevada, had an enlarged heart but seemed to have been spared the exotic disorder that caused a runaway cholesterol buildup in his brothers. There was no way to control it, not even diet. Three years ago, doctors had performed a triple bypass on Harvey, but he still had a bad heart, and cholesterol had massed and settled throughout his body. It was in his fingernails and in the tissue of his eyeballs.

Donna and Harvey were active members of Bethel Baptist Church, where Harvey was deacon. Recently, Harvey had become a local Christian radio deejay and demagogue, railing out against what he and other fundamentalists clearly saw as a resurgence of satanism. Harvey also was spending a lot of time preparing to become the permanent pastor of a church in Stevensville. They had put their house on the market as part of the plan to relocate "down the Bitterroot," as the local saying goes—south of Missoula in the beautiful Bitterroot Valley. Harvey's employers noticed that his preoccupation with the church was undercutting his performance. In fact, while they didn't say it to his face, he really wouldn't be missed if and when he accomplished his move south.

As Donna rode east along state Route 10–200, a two-laner that parallels Interstate 90 most of

the way to West Riverside, a wet snow began
to fall. The dime-sized flakes crashed against
the windshield, materializing for only a moment as a liquid, translucent blur, awaiting the
wiper blade's inexorable return. Donna and her
friend passed through East Missoula, past the
truck stop, past the roadhouses. And as the
now oatmeal-sized flakes intermittently turned
to a cold rain, the sterility of the brown and
gray landscape was transformed, softened beyond the windshield. It seemed dirty, muddy,
a blunt reminder that the first flush of green
that would appear suddenly—as if overnight—
with the arrival of Spring, was still weeks off.
Had anyone looked at their house today?

As a name for a place, West Riverside has an
upscale ring to it that suggests there is more
to be found in this pancake of land under the
mountain than a clot of trailer homes, arranged
singly or in rows, and an odd-man-out single-
family house. What Donna Pounds saw as she
approached home on a Thursday afternoon in
mid-April, was a vast, early spring mudscape,
intersected by the meanderings of a half-frozen
river, braced by snow-covered hills all around.
Like so many tiny markers on a large map, the
spots where man had built shelter and settled
in would appear miniscule against the expanse
of the land. Man was a mere trespasser here.

Just eleven days before, on March 30, Donna
and Harvey had celebrated their twenty-second
wedding anniversary. He gave her a Waring
blender. They had cake at home. Kathy, twelve,
the youngest daughter, and Karen, twenty, the
oldest, were there. And ten days before that,

Kenny, their son, had returned to Army duty at Fort Bliss, Texas.

The car turned left onto Tremper Street. Donna said good-bye and headed into the house, a one-story stucco ranch. The door was open, as it should be, so the real-estate agents could come and go. And the house was empty, as it should be, with Kathy still in school and Karen at work. It was just after 1:30 P.M. The house was quiet, except for the audible hum of the Kelvinator in the kitchen. It would be her last hour of life.

Police theorize that Donna first encountered her attacker in the master bedroom, most likely as she entered the room.

He was wearing gloves, and in his hand he held Harvey's .22-caliber Luger. He would have used the gun to force her into submission on the bed. If she recognized her husband's gun, which she probably did, she would have realized that her attacker had gotten it from a hidden, built-in cabinet drawer in their bedroom.

He fired at least once into the corner of the bedroom. The slug disappeared somewhere near her sewing machine. It would have been intended to show her that he meant business.

The gloves he wore were made of amber-colored latex rubber. He ordered her onto the bed, where he tied her wrists and ankles to the bedposts with short sections of white, knotted clothesline that he produced from a black gym bag. After removing her slacks, he then pulled a knife and cut off her undergarments, slitting her underpants down the middle. He removed her sanitary napkin and dropped it on the bedroom's linoleum-tile floor. Then he raped her.

Afterward, he untied her feet and led her, still naked from the waist down, into the unfinished basement, forcing her to kneel on her hands and knees under the stairwell in what was a semifinished furnace room. There, after retying the rope restraints on her ankles and taping her mouth shut, he stood behind her and squeezed five rounds from the Luger into the back of her head at point-blank range. Her body fell forward into a crouch. Her killer then shoved the gun between her legs and inserted the barrel into her vagina, where he left it.

The house again fell silent. No one in the neighborhood heard any of the gunshots. The killer ascended the stairs and turned off the basement light, leaving Donna Linebeck Pounds in her cool, dark, concrete tomb.

The furnace fired now and then, sending a rush of heat upstairs, where the room temperature was kept at the nationally recommended sixty-eight degrees.

Chapter 4

The Husband

It was close to six o'clock when Harvey pulled his old Rambler into the driveway. As he came through the door, he said hello to Kathy, who was huddled in front of the TV with a friend, and the first sign that anything was amiss came with her response.

"I don't know, Dad, why, but there are ropes on all the beds and the rug is messed up in there," she said. Her tone was nonchalant, her attention fixed to the tube.

Harvey went to look. Maybe it was a game. Something they had done to her room.

As he peered into Kathy's room, he found ropes tied in half-hitch knots to the bedposts of her bed. Then he stepped down the hall to look in Karen's room, where it was the same. Ropes tied to the bedposts. As he turned, his eyes caught a glimpse of the bathroom. He could see more rope had been oddly laced around the base of the toilet. The same piece of white clothesline reached up and had been looped over the hinge pins on the bathroom door.

Though a 12-year-old, Kathy was, Harvey knew, immature for her age, and he was not surprised that she was so casual about this. She was perplexed about it, but she quickly allowed the mystery to fade when her friend arrived. They were eager to watch TV. But Harvey's heart was pumping faster now. He skipped Kenny's room at the farther end of the house and headed for the master bedroom.

His eyes fell first on the ropes, and then on the bloodied sanitary napkin on the floor. Donna's clothing was strewn on the floor. A pair of underpants, slit in half, stared at him. A single shoe had been left at the foot of the bed. Then his gaze locked on the empty holster that belonged to his Luger. There it lay in plain view on the bed. He could see that the gun had been cut off the holster. Someone had sliced through the leather to remove the weapon, which he didn't immediately see.

All he knew was that he had to get Kathy and her girlfriend out of the house.

"Kathy," he called, reentering the living room, "why don't you go over to your girlfriend's house. I'll call you later."

"Aw, Dad," she whined. "Right in the middle . . ."

"I'll explain later," he said, stopping her. "Just please, do this for me. I'll call you. Just . . ."

"Okay," she said in a downturn. And in the time it takes two preteen girls to assemble and leave, they were gone.

Harvey waited patiently as they pulled on their overcoats and he watched as they walked to the street and headed away. Hurriedly he checked Kenny's room. He noticed that his son's guitar had been left on the bed. That was odd. Who would have taken it down? But there were no ropes, and no other sign of disturbance.

There was only one place left to check—the basement. It was exactly 5:59 P.M. when he telephoned the Missoula County Sheriff's Department to report what he found down there.

As the setting sun cast its diminishing light through the maw of Hellgate Canyon, the house on Tremper Street would become surrounded by nearly every available police vehicle in the county. Every sheriff's deputy on the force who wasn't already on duty would be called in on overtime.

Among the first to arrive was County Attorney Robert L. "Dusty" Deschamps III, the chief law-enforcement officer of the county. Known universally as Dusty, a boyhood nickname that stuck, Deschamps had just filed for a second term in office. Though only twenty-nine years old, he had been hired for the job three years before, when he was a fresh graduate of the University of Montana Law School. For one thing, he was a Democrat. For another, he was the only applicant. Now, this evening, he was summoned to investigate a homicide whose degenerate ferocity was unprecedented in this part of the country.

Right behind him was Missoula County Sheriff John C. Moe. He too had filed for a second term on this very day as a Republican in a predominantly Democratic county. Sheriff Moe had won election to his first term after the county commissioners had asked him to run. A lawman first and a politician second, Moe actually had to ask what party affiliation he should assume. It was an easy decision, the commissioners advised him. The incumbent was a Democrat, so he would be a Republican.

After surveying the scene, Sheriff Moe had a few words to say to the *Missoulian* reporter, Steve Shirley. He said that without a doubt this crime ranked as one of the most vicious he had ever come across. Those words, coming from this white-haired authority figure, carried a lot of weight in Missoula. Moe was more than a elder townsman who wore the badge because someone had to run on the Republican ticket. Moe's law-enforcement career spanned thirty years. He had been a member of the U.S. Border Patrol for seven years, had served in Naval intelligence, and, more significantly, had been an agent for the almighty Federal Bureau of Investigation. After nineteen years with the FBI, he had retired to Missoula.

Moe's deputies fanned through the neighborhood, searching the backyards and the outer perimeter of the neighboring fields, going door to door, interviewing everyone who lived in the environs of West Riverside. The deputies asked basic questions of the residents. Were they all right? Had they seen any vehicles come or go? They were instructed by Moe not to disclose that there had been a murder. All they were allowed to say was that there had been a violent crime. Had anybody seen anything out of the ordinary?

Deschamps and Moe were joined by Ray Froelich, chief of detectives, and the three of them huddled under the floor joists, leaning against the cool steel of the lally column that held up the house, waiting for Lawrence Livingston, the funeral director who was also the coroner.

A detective descended the stairs. As he turned and came more directly under the bare-bulb lighting, they could see he was carrying something in his hand. He told them Sheriff's Patrolman Weatherman had found it on a dirt road that runs along the base of the mountain, connecting eventually to Tamarack, a trailer village approximately one-half mile away. It was a light-brown surgical glove. On the back of it was the inscription: "amber + LARGE No. 366." It appeared to be stained with blood.

Dangling there before their eyes, the object seemed to suddenly distill a hideous new knowledge that was even more difficult to bear than the sight of poor Mrs. Pounds, bent over, backside out, under the stairwell. Up to this point, they had been absorbed in the intense first canvas of the house, seeing what was there and making certain Harvey would stay upstairs, where he was on the phone to relatives, giving them the news. The surgical glove would lead them outside again, into the community, where somewhere they had to find the killer who had done this.

They could see the headline on the front page of tomorrow's *Missoulian*: "West Riverside Woman Is Slain." The story would conclude, they knew well enough, with the sobering statement that no arrests had been made. Only yesterday, in the Wednesday paper, displayed above a couple of Easter advertisements, was an update on the Siobhan McGuinness murder investigation, another recent unsolved case.

City Police Chief Ray Roehl said that despite
investigating thousands of leads and bits of information, the department had not added any
significant information to the McGuinness file.
Police still had no suspect. They had theories,
which they hoped to bear out with FBI tests. In
fact, yesterday's headline played off the labora-
tory angle: "Policemen Hope Science Can Find
Siobhan's Killer."

The murder of five-year-old Siobhan McGuinness still tore at the community's heart. The
Missoulian, attempting to restrain a vengeance-
minded public, printed an editorial on February
13, a little more than a week after the girl was
snatched from the sidewalk on Missoula's North
Side, an older part of town situated between
the Clark Fork River and Interstate 90.

"It is important that people keep a grip on
themselves," the editors wrote. "It would be
very wrong to allow a lynch mob atmosphere
to form. The killer, loathsome as he is to all, is
a sick person. By no means does that excuse
what he did or render it less dreadful. But he
IS sick, and it is important that we treat him
with the humanity which he is too sick to give
to others." The advice to the community ended
with an aside that appeared to be written for
the benefit of Deschamps and Moe. "That
hinges on catching him, of course," it concluded.

Siobhan, pronounced "She-VON," was last
seen on February 5, 1974. Her mother, Bonnie
Tarses, had last talked to her precocious and
friendly daughter at six-thirty on that Tuesday
evening. Siobhan as visiting with a friend a few
blocks away, and her mother had called to tell

her it was time to come home. A friend of Bonnie's would escort Siobhan as far as Whittier School, and the girl would continue alone from there. It wouldn't have struck anyone as out of the ordinary for Siobhan's mother to expect her to walk the three blocks from Whittier alone after seven o'clock, which in early February was well after dark. There was no reason to think anything could happen to her in this safe community.

Home was at 501 North Second Street, but Siobhan never made it there. Her disappearance, reported by her mother after she failed to arrive home, led to a two-day manhunt. City police teamed up with the sheriff's department. Everyone worked double shifts. The FBI joined in. State fish and game wardens were enlisted. Police teams canvased the North Side all night long. The following morning, approximately 130 volunteers gathered at Whittier School and made a daylight search of a wide area, checking outdoor sheds, abandoned cars, and the riverbanks. By noon, city police captain Richard Golden decided to send the volunteers home, telling them he would call them back if he needed them again.

Blood discovered on railroad tracks on the North Side that afternoon turned out to be from an animal. A bloodhound, which had sniffed two pieces of Siobhan's clothing, couldn't detect a trace of the girl after circling the schoolyard. The search intensified after police, during their house-to-house search, turned up a report of an attempted assault on another five-year-old girl in the same neighborhood earlier on the same day. A man had coaxed the girl into a shack and had tried to molest her. She escaped unharmed and was able to provide her parents and police with enough of a description to enable Steve McGuinness, the father of the missing girl who was also a bit of an artist, to make a sketch. The suspect was a man of medium build, about five foot eleven, between the ages of eighteen and twenty. He had red, curly hair.

The day after Siobhan disappeared, an unidentified woman who claimed to be a psychic telephoned the police department. She said she had a vision of a child in a culvert. The following day, on Thursday afternoon at approximately three forty-five, that vision was no longer the stuff of some other dimension. Vern Berezay, assistant county roads supervisor, spotted something as he drove along the county road that hugs the interstate near the Turah exit, approximately ten miles east of Missoula. As he approached, in the snow by a culvert, he could see it better. It was the facedown body of a child. It was Siobhan McGuinness, still clothed in her blue jeans and purple corduroy coat.

A heavy snow that morning had covered a trail of blood from the roadside to the culvert. By the time Dusty Deschamps arrived at the grim scene, an army of detectives had plowed their way through the snow, searching for clues, puzzling over this telltale trail of blood. Deschamps was horrified at the city police department's approach. There, hunkered down in the blood-splattered snow, was a detective, churning it up with his hands, sifting for anything that was there. He and the others had waded into the snow cover, contaminating the crime scene, which Deschamps knew should have been cordoned off, handled with the utmost care. But it was too late. The trail of blood was now intermingled with dozens of detectives' footprints. The investigation would have to rely almost completely now on the physical remains of the body.

While it was officially a city case, Deschamps took charge, deciding to send the body to Great Falls, where Montana's only forensic pathologist at the time, Dr. John Pfaff, would perform an autopsy. The girl's body was removed from the scene, fully clothed just as she had been found, and bagged and loaded into the baggage berth of a Greyhound bus. Deschamps drove to Great Falls himself to watch the autopsy. It was his decision to ship the body the 168 miles to Dr. Pfaff's lab, instead of having it done by a local pathologist, who probably would have done the work right at the funeral home. There were real questions about cause of death. Siobhan had been stabbed in the chest and also hit on the head. The trail of blood left unanswered the question of time of death. And then there was the question of sexual assault.

The headline atop the front page of the *Missoulian* the day after she was found read: "Missing Child Is Dead." The story reported that City Police Detective Herb Woolsey surmised that the trail of blood in the snow, plus the absence of footprints, suggested that the body had been put in the culvert and then dragged out by dogs. There was no sign that the dogs had mauled or otherwise disturbed the body, the detective added.

Berezay, who had found the body, also told

police he had driven past the Turah exit on the previous Tuesday night, and remembered seeing a car parked there. It was an older-model Cadillac, vintage 1958 to 1960, and it was green, bearing New York license plates and missing a left rear fender skirt. He also gave a description of the driver—a middle-aged white man wearing dark clothing and a baseball cap. Berezay had reported this to the police the following morning, a Wednesday. His report was taken down, catalogued, and scheduled for systematic checkout, along with dozens of other leads and tips that were swamping the city police and sheriff's deputies in the early hours of the search. A master list of all leads was started, but soon abandoned as the number of entries began to stretch out across three pages, with two columns on each page.

By Thursday night, after Siobhan's body had been found, Berezay's report of the man and the Cadillac had suddenly become very significant. Police conducted a block-by-block grid search of Missoula on Thursday night, but no green Cadillac turned up, and city police chief Ray Roehl was not optimistic that the car would be found two days after Siobhan's disappearance—especially now that the body had been discovered.

And the curly redhead that city police had been looking for turned himself in on Friday night, but he was not linked to the McGuinness case. The fifteen-year-old was booked on the molestation charge, but a week later he would take a polygraph test that would eliminate him as a suspect in the slaying of Siobhan.

By Saturday, County Attorney Deschamps

knew the child had died as a result of two stab wounds to the chest. The autopsy revealed that she had also received two blows to the head of sufficient force to produce unconsciousness, and that she had been sexually assaulted. The two blows Siobhan had received on the head were on the very top of her skull, suggesting they were delivered as she struggled with a captor who towered over her.

While the stab wounds had been fatal, death was not quick. Dr. Pfaff hadn't yet determined the time of death with any degree of accuracy, but eventually he would conclude that Siobhan had lived a minimum of eight hours and a maximum of twelve hours after she had been attacked.

The detectives who were privy to the details in Dr. Pfaff's report dreaded to think that the little girl may not have been moved by dogs at all, but may have crawled into the culvert for protection and then back out again to be by the road where someone might find her. It was within the realm of speculation, for by the time someone did find Siobhan, she was a frozen corpse.

The echo of that tragedy was not missed here in the basement on Tremper Street, and Deschamps knew the *Missoulian* could not report this latest murder without introducing matter of factly in the patchwork of the story that it was the second murder to have occurred in the span of two months. It wouldn't help that the little girl's body was found in the same general vicinity of this second murder, just ten miles east of the Pounds' home. By tomorrow morning, the community's jumbled feelings of horror, sadness, and pity would again be electrified by this new atrocity.

The body of Donna Pounds was not moved for hours. One of the deputies who was initially assigned to door-to-door interviews, Sheriff's Deputy Harry Northey, was now searching for and collecting evidence in the house, focusing on the four bedrooms. He collected the lengths of rope that had been tied to the bedposts in the master bedroom, and in the two girls' bedrooms. In one of the girls' bedrooms, there were rope ties on only three of the bed corners. Northey collected the bedding from Donna's and Harvey's bedroom and combed the rooms clean. It was after 2 A.M. by the time he was finished. Harvey was gone. Deschamps had left. Donna was still down in the basement.

Moe and his chief detective were left in possession of the corpse of a middle-aged, overweight woman, a single .22-caliber bullet retrieved from the corner of the master bedroom, a single rubber glove, sections of ordinary clothesline, a knife from the family's kitchen, a bloodied sanitary napkin, and a single pubic hair found near a large bloodstain on the couple's bedsheet. They theorized that Donna was killed sometime between 1:00 P.M. and 3:30 P.M.

Sheriff Moe began to assimilate the evidence before him, and to keep the lid on as much as possible. He made it abundantly clear what his deputies could say about this one.

"Number one, how many shots were fired into the back of the head. If you were asked," he said, "she was shot. I mean if anybody asked, she was shot. Not how many shots, where she was shot, or anything else.

"And definitely not the placement of the gun. The placement of the gun can be the breaking point of the case. You can have a million suspects, and all of a sudden you have somebody confessing. And you ask, 'Where did you leave the gun?' That could be the critical issue in a confession."

As he left the scene, only Sheriff Moe knew he already had a suspect in mind: the husband.

The next day, the *Missoulian* carried a six-paragraph story about the Pounds murder. It was a fact-filled account, with only one interpretive statement from Dusty Deschamps. He noted that the slaying appeared to have occurred under bizarre circumstances. On Easter Sunday, the headline writers at the *Missoulian* were a little more suggestive of the problem at hand: "Lawmen Have Theory, But Killer Still Free." The story documented the West Riverside neighborhood's fears, quoting residents who said they were loading their guns and keeping them handy. Some were changing their door locks. They nervously speculated to reporter Steve Shirley about whether the killer would revisit West Riverside. Sheriff Moe was on the record, too, saying that there was no reason to believe that the Pounds murder was in any way connected to the slaying of Siobhan McGuinness. But the word on Tremper Street was otherwise. No one who knew Harvey Pounds had any reason to suspect him of such a diabolical crime. There had to be another explanation, and the collective imagination of the anxious neighborhood residents found it soon enough.

During the first few days after the murder, a rumor linking the two killings to a satanic cult swept West Riverside. In no time, it had found its way downtown. What had been viewed by local law enforcement as a classic kidnap–murder case, likely the work of a child molestor, the McGuinness case was now construed by an agonized public as Phase I of a diabolical satanic triad. Whoever the killer was, he had to kill a virgin, a Christian, and a betrayer. It had to be in that order. Supposedly Donna Pounds, a devout Christian, was sacrificed by this devil-worshipping psychopath who was satisfying Phase II. Supposedly a book had been found in a trash can behind the house, detailing the ritual by which she had been murdered. Some contributors to the rumor mill claimed that the ropes found in the house stood for Salem witch-trial nooses. A devil sign of some sort was said to have been painted on a wall in the basement with Donna's own blood, and similar signs were said to have been cut into her body. Somebody told somebody that parts of her body were found in Pattee Canyon, a picturesque recreation area south of Missoula.

Sheriff Moe was aware of the rumors, and he knew, too, that Harvey Pounds was an avid proselytizer against satanism. On a local Christian radio show, his fundamentalist, God-fearing ministry sermonized on the question: Was Satan marshaling his forces for the inevitable confrontation? But Sheriff Moe was not going to believe that some murdering madman following the precepts of a black cult had singled out Harvey's wife because of his radio program.

Still, the public-relations aspect of the case—aimed primarily at defusing the cult theory—was a problem. And Harvey and his church were making things harder, not easier. Perhaps the most ardent contributors to the escalating rumors were the members of Missoula's Christian fundamentalist community, who lumped all forms of the occult, even astrology, in with the powers of darkness. At the Christian Book Store downtown, best-selling books warned of the dangers of the occult, tying America's rising interest in the subject to the apocalyptic prophesies of the Book of Revelation. In some local churches, the congregations were educated on the subject by films such as *Satan on the Loose*, which portrayed scenes of devil worshippers dancing in hypnotic trances that built to a final fusion, a demonic frenzy. The fundamentalists also campaigned against the discussion of psychic phenomena in high school classrooms, and were especially opposed to an English class being taught at Sentinel High School that dealt with literature of the occult. The threat was real, as they saw it. And, indeed, Americans as a whole definitely showed a new popular interest in satanism. The subject was enjoying a resurgence not seen since post-Civil War days.

To the sheriff's department, Harvey was just one more part of the problem. He supposedly was spreading the word about witchcraft involvement in Donna's death. Detectives heard that he described the ropes as being laid out in the form of a peace symbol, which they knew to be untrue. The restraint ropes had been tied to the bedsprings. When Donna was found in the basement, the rope ties on her legs were distinguishable by small, cut tails, suggesting that they had been cut from the bed ropes. There was no other symbolism here. No peace symbol. The ropes were just one practical aspect of a homicidal frenzy.

Harvey's alibi was another problem. No one could corroborate his statement that he was at Yandt's, the clothing store on North Higgins where he worked, all day. He said he had gone upstairs at lunchtime to what was a makeshift mezzanine. There, he said, for a period of about forty-five minutes at midday, he ate his lunch. Nobody in the store could verify where he had been during his lunch break. As far as Sheriff Moe was concerned, three quarters of an hour was enough time for him to have driven home, killed his wife, and returned to the store.

But Harvey had a still bigger problem. The decision to pursue him as the number-one suspect was made after it was learned that the Poundses were having marital difficulties. Authorities were not going so far as to label it an affair, but Harvey, they discovered, was zeroing in on another married woman. She was a member of Harvey's self-styled congregation.

Sheriff's deputies interviewed the woman at her home, and they treaded carefully. She already had experienced enough tragedy in her life. Only two years before, her sixteen-year-old son had committed a brutal murder. He was a student at Hellgate High School and a strapping body culturist who worked out regularly with weights. One night, after refusing a babysitter's command that he go to bed, he flew into a rage and attacked her with the metal rod of his barbell set. He beat her mercilessly about the head, so vigorously that her blood washed through the carpet and the carpet padding and into the plywood subfloor.

By interviewing the supposed other woman, the deputies were trying to establish a connection to Harvey. Because of his religious beliefs, Harvey couldn't have divorced Donna. But deputies never really made much progress. In the final analysis, all they had was conjecture.

Harvey's behavior as a prime suspect in the murder of his wife also baffled Sheriff Moe and his detectives. It seemed out of sync. For one, he wasn't particularly emotional about the consequences he faced, or, for that matter, about the sudden void in his life. He showed concern, but not once did he seem the slightest distraught. Sheriff Moe and Dusty Deschamps expected to see more anguish. In fact, Harvey was so together about matters at hand that he even assisted in the investigation, becoming initially an irritant, then ultimately casting even more suspicion on himself.

In the days following the event, Harvey was finding things in the yard and calling the sheriff's department or coming in to hand over new evidence. The most startling new information he turned up was a second bullet, which he said he found lodged in a dictionary on a bookshelf in one of the daughter's bedrooms. How could they have missed it? The dictionary, Moe and Deschamps and Deputy Northey knew for sure, was found lying on its side on top of other books. Its binding was to the wall, out of sight, but the face of its pages was in clear view, and so was the obvious bullet-entry mark. No, they couldn't have missed it.

When Harvey stated that he had made love to his wife the night before she was killed, he not only canceled the validity of any semen typing that could have been performed, he made himself look more the liar, and Sheriff Moe decided to ask him if he would submit to a polygraph test. True to character, Harvey readily agreed.

The geopolitical ground-zero of Missoula County is the courthouse, located only a block away from Higgins Avenue, the main business drag. It is an impressive turn-of-the-century, Neoclassical structure, anchored on a massive granite layment and crowned with a period favorite, the Italianate bell tower. It genuinely measures up in physical presence to the spiritual stature it presumes. And its muraled terracotta walls, like those in all places of human activity, serve as ready backboards for all the tidbits of news or gossip of the day: There had been statements made about satanic involvement in the Pounds case, and these had been repeated by law enforcement. The echoes off the courthouse walls told it so.

Sheriff Moe was getting tired of all the loose talk, and when he was ready to move with an arrest warrant, he sent one of his deputies to see the county attorney.

When Phil Nobis walked in, Dusty Deschamps knew what was coming. The sheriff had been leveraging heavy pressure on him for days now.

Nobis sat down in the antique oak chair in front of the matching antique desk where Deschamps sat, elbows at rest in front of him, ready.

Then Nobis began to beg.

"Just give me a warrant, Dusty. I can get a confession. Please give me a warrant."

The frustration hung in the air. Both men wanted the case to proceed toward a solution, but the distance between these two country lawmen was far greater than the span across Deschamps's massive desk.

"Look, Dusty . . ."

Deschamps was half-listening. His mind was weighing the other possibility. The other suspect. While the sheriff's department had made little of it so far, the canvassing of the West Riverside neighborhood on the night of the murder had turned up some interesting observations. While one woman said she saw Harvey's Rambler in the driveway sometime during the afternoon, she wasn't really sure when. But a next-door neighbor was certain that she saw Wayne Nance, a neighborhood boy, in the Pounds's backyard that day. Then another neighbor reported that she saw someone who fit Nance's general description in the West Riverside vicinity on that afternoon. Yet another neighbor witnessed a man walking away from the Pounds's house on the day of the murder, carrying a black bag as he walked in a southwesterly direction through the field beyond the house—toward Tamarack Trailer Park, where Wayne Nance lived.

To the neighbors, none of this was unusual. To Sheriff Moe, it was equally hard to believe that an eighteen-year-old high school senior could be capable of a crime of this scale. Besides, Wayne knew the family and was a friend of the son, Kenny, from the time when the Nances and the Poundses were next-door neighbors at Tamarack. When it was revealed that Wayne actually knew where Harvey hid his Luger, knew how to operate it, and had actually fired the weapon once on a lark with Kenny, Sheriff Moe was still unconvinced. What possible motive would Wayne have had?

But Deschamps, who had grown up and lived all his life on the outskirts of East Missoula, where his family had settled four generations ago to farm the land on both sides of the river, knew something else about Wayne. Eleven years older than Wayne, he had preceded Wayne in the same schools and, as a boy, banged around in the same flat by the river, and clambered up the same ravines that lead to the ridge tops. He had a sister in Wayne's class at Sentinel, and because the West Riverside kids who start school together at Bonner Elementary are the same kids who graduate together from Sentinel High, there is little room for anonymity. He knew that Wayne had a reputation as a strange kid. He had heard stories.

"I kinda think it's possibly Nance, Phil," he finally answered.

But Nobis didn't relent.

"Look, Dusty, if you will simply give me a warrant, I know once I arrest Harvey, I can get him to confess. I know I can solve this case," he pleaded once more.

"Phil, I mean, the next-door neighbor saw him in the yard," Deschamps replied. "I know

Ray [Chief of Detectives Froelich] found the guy who kinda looks like Wayne, the guy collecting the scrap, who, I agree, bears some resemblance. And I know Ray thinks the woman saw this guy, not Nance. Maybe that's so. But someone else out there saw someone who sure fit Nance's description, who was in the general vicinity. Someone else saw the guy with the black bag. Plus the kid had been in the house, knew where the gun was, had fired it. Plus he wasn't where he was supposed to be. In school."

He could see Nobis's disappointment.

"I can't give you a warrant. Not at this time. The trouble, Phil, is there's no clear suspect here."

Wayne's alibi was that he had stayed home from school that day to work on a class project. It was true. He had skipped school. They knew that much. The next step was a search warrant.

Chapter 5

A Prime Suspect

The deputies drove out to Tamarack Trailer Park, a spit of a place under a mountain in a no-man's land just a half-mile west of West Riverside. It is more identifiable as being on the eastern outskirts of East Missoula. They were armed with a search warrant, and it was midafternoon as Patrolman Larry Weatherman pulled into the macadam drive and up to the Nance trailer. The focus of the search would be Wayne's room, and he hoped they wouldn't have any trouble.

Just as he expected, Wayne wasn't at home. He was still in school. Wayne's mother, Charlene, answered the door.

"Mrs. Nance," Weatherman said, the words coming out flatly, "we're here to take a look around. If it's okay with you."

"You have a warrant?"

The deputies showed a folded sheet of paper.

And there was no trouble. Charlene pushed on the door, letting them in, and as they walked inside, their eyes scanned the living room.

"We'd like to see Wayne's room," they said.

She understood. By now it was no secret to her that her son had been sighted near the Pounds home and that he had drawn further suspicion by playing hooky on the day of the murder. Besides, there was nothing she could do.

Wayne's room was a mass of organized clutter, and as Weatherman viewed the scene, his first order of business was to look for white clothesline rope.

Though he was low on the totem pole at the sheriff's department, as a rookie Weatherman had been recognized by his superior, Ray Froelich, and by Sheriff Moe as a promising detective. It was Weatherman who had found the rubber glove out behind the Pounds house. With that feather in his cap, he was assigned to be part of a team with Deputy Northey to run down the source of the ropes. They had gone to every hardware store in town, hoping to match the individual color of the rope's inner core. When they finally tracked down a sample of rope with a matching inner core at a hardware store in the Holiday Village Shopping Center on Old U.S. Highway 93, no one there remembered selling any of it.

Harvey Pounds couldn't help them either. He couldn't say whether it was from the house or not. He told them it might have been pulled out from under the kitchen sink. He wasn't sure. He did, however, recall that about a year earlier, he and Donna had noticed that some clothesline was missing from the line out back. It seemed insignificant then, and it gave Weatherman little insight now as he pored through

Wayne's things, looking also for a mate to the surgical glove.

The single glove had been sent to the FBI in Washington, where it was hoped that the stain that appeared to be blood would be identified and typed. At this point, there was no guarantee that it would yield any forensic truth, so the search for the mate had become a high priority.

In a call for help from the community, Sheriff Moe asked residents of the West Riverside area to be on the lookout. Dogs may have carried it away. Photographs of the single glove were put on display at the courthouse. The appeal netted two samples. One, which someone found along South Avenue, was of extreme age. A second, discovered near the Bunkhouse Bridge downtown, wasn't of the same type.

Weatherman was a towering presence in Wayne's small bedroom, standing at the center of the four walls, his eyes piercing methodically through his eyeglasses at all the trappings of a teenage boy's life. There was something odd here, he realized, though he said nothing. Charlene was lingering quietly in the doorway. Weatherman began to understand that the high school senior whose life was before him was more than just a pack rat. There seemed to be a settled order to things. The *Weekly Readers*, which had to be holdovers from Wayne's elementary school days, were neatly stacked up. Why would he keep those?

Then he saw it: a black, grip-type gym bag. It appeared to be of the same type described by one of the eyewitnesses. Weatherman grabbed it to make a closer inspection, and before even pulling open its zipper he could tell there was something inside.

The detective was anxious. He knew that hard physical evidence was crucial. In fact, the whole problem so far was that they had none, no tangible thing to carry into court that would prove, as an unimpeachable witness might, who had murdered Donna Pounds. Wayne's mother showed a heightened nervousness as Weatherman opened the bag. Inside, Weatherman and the other deputies found a variety of .22-caliber bullets and shell casings. They recognized them as the same brand as the ones used in the murder weapon.

"We'll be taking these," he muttered, turning to continue his search.

Then Weatherman found the jackpot. He opened a dresser drawer and his eyes fell on a pair of Wayne's underpants. A large dark-colored stain was visible, and his experienced eye told him it was blood. Anyone could tell, by what was now a rust-colored stain, that they had been washed since they had been soiled, and he hoped that the FBI would be able to determine—if this was human blood on these shorts—whose blood type it was.

"We'll take these, too," he said matter of factly.

Charlene spoke up. She didn't object to the removal of things from Wayne's room. She instead volunteered that she had recently washed that pair of underpants.

Weatherman and the other deputies thanked her and left. They had to get back to the courthouse with this evidence. Weatherman was sure that Sheriff Moe would request a blood sample from Wayne and that this new evidence would demand that Wayne be interviewed.

"You know, I'm the sheriff's number-one suspect," Wayne blurted out.

It didn't register right away to Stan Fullerton, his biology lab partner, what he was talking about. The two of them were surveying the open carcass of *Rana pipiens*, the North American leopard frog. It was dissection time.

"What do you mean?"

"The sheriff's detectives have had me in and interviewed me." Wayne had his classmate's attention now.

Fullerton now knew exactly what he was talking about. The Donna Pounds thing. There was a lot of talk about it in school. Students were upset about it. And Fullerton, in a flash recalling Wayne once telling him about hanging cats on a clothesline and skinning them alive, also knew where Wayne lived—out there by the Poundses.

"Well, you didn't do it, did you?" he asked Wayne point blank.

"No," Wayne answered, head down, picking now at the exposed heart of the frog. "See, one, two three chambers. A three-chambered heart." After a pause, he continued, "They're just bringing in everybody out there and talking to them."

That's how Wayne ran it by Stan Fullerton, a senior with curly hair that he groomed the only way he could. Trouble was, the end result was a lot like a Julius Caesar hairdo—thus the nickname Julius.

Stan thought it a strange thing to mention,

that you were a suspect in a murder. Isn't that something you wouldn't want known? Wayne seemed proud of the fact, brazenly talking about it even though a local radio talk-show host was running a vigilante campaign to find and punish the killer. And a group of leading citizens and officials, who had started the Missoula Reward Fund to help solve the Siobhan McGuinness murder, now was offering a similar thousand-dollar reward for information that would lead to the arrest and conviction of Donna Pounds's killer.

But Stan was not one of Wayne's closest friends, and not the first classmate to have a private audience on the subject of his involvement in what by now was easily the most sensational murder case in modern Missoula's history.

Chapter 6

The Pentagram

The words came out of the dashboard speaker.

"Israel's Premier Golda Meir formally re-signed Thursday before a packed parliament . . ." The voice was colored by the familiar and distinct accent of a foreign correspondent, and the queer echo-chamber distortion of it was not made by Bill Van Canagan's car radio but by its travel across half a world.

Bill was in a hurry. It was one-fifteen in the afternoon and he had a one-thirty class at Sentinel.

"Former United Mine Workers president 'Tony' Boyle has been convicted of three counts of murder in the slaying four years ago of union rival Joseph 'Jock' Yablonski and his wife and daughter," came the next report.

Bill was turning onto South Street now. Traffic was lighter than usual. It was Good Friday. Many of the town's offices and businesses were closed for part of the afternoon to allow time off for church services. The traditional community union services were under way downtown at the Wilma Theater, and it was probably packed. He would definitely make it to class on time.

The next report on the radio was the big local story of the day.

"Missoula County Attorney Dusty Deschamps said a thirty-nine-year-old West Riverside woman was fatally shot in her home last night. She is identified as Donna Pounds. She was found by her husband. Authorities said she had been shot in the back of the head several times with a .22-caliber pistol. The slaying appeared to have occurred under bizarre circumstances."

It was a clipped report, a succinct summary, a dot on the consciousness of the announcer and the listener.

Bill didn't make much of any of this. He had heard about it on the news earlier in the day, and he was in a hurry. As he neared the high school, the weather forecast was being aired: "Continued cool with scattered rain or snow . . . decreasing tonight . . . temperatures will be in the low thirties."

As he parked in the student lot and got out, he grabbed his books and looked up at the clouds overhead, evenly painted gray as if this were a seamless artificial ceiling over a crucible of ice and hard-packed earth. He walked toward the door that led to the gymnasium, realizing that this was his last term at Sentinel High, knowing already that he would be a freshman at Stanford in the fall.

Inside, he immediately spotted his classmate Wayne, sitting at shoulder's height on an indoor, concrete-block ledge that overlooked the parking lot through a large window. Bill stopped to look. Wayne was enthroned there, staring out the window. He seemed to be in a trance, but then he spoke.

"It's been done," Wayne said, somewhat royally, and without looking directly at Bill. Bill was surprised that Wayne interrupted his reverie to even talk. He usually played this kind of thing—the trances, the stares—to the hilt.

"What's been done?" Bill asked, going along with it. Wayne seemed unable to snap out of his suspended state to answer back. Wayne then adjusted his position ever so slightly. "What are you talking about?" Bill played along, once again feeling himself getting tired of this.

"It's been done," he said again, this time turning to show Bill something on his arm. It was a brand mark of some kind, a five-pointed star, and it was still bleeding and appeared in the glimpse of it that Bill got to be slightly infected.

Bill felt a wave of nausea push up from his stomach, rush to his head. It was a sickening moment of truth, arriving as a multiple fusion, a sudden synthesis of all of Wayne's nonsensical threats about killing someone before his nineteenth birthday so he could join some cult, which was part and parcel of all his bullshit black magic stuff and his obsession with what he called the dark side. For Bill, it all merged at once into something that was utterly fantastic but absolutely real. He could see it clear as day. Wayne had killed Donna Pounds. Wayne had just told him so.

Suddenly there came a high-pitched laugh. It was hysterical, eerie, a banshee's cry that filled the stairwell. Wayne seemed crazed, and Bill rocked back on his heels. The second it took to get out of there, he ran up the stairs, bolted through a door, and was running frantically down the hallway, where he collided into Ryan Ushijma, a classmate and close friend.

"Hey, what's the matter?" Ryan wanted to know.

"Ryan. Ryan." Bill was too agitated and panic stricken to talk, and he didn't want Wayne, if he had followed him, to see him talking to Ryan. So Bill dragged Ryan into an empty classroom, where he told him what Wayne had just said.

Wayne was the kind of student whose teachers would remember him, but not for all the same reasons they would remember Bill Van Canagan. Bill was a leader who embodied the very values the faculty was trying to foster. When he adopted a cause, speaking out either for himself or as president of the student body, they listened. He would distinguish himself at college, then go on to earn a law degree. Wayne, on the other hand, would be remembered by his teachers mostly for his art.

Everyone knew Wayne could draw. What Darlene Smith, his senior-year counselor, saw in him was a young man who was clearly unique, who was a strong student with the potential to pursue a career in art, who came from a background that might not be able to either finance or embrace the concept of college. But the latter circumstance hadn't deterred others like him before, and it didn't cancel her recommendation to Wayne. Government monies were available, and they were very easy to get. This would not be a problem.

"The thing I can visualize about Wayne

Nance's face as he was as a senior," she recalls today, "was his very curly red hair, his very steely eyes, very penetrating. I don't mean to say cold, but really they didn't have a lot of warmth to them. His skin was very pale. So he was a lot of contrast of colors, or lack of them. And I remember his fantastic art."

While technically accurate, tight, and crisp, it was also freakish, dark, and violent, character- ized by the ubiquitous bloody swords, daggers, and battle-axes and monsters of all sizes and shapes.

"It was not art that an average kind of indi- vidual would appreciate or enjoy, because it was sort of far-out and a little weird," Smith remembers. "It was certainly negative. It was wild in form. Lots of disorder. Nothing was in order or was peaceful. There was no peace- fulness.

"From the standpoint of another person, it was conflict. Maybe it wasn't conflict to him at all, but when I would look at it, I would react that 'I don't like it. I don't like that disorder and chaos.' "

Wayne joked around with his art, too, always remaining true to a macabre theme. When Stan Fullerton asked him to sign his senior year- book, Wayne made a small drawing of Stan, exaggerating the Caesarlike curly hair and giv- ing Stan a pair of devil horns. There was a knife sticking out of Stan's back, and Wayne signed it: "Make it good, Julius! I really hope you do! Brutus: alias Wayne Nance."

Stan always believed that Wayne was on the cutting edge of the Conan the Barbarian craze. When Wayne showed up in biology class with a five-pointed star branded on his arm, Stan didn't know what it was. It was a little bigger than a baseball, about as big around as a coffee cup. It was infected.

"What's that?" Stan asked.

"I was playing around with my knife, and I put this in my arm."

"What the hell?"

"Well, I didn't mean for it to get infected. I figured it would go away." Wayne begged off.

The mark on his arm was a pentagram, a common occult sign that when inverted, with its two star points at the top, is supposed to symbolize the devil-goat's horns. The three points below represented the Holy Trinity denied.

The story Wayne told Kim Briggeman, another senior who had known Wayne since the third grade at Bonner School, was that he had moulded a piece of wire into this shape, and that he got it red hot and branded himself with it. Briggeman was shocked, but not that shocked. He had ridden the same school bus with Wayne for nine years, since they lived in the same eastern side of the county. In fact, they were neighbors, although they didn't socialize out of school. Kim had seen enough of Wayne to know that Wayne didn't care what other people thought of him. That Wayne was a monster-buff, who drew scary pictures all the time, whether he was on the bus or in study hall.

Wayne loved doo-wap songs from the Fifties. "Blue Moon" was his favorite, which he would break out singing, bridging his bass baritone voice with flying falsettos, in the hallways at Sentinel. But Wayne had a deeper fascination with another lyric, and he was capable of giving flawless recitations. It was Lewis Carroll's non-sensical verse. "The Jabberwocky," a parody of the White Knight's song in which a son gains inspiration from his father to slay a monster, the Jabberwock, with a blade. It was no small feat, but Wayne made it seem easy:

'Twas brilling, and the slithy toves
  Did gyre and gimble in the wabe:
All mimsy were the borogoves,
  And the mome raths outgrabe.

'Beware the Jabberwock, my son!
  The jaws that bite, the claws that catch!
Beware the Jubjub bird, and shun
  The frumious Bandersnatch!'

He took his vorpal sword in hand;
  Long time the manxome foe he sought—
So rested he by the Tumtum tree,
  And stood awhile in thought.

And, as in uffish thought he stood,
  The Jabberwock, with eyes of flame,
Came whiffling through the tulgey wood,
  And burbled as it came.

One, two! One, two! And through and through
  The vorpal blade went snicker-snack!
He left it dead, and with its head
  He went galumphing back.

'And hast though slain the Jabberwock?
  Come to my arms my beamish boy!
O frabjous day! Callooh, Callay!'
  He chortled in his joy.

'Twas brilling, and the slithy toves
    Did gyre and gimble in the wabe:
All mimsy were the borogoves,
    And the mome raths outgrabe.

When Kim first heard Wayne cut loose with this one day at school, he thought Wayne had made it up. Wayne taught Kim the verse, and then they together tried to write something together in *portmanteau* for an English poetry class, but it didn't work out. These two weren't made to write poetry together. Kim ran with a jock clique. Wayne was a loner. Though he had the size and speed to make a linebacker, he didn't fit in with the crowd.

During junior year and for some of his senior year, Wayne wrestled on the junior varsity squad. Duaine Rieker, an underclassman, wrestled with Wayne during practice, since they were both in the 145–155-pound class. Wayne never really objected when Duaine pulled an occasional dirty move on him. On the mat, they got along fine. Otherwise, as was the case with Briggeman, Duaine didn't associate much with Wayne.

After all, Wayne had begun to wear a novelty-store shrunken head, looped around his neck on a rawhide lanyard. It was an ugly charm: a plastic human skull with stringy black artificial hair that was made, through some mundane manufacturing process, to appear as if withered muscle tissue and dried gore still clung to the bone.

And he always carried a knife, which was strictly taboo at school.

Once when he was in a hurry to leave the

locker room, he rushed away in such haste that his knife fell out of his pocket. There it lay, a large jackknife in a leather sheath case.

Wayne was a junior then, and a class of freshmen were just finishing getting dressed when they watched him fly out of the locker room, his knife laying there on the floor.

"Everybody knew it was his. Everybody saw it fall out, and they didn't want to screw with it," recalls Mark Lyman. "They knew who he was."

Inside five minutes, Wayne was back. Everyone pretended not see him pick the knife up and stuff it into his jeans. Then he was gone.

All pointy objects fell within the purview of Wayne's keen interest. Once during senior year he somehow got his hands on a hypodermic syringe, and he bragged to his friends that he would stab somebody with it. Right in the school hallway, he was going to run up behind someone and jab the needle in. One day he did run up behind a student at random, and with one quick thrust, drove the syringe into the boy's leg, laughing hysterically afterward.

Bill Van Canagan knew that Wayne was a card who could deliver a one-liner and get someone's attention, but he also could see beneath the surface of Wayne's laughter, and it made him uneasy. It was a sixth sense that told him to keep his distance. Bill knew that Wayne's intelligence and his flashing temper could be a dangerous combination. And Bill was not comfortable with Wayne's growing, creepy fascination with knives. He brought them to school. He even brought them to work at his after-school job at Taco John's, a fast-food joint across from Sentinel where both Bill and Wayne worked, along with Greg Baringer, another serious-minded, straight-arrow student.

Bill and Greg had gotten their jobs there first, and they didn't really care much when Wayne got a job in the Taco John's kitchen, until a friend of Wayne's started showing up a lot. His name was Dale Nickelson. He was a senior at Sentinel who went by the shortened "Nick."

They had learned to tolerate Wayne's nasty style, even when he pulled out a big, obviously cheap knife fitted with a long serpentine blade, which he said he had given the name of "Hook." But Nickelson was on heavier stuff. His hip pocket was always stuffed with a pint of sloe gin, and he would frequently show up drunk. He was a wild specimen of Bonner–Milltown heritage, a throwback who claimed he was half Indian-blooded, claimed he was a shaman, a medicine man. He also promised he would marry his girlfriend, Barbara, after she became pregnant—and he did, though they were both only seventeen.

One night, Nickelson, swaggering and boisterous, showed up ready to shoot up the place. He physically dragged Bill outside, where with one hand holding his pint of syrupy red liquor and the other brandishing the .22-caliber pistol he often carried around, he aimed and fired at the chicken broaster, pumping its outer tin skin with holes. Then he started shooting the outdoor lights, and then Taco John's plate-glass window.

Greg and Bill had already begun to believe that these two bullies were actually dangerous.

What would they do next? Greg's parents started picking him up after work. It seemed the after-school jobs that they had taken to earn their own spending money had turned into a life-threatening nightmare.

The facts were that Wayne had been boasting that he would kill someone before his nineteenth birthday, which was still months away, and he seemed to take pride in his notoriety as a principal suspect in a murder case. Though most of his friends didn't believe for a minute that Wayne was actually capable of murdering anyone. He was still weird old Wayne, the guy who had bragged since he was in elementary school that he skinned cats alive, though there never was any proof. But some of them had glimpsed enough of his negatively faceted personality to give them a new, ominous respect for him.

Chapter 7

A Sadistic Little Boy

Julie Frame, a second-grader, was fidgeting in her seat when her glasses fell off and banged along the floor of the bus. They landèd somewhere under her seat.

Across the aisle, sitting one row back, her classmate and neighbor, Wayne Nance, a freckled, redhead who was also eight years old, reached down to pick them up.

Julie and Wayne were on the schoolbus, headed home. In the seconds that it took for Julie's glasses to slide across the floor underneath her, she hoped they hadn't been broken, because maybe her mother would be mad. Wayne could see as he lifted them from the floor that they were intact. But Julie's relief just as quickly evaporated. She saw the tease in his eyes.

"Give 'em back," she demanded.

"Sure," said Wayne.

"Give me my glasses!"

Wayne held her plastic frames up in front of him. And somehow Julie knew what he was going to do even before he did it. She watched in anguish as he snapped her glasses in two and threw them back across the aisle, where they landed in two pieces—on her lap and on the floor.

Julie broke into tears, thinking for the rest of the short ride home about what her mother would say, and fitfully trying to protect what was left of her precious broken eyeglasses.

Marge Frame was indeed mad when her daughter walked through the door, sobbing, telling her what Wayne had done, reaching out her hand to show her. Elmer Frame, Julie's father, was angry, too, and he decided it was time to have a talk with the boy's father.

"Aw c'mon, Elmer, boys will be boys," George Nance said, standing in the doorway of the trailer. "What do you expect from an eight-year-old boy?"

Marge and Elmer didn't really know, because they had girls. But they knew there were many other boys Wayne's age at El-Mar Trailer Park, which they owned and operated, and none of them seemed to get into as much trouble as Wayne.

The couple had given their place its name, El-Mar, a shortened combination of both their names, out of the great pride they both took in the park they had started on a bit of unincorporated city land on Missoula's northwestern outskirts. It was the first of its kind in Missoula, because it was designed at the outset as a trailer park. There would be fifty home lots, each abutting a paved street. No other park in Missoula had paved streets yet. Elmer and Marge screened prospective tenants carefully. There was an application process, complete with interview.

When George and Charlene Nance applied
for a place at El-Mar, they were living in a
house at 540 Kent Avenue, on Missoula's
expansion-bound South Side. But their family
was growing and they needed more room.

To Marge and Elmer, George and Charlene
seemed industrious people. They both worked.
George was a trucker, Charlene a waitress.
Their children were attractive. There was no
hesitation. The family passed muster. The
trailer the Nances had purchased was moved
to a rented space on Tina Avenue, the main
artery of the park. They lived on Lot number
8, and in time they would trade trailers with
another family and move to a different lot on
Kathy Jo Street, one of the park's tidy lanes off
Tina Avenue.

Marge watched the redheaded, freckled Wayne
develop into a cute little boy, running around
their planned neighborhood, playing cowboys
and Indians just like all the other children. But
she detected something in Wayne that she
didn't see in the other children, or in her own
girls. It was a mean streak. She presumed it
was because he was a little boy, but it bothered
her. It didn't sit well, either, that Wayne's father always explained away Wayne's misbehav-
ior by saying that it was somehow Julie's fault.
Julie was picking on him, he would say, because her dad owned the park. Julie and her
sisters had gotten on Wayne's case. That was
the explanation.

The Frames were not privy to the goings-on
in the Nance household. While they sometimes
got to know families quite well, there were fifty
families living in El-Mar. Whole towns in Mon-

tana sometimes had fewer people to get to know. And there was no reason to inquire. There was no trouble with the rent. But when the time came for the Nance family to move on, Marge and Elmer weren't sorry to see them go. It wasn't because of anything to do with George and Charlene. It was because of Wayne. It was something he once had done. Elmer had witnessed it.

It was a bone-chilling winter day. The sky was crystal clear, a light sapphire blue overhead that turned a shade darker, almost cobalt, as it reached to the horizon. Elmer was outside, performing one of the many chores that had to be done to keep everything ship shape, which was just the way he liked it.

Out of the corner of his eye he saw Wayne coming, though Wayne didn't see him.

The boy seemed to be more or less aimlessly making his way down the street, and he was about to pass by the incinerator, a cone-shaped affair with a hinged door near the top of the firebox, where everyone burned their trash. The box was pretty well stoked when Elmer left it, and he hadn't bothered to close the door. He knew that the family of kittens that scampered around his feet would soon climb up to the makeshift shelf that was created by leaving the door open, and that there they would huddle against the cold, staying warm by the blazing fire.

Elmer saw Wayne stop to take a look. The kittens were curled up, just as Elmer knew they would be. In the same moment that Elmer felt a chill, as he wondered what Wayne was thinking, his mind was horrified. The boy walked over to the firebox. Elmer had no time to shout at him. In the blink of an eye, Wayne lifted the door on its hinge, and the kittens slid down into the fire.

Elmer wasn't sure whether to tell his wife about it, but he did.

"Maybe boys do that," she said, her tone resigned. She was trying to understand. "But maybe he has a sadistic streak."

It was difficult for the hard-working, value-driven Frames to understand. After all, weren't George and Charlene hard working, clean people, who just like everyone else were trying to scratch together a life in these promising times? These heady Eisenhower years.

In the 1950s, even Hollywood had come to Missoula to make a film that would romanticize the place. *Timberjack*, a story about life in America's logger camps, starred Sterling Hayden, Vera Ralston, Hoagy Carmichael, and Chill Wills. And on Missoula's main thoroughfare, in the fall of 1955, the making of this movie, which portrays a son's search for his father's killer, was the talk of the town. While the movie entertained a nation at large that ate up its gee-whiz true grit, it also served to commemorate a historical *fait accompli* that Montanans were well aware of. These were boom times. Montana's vast stands of Douglas fir, spruce, and Ponderosa pine had steadily become more and more important to a building boom and had provided a growing source of employment. By 1955, the lumber industry was at its peak. The number of men working in the woods and in the mills would decline as the decade closed out, but the foundation had been laid for a diversified wood products industry. Big money was once again discovering Montana, just as the rich copper kings had done before.

In the midst of this emerging prosperity, on October 18, 1955, Wayne Nathan Nance was born. To Wayne's parents, this was the big event. George had a son. They had been married nearly three years earlier, on December 28, 1952, in a small ceremony at the North Side home of Charlene's parents, Nathan and Marva Mackie. Charlene Mae Mackie was a child bride. She was sixteen. George Edwin Nance was twenty-four. The announcement of their marriage appeared in the society pages of the *Missoulian*, right along with the photographs and marriage notices of other high-school girls who had recently been betrothed. These were simpler times. Eisenhower would soon be sworn in as president, setting the economic pace for the decade.

Eight and one-half months after their marriage day, on September 10, 1953, a first child, Desiree, was born. Charlene was now seventeen. When Wayne was born, almost two years later, his then nineteen-year-old mother gave him her father's Christian name as a middle name. On September 9, 1960, a second boy, William, was born. On November 15, 1962, a second daughter, Veta, arrived.

By the time George and Charlene had moved their family from El-Mar, in the early years of the new decade, it would be a significant step. The move took them beyond the immediate environs of Missoula, out beyond Hellgate Canyon, past East Missoula, and into the unincorporated tracts of the county. There, in another trailer park, Tamarack Court, named after a tree, the larch, they would make their new home. The neighborhood was called Pine Grove, and Tamarack Court was a shade downscale from El-Mar. It was located nearer to the roadside and its orientation was to the east, toward West Riverside, Milltown, and Bonner, home to mostly blue-collar families, many of whom also lived in mobile homes but who aspired to live in the sunny suburb of Missoula's South Side.

George continued to work as a trucker. Charlene still worked as a waitress. The family's life seemed as if it had unfolded from the pages of a dime novel. The teenage bride. The first child arriving before the requisite nine months had elapsed. The husband, a hulking brute, a truck driver. The wife, who sometimes drank a little too much, a hard-working waitress. More children. No permanent roots. All the routine ups and downs of a marriage not made of money. Charlene yelled a lot at the kids, especially at Wayne, who was always getting into trouble. She would complain to her coworkers in the kitchen at Ming's Restaurant downtown, as she threw her hands up in despair, that she ought to put him in reform school.

But Wayne always redeemed himself. Despite all his run-ins, he was a good student. His grade-school teachers recognized right away that he was academically inclined. And because he got good grades, he held a certain sway over his classmates. He read a lot. He knew things. He knew more than anyone else did about sex. Whenever anyone had a question on that taboo subject, Wayne seemed to know the answer.

Wayne was physically precocious, too. Though he was of average size and weight, by the time he reached the eighth grade his biceps were as big around as cantaloupes. He was stronger than his overall appearance would suggest, but he lacked athletic finesse to match his strength and he wasn't much of a team player. Wayne would often throw a basketball too hard at close range for a teammate to catch. But he was a fleet runner and he definitely had a hard head. Once, when he accidentally flipped head over heels on his bicycle, vaulting over the handlebar and landing smack on his head, he skidded across the pavement on his skull. But he just rolled over, stood up, and got right back on the bike. His buddies were amazed one more time.

Most of all, he was provocative. At show-and-tell, he often brought in snakes. When his younger brother Bill had friends over on Saturday afternoons to watch creature films, which they enhanced by pulling the curtains in the living room to make the room darker, Wayne invariably pulled a stunt. Often he would wait for the right moment, and then leap through the door, hoping to spook everyone a little bit more.

Charlene's big problem was Wayne's temper. From the early grades on, he was a belligerant troublemaker, and she didn't know how to stop him. Her bright, studious, oldest son was prone to fistfights, ready to swing at the slightest queer sidelong look. George didn't help the situation by laying the fault on the outside world, as he did the time Wayne got kicked off the bus for fighting.

When Leo Musberger, the principal of Bonner Elementary School, where Wayne had been enrolled the year before as a third grader, called George to tell him that his son was going to have to find some other way to get to school, because he was being temporarily suspended from the bus for fighting, George blew his stack.

"What authority do you have to kick my son off the bus?" the father blasted back.

"I'm sorry, Mr. Nance, but your son has caused trouble more than once on the bus. He'll have to get to school some other way for a while."

"Well, I'm gonna put him on that bus myself. Tomorrow morning. And you better be on that bus yourself if you wanna do anything about it. Just try to stop me," George warned, hanging up the phone.

Musberger had been told about the latest fight on the bus by the driver, George Otto, who was also the school's janitor. In both these jobs, he had contact with Wayne throughout the day, and he, too, had lost control of this incorrigible troublemaker. He was rough and mean to the other kids. Otto said he couldn't manage him on the bus anymore. After Musberger heard George's antagonistic challenge, he decided to ask the members of the school board whether he should ride the bus himself to enforce the sanction.

On their advice, Musberger decided not to ride with Otto the next day, and when the bus pulled up at the Tamarack stop the next morning, there they were—George and his ten-year-old son Wayne, standing in the snow. George peered through the windows, looking for Musberger.

"Is he in there?" he called up to Otto.

"Nope," answered the driver, one hand on the wheel, the other at the ready on the door guide.

A nervous moment passed, and George thought the better of it. He turned to Wayne and signaled that it was over. The bus pulled away, and George put Wayne in his pickup and drove him to school.

But whatever lesson Musberger hoped to give Wayne was soon revealed to be a lesson unlearned. Later, as Wayne swaggered past Otto in the hallway, Wayne stopped and looked him right in the eye.

"My dad told me, you gotta get them before they get you," the little boy said, turning to walk away, speaking now over his shoulder. "That's my motto."

Chapter 8

A Father's Exit

It was shortly after nine in the evening as Howard Brein began tabulating the day's receipts at the Super Save Store, where he was assistant manager. He was alone in the store and eager to get home.

He looked up as a customer, a man, entered the store, then turned his focus back to the adding machine. Brein had to get the money bag ready for Mike, the armored-car driver who would be pulling up any minute, because Mike Cantrell was always on time.

For a second, Brein looked over to see if the customer, a largish middle-aged man, needed help. But it didn't seem so. The man was hovering over the salt blocks by the windows up front. Brein glanced back at the pile of receipts. He didn't think twice about this last-minute customer until he saw the gun, which had been suddenly shoved in his face.

The date was December 14, 1968, a Friday night, and George Nance needed money. George told Brein to do as he said. He wanted the money, which Brein had already stuffed in a gray canvas bag for pickup.

89

But when Brein handed it over, supposing that would be the end of it, that this burly, menacing robber would be gone, he watched the man pull a roll of white adhesive tape from a jacket pocket. George then told Brein he was going to tape his hands and lead him to the back of the store. Brein complied, and after they got to the rear of the store, George then whipped him about the head with his pistol.

The assistant manager was in a daze as he watched his attacker make for the front of the store. He heard a loud crash. It was the sound of plate glass being smashed. On his way out, George decided to chuck one of the salt blocks through the window, and just as he was making his way through the door, the armored pickup arrived.

In the same second he pulled to a stop, Cantrell saw the smashed glass window and noticed a large man inside, who was racing for the back of the store. He radioed for help.

While George holed up inside with his beaten captive, Howard Brein, a small army of law-enforcement personnel laid seige around the store. Cantrell had gotten help. First came sheriff's deputies, then city police. Highway patrol officers arrived, and members of the four-by-four patrol. City firemen responded, too. The Super Save place was surrounded as George sought somewhere to hide. It wasn't going to be a shoot-out, because George wasn't ready for that. So he wiggled himself into a corner, where he waited, crunched down out of view, for the dogs to find him.

Brein was rescued and taken to Community Hospital, where he was treated for multiple lacerations to the head. George was disarmed, handcuffed, and escorted to a police cruiser that would take him directly to jail. The massive police commotion surrounding what turned out to be an assault and bungled robbery attempt didn't escape the attention of the night editors at the *Missoulian*. So the story of the robbery, and a two-column photograph of a handcuffed George, ran the next morning. It was front-page news, and in a quirk of juxtaposition, the story and picture appeared adjacent to a yule-tide cartoon, a reminder of the upcoming holiday. It showed Snoopy advising: "Cheer up! You've got 9 big shopping days left."

Nance was released on bond. Five months later, then forty years old, he was sentenced by District Judge E. Gardner Brownlee after he pleaded guilty to the felony charge of robbery. Prior to the sentencing, Nance was called to the witness stand, where he testified that he had learned his lesson. Other character witnesses asked that he be given a chance to lead a productive life in the community. Their bidding didn't sway Judge Brownlee, who sentenced George Nance to five years in Montana State Prison at Deer Lodge. Wayne, his 13-year-old son, was nearing completion of the seventh grade.

The teachers at Bonner School felt there was no reason to doubt that Wayne, despite the family's current circumstances, would still have a bright future. They knew Wayne possessed an above-average intelligence and a clear ability to focus on the work. They expected these assets would serve him well in the future when he would become a freshman at Sentinel High School. Perhaps the puzzling parts of Wayne's personality—the loner side of him, the fomenter of trouble—would fade as he grew into manhood, to be replaced with the kind of gregarious and harmonious character that would seem to match the appeal of his fresh face framed in that curly red hair. He was a beguiler, they knew, and they could only hope, as teachers are wont, that he was a good boy, deep down.

They were shocked and disturbed by what Wayne's father had done but they still looked forward to the days when Wayne would outgrow his combative ways, even as they tried to corral him in the very final days of grammar school. Eleven days before graduation, after his father had already returned home—paroled after serving less than a year of his five-year term— Wayne vowed to beat up a certain boy every day until school was over. There would be eleven beatings in eleven days. Wayne was doing this because he himself had gotten into trouble over another, different fight. He had picked this poor kid as a random target to vent his anger. It was pretty sophisticated. And so was his decision to suspend the punishment. After two days and two pummelings, Wayne just stopped.

The year was 1970. A new decade was born, and the conventions of the times were being scrutinized, challenged, or thrown out the window by a youth culture that seemed to be taking over. Eisenhower was now dead, having taken with him the mantle of most popular president during a peaceful, hypnotic decade. Now the message of the Sixties decade was coming to a head. Hundreds of thousands of Americans protested in cities across America against the war in Vietnam. Wrongs were being righted. Young America, like lemmings on the march, wanted to get at the truth. For educators, the challenge in the early years of the Seventies became primarily one of negotiating student viewpoints. The taut fabric of tradition was being stretched to new and different lengths, and the hard-jaw approach was out. Principals and teachers had to become masterful listeners.

By 1974, the Sentinel High School student body that Wayne had become a part of represented the largest single population of teenagers in all of Missoula County. The anti-ROTC protests at the University, which was only blocks away, were not ignored by the high school students. Neither were the sit-ins. The liberal college campus newspaper was distributed daily at Sentinel's doorstep, chronicling an explosive unrest, reporting on the latest sit-in, or maybe just announcing the plans for an upcoming concert. Back then, if Sentinel students weren't found at Sentinel, they could just as well be at the University, participating. Or mellowed out somewhere, with a joint and some Chicago, or Steely Dan. Daydreaming about a Yes concert. Or seeing Santana or the Eagles live. Or listening to Utopia's new album.

Sentinel was so bulging at the seams—there were two thousand students in a building that held only eleven hundred at one time—that the students could pretty much come and go as they pleased. The school day was segmented into nine periods, and the students had to attend at least four of them. They could realistically be anywhere else for the other five class periods of the day.

The open, collegelike atmosphere that was mandated by the overpopulation served to precipitate a kind of early maturity among some of the students. As they learned to fend for themselves, some still could rely on the traditional values instilled in them by their parents. But those students who weren't so well equipped found other ways to spend their free time and deal with their responsibilities, and their parents and their teachers just had to cope. They had no choice. Weren't they already hostage, in a sense, to a climate of public opinion that had been irreversably altered by Watergate, by the Vietnam war, by runaway inflation, and by one energy crisis after another?

These new facts of life lent credence, if merely by default, to a blander, more tolerant approach. If Wayne's high school teachers didn't like his artwork, they certainly would tolerate it. His classmates didn't swallow his fantasies, but they didn't question for a minute his right to experiment with the unconventional. Had it been twenty years earlier, someone might have noticed and been alarmed that such a bright young student was so obsessively distracted by a need to escape.

Starting in their junior year at Sentinel, Wayne's classmates had noticed that he seemed to be undergoing a change, and it was for the worse. Though he had always been from the other side of prosperity, compared to most of his classmates, who were for the most part the children of middle-class families living in Missoula's suburban South End, Wayne still competed with the best and brightest in his class. And because of the academic skills he possessed, he shared the same classes. He took the difficult, college-prep courses. He maintained a better than 3.0 grade-point average. He was focused and interested in his studies. But he was also getting to be a bore with all his yakking about black magic and dark spirits and devils and the dark side.

There were many times, when huddled around one of the square lab tables in the back of the chemistry classroom, Bill and Ryan listened as Wayne spun another of his medieval tales of sorcery. It was always fascinating, until the end, when Wayne began to unveil the dark side's predictable victory. Then it seemed trite, and it became somewhat tiring.

"You're full of shit, Wayne," was Bill's frequent response to one of Wayne's oratories.

Bill, Greg and Ryan, along with Eric Visser, Sara Shannon, and John Wagner, as a group of close friends who each knew Wayne, found their friendly gatherings directed into a discussion about Wayne on many occasions. About his witchcraft obsession. What they should do about it, or not do. But it wasn't until senior year, when Wayne's thing with the occult began to escalate, that their somewhat idle concern turned to fear.

"I had this dream," Wayne told Bill one day. "I was visited by a spiritual entity. It was a queen."

Bill tried not to roll his eyes.

"She was from the dark side," Wayne continued, "and she told me, gave me specific instruction on how to become, how I could become a warlock.

"This was a gift from the queen." He showed Bill a large star-shaped, gold-colored medallion he wore around his neck. "I obtained it on instruction from the queen."

"This is stupid, Wayne," Bill hissed back.

"No, I have been ordained a third-degree witch. My goal is to become a warlock. I am moving up the ranks. I'm in a coven."

Not being a student of the medieval origins of witchcraft, or Wicca, Bill didn't know that anyone who aspires to practice the craft also presumes a vow of silence on the subject. The closed-mouth tradition is carried on today. There is such a thing as a third-degree witch in the hierarchy of modern-day covens. It is the highest station and is usually reserved for the high priest or high priestess.

Wayne was familiar with the lingo, the symbolism, and the rituals, and he indulged his fancy on the high holy day of witchcraft, Halloween, by declaring it to be his birthday, which was actually on October 18. But Wayne, it was clear to his friends anyway, was just dabbling, borrowing whatever happened to suit the needs of the goofy mosaic of his maturing personality. Like his new interest in the Vikings.

While he learned about these Scandinavian shipbuilders and pirates in a medieval history class at Sentinel, he also carried out a leap of imagination. In the fall of his senior year, he and his friend Nick Nickelson executed a make-believe burial at sea by torching some floats from Sentinel's homecoming celebration. After the parade, the floats were parked in the fairground lot across from Taco John's. Wayne and Nick bragged to Bill and Greg about how they had pretended they were Vikings and had conducted, according to Norse legend, a burial at sea.

Bill and Greg shrugged in disbelief, until they read about it in the paper, which reported on the minor fire damage to the flotilla.

Viking religion was mythological. Their pagan raids, which gave them the unmerciful and marauding image that history would largely remember, was what intrigued Wayne the most. The snarling, carved dragons that the Vikings placed on the prows of their ships as totems of mythical sea monsters fit the milieu of his own gory, fantastic art. Wayne would disclose to anyone who inquired that he followed Odin, the supreme, one-eyed Viking god of battle, magic, inspiration, and the dead.

But he also took a sharp interest in satanism and all matters of the occult, which was not out of the ordinary among students at Missoula's two high schools, Hellgate and Sentinel, at the time. Along with their textbooks, many students toted paperback copies of *The Exorcist*. After school, they huddled with Ouija boards and Tarot cards, and talked of witchcraft and magic spells. At night, they would venture up Pattee Canyon in search of spooks.

The publication in 1969 of Anton LaVey's *The Satanic Bible* had transformed the author, a onetime lion tamer in the circus and lecturer on dark esoterica, into a veritable media celebrity. His book sold more than five hundred thousand copies. For those who followed Satan, it was the gospel. Initiates were encouraged to receive a mark, a permanent scar or tattoo—a pentagram would be particularly apt.

Chapter 9

The Great Escape

Ronald MacDonald had been to the sheriff's department. He knew exactly why Wayne was being asked to consider taking a lie-detector test. Now, as he sat behind the desk in his spartan law office, he was taking a closer look at the subject himself, who sat across from him. Wayne was cool and matter of fact.

"Will you be my lawyer?" Wayne wanted to know.

"Well, Wayne, let's talk about that," MacDonald began.

It was the third time Wayne had visited MacDonald's office since the Pounds murder. First Wayne had called up to make an appointment. He came alone and described briefly to MacDonald that he was being asked to take a lie-detector test. Wayne hadn't come to him on a referral from another attorney, and MacDonald wasn't surprised that Wayne had picked him out of the phone book. In his three short years out of law school, MacDonald had made somewhat of a name for himself trying criminal cases. In the first year he tackled what later turned out to be the number-two story in the state for that year. The following year, he succeeded in getting some evidence suppressed in a major case, which landed him more publicity—a lot more than anyone would expect for someone who had been practicing law for such a short time.

"As I told you when you came in the first time," MacDonald continued, "I wanted to look into this a little, to find out exactly why they want you to take a lie-detector test."

At that first meeting, Wayne told the lawyer that he was a neighbor and friend of the Pounds family. He said that he knew Donna Pounds and was a friend of her son, Kenny. He said that he had been in the Pounds home many times and that he had been in the neighborhood the day she was killed.

MacDonald theorized to himself that the sheriff's department wouldn't move to a lie-detector test until it had pretty much garnered whatever physical evidence it could. He initially concluded that Wayne must be a collateral witness whom the sheriff fully expected to exclude as a potential defendant via a routine polygraph test.

MacDonald was intrigued by the fact that Wayne had come by himself. Where were his parents? But his principal observations of Wayne lingered elsewhere: Wayne seemed so disconnected from any concern that he could be a prime suspect in such a violent murder, so oblique to his circumstance. Wayne's nonchalance tracked with MacDonald's first response that it wasn't a serious matter. The kid obviously wasn't sweating it.

After Wayne raised the subject of satanism,

telling MacDonald that it was something in which he took an academic interest, displaying a shade of agitation and indignation that his study of the subject had made him a target of the investigation, MacDonald nodded. The lawyer was aware of what he viewed as the dubious speculation around town that there was a satanic link to Donna Pounds's murder.

"Could you bring me some materials to look over?" he asked Wayne.

"Sure."

Later, when Wayne dropped off a handful of books and pamphlets, MacDonald thanked him and told him he still hadn't found time to inquire further at the sheriff's department, but that he would by their next meeting, which was then scheduled. It was during this second visit that MacDonald got his first shocking view of Wayne's pentagram tattoo. The first time he had seen Wayne, a green Army fatigue jacket and long-sleeved flannel shirt covered Wayne's forearm. This time, Wayne, in a short-sleeved shirt, showed off the pentagram.

By now MacDonald was beginning to see Wayne as one of the typically disenfranchised teenagers who could be found on every street corner in America during the spring of 1974. The Army fatigue jacket, the untucked shirt draped over a pair of well-worn Levi's, and the cloddy boots were all of a type. Wayne was coming from a counterculture position, a boy dressed in the garb of a dirthead to certify his antithesis position, to show that he was not a belonger. MacDonald presumed that Wayne had adopted the satanic interest as a sort of conversational currency, which could be used to sustain interpersonal relationships. And it was something that people were, at the time, interested in.

As a potential case, this one had what lawyers call largesse. It was big enough to pose significant downside risk for any defending attorney. But Ronald MacDonald wasn't afraid of that. He wasn't afraid of the scale of this one, because much of the energy in his practice in the early years of the Seventies was directed at the presumption of innocence. Didn't the high school kid who had called and made an appointment in fact personify the Everyman around whom all of America's legal structure is built? Moreover, he was privy, as a frequenter of the courthouse corridors, to Sheriff Moe's predisposition to arrest Harvey Pounds for the murder of his wife.

But MacDonald decided not to represent Wayne. The decision was made during his visit to the sheriff's department, where he met with deputies who were working on the case. Sheriff's Deputy Weatherman had shown MacDonald the crime-scene photographs. Then Weatherman explained what evidence they had collected in Wayne's room: the black bag, the .22 shells, the bloodstained but now-washed underpants. Then he learned that Wayne was also under some suspicion in the murder of Siobhan McGuinness, and that's what stopped MacDonald. He knew the little girl's mother, and he had been instrumental in helping the family cope with funeral arrangements after the tragedy. There was no way he would represent anyone who might be remotely connected to that hideous crime. It was strictly personal.

By the time Wayne walked up the two flights of stairs to MacDonald's office on Higgins Avenue, coming for his third meeting, the decision had been made. MacDonald would meet with him today, but he would not represent him. The occult books Wayne had dropped off rested on the windowsill, staring out into an alleyway. MacDonald made a mental note to remind Wayne to take them when he left.

After Wayne came through the door and sat down, MacDonald realized again that this eighteen-year-old suspect in a murder case was here without his parents, and it surprised him once more, especially knowing now what he hadn't known before. This was not a collateral witness. Wayne was a prime suspect.

In the days since MacDonald had last seen Wayne, the figure in the work boots and the fatigue jacket seemed to be emerging from a chrysalis stage, developing the prowess of a professional crisis manager. It was unprecedented in MacDonald's short but active career to see anyone deal with this kind of criminal dilemma the way Wayne did. Ninety-nine out of a hundred times, the client wants to hand the matter over, go home, and not have to deal with it. But not Wayne. Instead, he was calling the shots.

It was as if Wayne were conducting himself as a businessman might, coming to MacDonald with a secretive deal, which he didn't want anybody to know about. Wayne seemed to want to isolate certain aspects of the deal. He was letting MacDonald know at the front end that the attorney's role was limited.

There was no reference to parental involvement. There was no mention of any other attorney. Wayne was here to collect data. He had come to someone whom he had heard would know something about evidence testing and lie-detector tests, and it was essential to pick this expert's brain. He was going to assimilate whatever he gleaned on his own. He was going to make his decisions on his own, and he certainly wasn't handing MacDonald any of the variables that were on the surface—in terms of how he might handle it.

MacDonald asked him whether he had bought any rope. He asked him questions about his interest in satanism, and in particular about the pentagram mark on his arm. But Wayne directed the conversation elsewhere. Without spelling anything out in response to MacDonald's question about the rope, Wayne left the attorney with the impression that the rope issue wouldn't lead anywhere. He seemed confident of that. And the pentagram, which he talked about extensively, was equally meaningless. The satanism stuff, MacDonald should understand, was something that interested him. He was studying occult literature in an English class at school. The Pentagram was something he carved into his arm to goof on his friends. It wasn't something to be taken too seriously. What Wayne wanted to know about was the lie-detector test.

In MacDonald's experience with polygraph tests, he had come to observe among those who claim innocence at the outset a certain patterned reaction when it is suggested they consider taking such a test. The reaction is frequently of one vein, and it is immediate: "Well,

I know a lot about that and I'm not going to do that, because all these things are wrong with them and they make mistakes and . . ." Not Wayne.

He wanted to know if it could be beaten. Does it sometimes misread? Do drugs or alcohol affect it?

He asked MacDonald for an exact description of how it worked. He wanted to know what MacDonald thought of the operators. He wanted further to know whether the proficiency of the operator had something to do with the validity of the results.

MacDonald was struck by the marmoreal whiteness of Wayne's skin, the shock of thick curly red hair, and the combination they made with his darting, interrogative, and anticipatory eyes, flashing through gold wire-framed glasses, always avoiding contact. Wayne was manifestly cerebral as he quizzed MacDonald, betraying no body language that might signify what it was he was trying to get at, that might suggest some sense of familiarity, some bit of human frailty. To MacDonald, it was as if Wayne were looking off in the distance at an imaginary chalkboard on which he had written the components of this case. And instead of sitting down to start at the foundation of this problem, and proceeding to comprehend its entirety step by step, MacDonald could see that Wayne was impatient about getting to the point. He could see that his mind was taking things that he had already exposed himself to and adding and subtracting what MacDonald was saying, always having a conclusion right on the tip of his tongue, a running subtotal of his status. Donna

Pounds was a nonentity. They weren't even dealing with death in the abstract. She had no persona, even though he knew her. *Not even a poor Mrs. Pounds*, MacDonald thought to himself.

The impression Wayne left was that if he were involved in this murder, he alone was going to take care of it. He didn't really need help from anybody. For now, matters were more or less in his control. He was being asked to take a lie-detector test. He could decide whether or not he was going to do it. He could postpone making that decision, but he also felt pretty comfortable that the sheriff's department hadn't developed anything that could get to him. He was confident he was going to be all right. As long as he stayed on his toes.

If he had committed Donna Pounds's murder, MacDonald was certain that Wayne was not about to tell anyone about it. He wasn't going to trust anyone, including a lawyer, and MacDonald was also certain he wasn't going to be that man. As he sat there, answering Wayne's questions, trying to divine Wayne's approach from the scorecard he couldn't see, MacDonald also realized that if this were himself at age eighteen, there would have been no way that he could have accomplished what Wayne was doing here.

In the end, MacDonald told Wayne that he wouldn't be his attorney.

"The circumstances are very serious," he advised him. "You shouldn't do anything without an attorney."

As Wayne got up to leave, MacDonald recalled how precise Weatherman had been in stating why they thought he was involved, and the gruesome photographs flashed across his mind. There was something seriously wrong with this kid, he thought, because guilty or innocent, he knows he's a prime suspect and he's unaffected by it. Why, he wondered, if he's being suspected in the murder of a woman, the mother of his friend? For it to turn on him in this way, wouldn't there be some indignation, some defensiveness, some demand that he not be treated this way?

Wayne didn't seem to mind.

Across MacDonald's desk, resting on the windowsill, were the books that Wayne had left.

In the week that followed Easter Sunday, Bill Van Canagan and Greg Baringer were back at school and still working alongside Wayne at Taco John's. The situation was fast becoming intolerable. Wayne seemed more and more out of control. He repeatedly threatened Bill with little menacing looks or remarks that were packed with double meaning. Bill might have shrugged it off, except that he knew Wayne was toying with him, playing off a fear that had been implanted on Good Friday.

For Greg, it was actually worse. Wayne had threatened to kill him. There was no reason given. It was just going to be. The two of them, Bill and Greg, and their friends, began to weigh what they knew about the murder of Donna Pounds, and about the murder of Siobhan McGuinness, in terms of the timing of Wayne's advancement in the cult, in terms of the fact that they knew that Nick Nickelson, a self-proclaimed shaman who packed a pistol and got shitfaced a lot, also just happened to drive an old Cadillac, which was the same kind of car that had been sighted at the scene of the McGuinness murder. The city police had turned Missoula upside down looking for such a car. Had they somehow missed Nickelson's Cadillac? Because he didn't live within the city limits, but out east of Missoula in the county.

Telling Wayne's parents would be a waste of time, they knew. Before any of them had gotten driver's licenses, Ryan Ushijma used to go to the movies with Wayne. Wayne's father, George, would drive them. George always made Ryan walk in front of him—so Ryan couldn't stab him in the back, he would say. It was a bigoted reference to Ryan's Japanese heritage. It wasn't funny. The plain oddity of it, however George may have meant it to be, registered indelibly on Ryan's mind, and it was unsettling.

Just as unsettling as it was to think that Wayne, with his Good Friday pronouncement, had cryptically taken Bill into his confidence, thus masterminding Bill's inescapable role as the one who might squeal, the one who could become the betrayer, the next sacrificial lamb. Was it an apocalyptic message of death, veiled by Wayne's weirdness? Bill and Ryan and their friends didn't have to catalogue the kinds of things Wayne did: They were all of a kind. His synthetic persona had become one-dimensional. He was the antihero. He was untouchable. And he killed Donna Pounds. They had to tell the principal, and Bill would do it.

Don Harbaugh looked over his horn-rimmed glasses at Bill Van Canagan, seated opposite him in the principal's office. Casting a dubious glance at Bill, Harbaugh was the affable, activist principal of Sentinel. He was quite at home in the superheated atmosphere of the Sentinel volcano, whose daily eruptions regularly spewed emotionally charged teenage debris in all directions. Today, he wasn't being any more circumspect than usual.

"There's a kid in our school who says he killed Donna Pounds," Bill blurted out.

Harbaugh's pulse quickened. Of course, he knew of the murder. In fact, he already had had some inquiries from the sheriff's department about Wayne. He had cooperated with the deputies who wanted to know whether Wayne was in school on a given day. He also tried to get some sense from them whether Wayne was a viable suspect, but he wasn't ready for this.

"What do you mean, Bill? I mean . . ."

"Wayne Nance is telling me he killed her," Bill barked, his voice rising above conversation level. He could see the glint of disbelief in the principal's eyes.

Harbaugh had been around students all his life and was familiar with teenage emotional highs and lows and with their tendency to sensationalize. But not Bill Van Canagan. Harbaugh had been Bill's adviser all year. He knew him well. Here was the president of the student body. This was not the kind of student one would dismiss out of hand.

"Everybody's scared of this. And he'll kill me," Bill continued.

Harbaugh quizzed him thoroughly. What he said. Where he said it. Wasn't he just pulling

Bill's chain? Did Bill believe it to be true? Who knows about it? By the time they had run out of more things to discuss, Harbaugh leaned into his desk, placing one hand on the phone.

"Bill, you've got to talk to the police."

Bill considered it, but he didn't pick up the phone. He knew the price of betrayal. Plus, Harbaugh seemed less than wholeheartedly receptive to what he had just told him. So how much would he back him up?

The meeting was over.

The next day, Harbaugh made sure he knew as much about Wayne Nance as he could. He talked frequently to the sheriff's department. He talked to Eric Visser, a student who associated with Bill and his friends. He talked to other teachers and counselors. Always he suspended judgment.

"We have a duty to protect the student body as a whole," he told his colleagues, "but we also have a duty to protect the individual student." Harbaugh was far from convinced that there was anything to the story. Everybody knew there was lots of stories going around. There was no doubt in Harbaugh's mind that Wayne had told other students that he was involved in witchcraft, that he aspired to be a warlock. But Wayne was regularly in class, where he was supposed to be. He was not a model student, but he was not a troublemaker.

After the sheriff's department advised him that there was more than one suspect, but that some people in the department thought Wayne could have done it, Harbaugh's antennae sprang to full attention. As it got into May and the Class of 1974 was beginning to see graduation day coming just around the corner, Harbaugh got another call from sheriff's deputies. They wanted permission to excuse Wayne from school so he could make the 230-mile round trip to Kalispell, where he would take a lie-detector test.

Harbaugh summoned Wayne into his office.

"They've called, Wayne," Harbaugh said, "and they want to take you out of school. Here's what's going on . . ."

They discussed the facts of this day off from school. As far as Harbaugh could see, Wayne definitely understood what was happening, and seemed also to express an understanding of Harbaugh's role, a sympathy that struck the principal as not suiting the moment.

"You have certain rights, Wayne," he told him, trying to walk the line. If he were innocent, this was a terrible rap being forced on an eighteen-year-old kid, he thought to himself. After all, he had no cause to suspect Wayne of anything like this.

But as time went by, and Harbaugh quizzed more and more teachers about Wayne Nance, it became harder and harder to hold the line, not to see that something more was involved here.

On the night of the senior prom, with the festive mood that is supposed to accompany this senior-year social finale, Wayne's classmates were huddled in conversation. What should they do about Wayne? Their teachers still seemed to be of one opinion: that their fears were unfounded. After talking to his father about it, Bill knew what he had to do. It was time to call the sheriff's department.

Bill dialed from home, and after he explained why he was calling, and that he had talked to certain fellow students about this, including Ryan Ushijma, he was told a squad car would be along shortly to pick him up. When it pulled up, Ryan was inside, and they were both driven downtown.

As they walked from the car to the courthouse, they were told that Wayne's mother, Charlene, was inside, in a different part of the office. She was being interrogated, too, but their presence would be kept a secret. Bill and Ryan were already nervous, and now they were being surreptitiously led to a separate office in the same building. What if she spotted them? The fact that they were being tape-recorded added to their apprehensions.

Sheriff's deputies listened as Bill and Ryan gave the account of Wayne's Good Friday edict, told them that Wayne had threatened to kill Greg Baringer, related Wayne's growing involvement in the occult, right down to his rank of third-degree witch, and described the trance-like states that he conjured.

Then one of the deputies spilled his own bizarre story about Wayne.

"You know," the deputy told them, "last night, we found Wayne under a bridge out in Milltown. He had some kinda altar set up. And a small fire, and he had killed some cats, sacrificed 'em, I guess. He was completely naked. Buck naked. And he was playin' with himself—masturbating—and appeared to be like he was in some kinda trance."

*   *   *

Kenny Pounds was walking along with three of his Army buddies, returning from supper, when he saw the Red Cross patch on the man's arm. The man was standing near the entrance to his barracks at Fort Bliss, and he asked for Kenny Pounds.

"Yeah."

"Can I talk to you, inside?"

Kenny's first thought was about his father, whose bad heart was a constant, mortal threat. It was his father. His father had died.

"There's been an accident at home. I can't say any more than that, but you are requested to go to Missoula immediately."

"Is it my father? What happened?"

"I'm sorry, I'm not authorized to say anything more. Just that there's been an accident and you are requested to go to Missoula immediately. I'm sorry."

When Kenny left El Paso, steeling himself for his father's funeral, he was trying to medicate a bad cold that lately just seemed to get worse and worse. By the time he got to Missoula, his bad cold was diagnosed as a case of mononucleosis, and he was told that it was his mother, not his father, who was dead. He didn't go home to West Riverside. He went from the airport directly into the hospital, where he stayed until Monday morning, the day of his mother's funeral.

On that day following Easter Sunday, Donna Pounds was laid to rest in Victor Cemetery in the Bitterroot Valley, in a Valhalla near Stevensville where she and Harvey had hoped to find happiness together. The springtime she had longed for would be especially wet this year, because the snowpack in most of western Montana's river basins, including the Bitterroot, was double the average. There would be heavy flooding when it all melted, but for now, the hardpack snow on the ground that received Donna Pounds served to endlessly extend the boundaries of this white grave. It was as if she were being swallowed by everything around her.

Two Baptist ministers officiated for the more than three hundred mourners, who included a brother from Bozeman and a brother who lived in Missoula, and Donna's parents along with a clutch of aunts and uncles from out of state and other nieces and nephews. The Reverend Robert F. Penner, pastor of Bethel Baptist Church, described Donna as "the epitome of modesty," a Christian soldier who devoted her life to church work through youth and women's groups.

Standing at some distance were Sheriff's Deputies Northey and Harold Hoyt, a senior detective. They were watching to see who showed, thinking, "Was the guy who did this waiting for the two girls to come home? Was he going to do the same thing to them? Maybe Mom came home and interrupted this guy planning all this out." Northey looked over at Karen, the eldest. He had seen her only days before, recognizing her as the bright, young, down-to-earth waitress at the Travelodge Motel restaurant. Many of the deputies stopped in there for coffee or something to eat.

Karen, Kenny, and Kathy Pounds stood by their father. The children were inconsolable.

They didn't know that their father would become a suspect. They didn't know that Wayne Nance was under suspicion. Kenny, who stood beside his high school sweetheart, Valerie Chaffin, now a junior at Sentinel, couldn't clear his mind of the knowledge that the only people in the world who knew where the Luger was kept were his father and mother, himself, and Wayne Nance. Kenny and Wayne had been friends since the third grade, when they lived in the same trailer court, Tamarack. Wayne was a year ahead of Kenny at Bonner School, and then at Sentinel. Kenny had shown Wayne the hidden drawer in his parents' bedroom. They had taken the gun out, handled it, even fired it once and put it back. They were not best friends, but when there was nobody else around, Kenny could always find Wayne sitting around in his trailer by himself.

After the funeral, while trying not to invade the personal tragedy but hoping to comfort her boyfriend, Valerie started to tell Kenny what was being said about Wayne at school. That morning, some of her friends had told her that everyone was talking about how Wayne had been bragging that he would kill someone before he turned nineteen. Now somebody was dead. Was Wayne the suspect Sheriff Moe was talking about in the paper? No one believed it, really. They knew Wayne was weird, but not that weird. Anyone who knew Wayne at all knew that if he really were going to kill anyone, it would be Kenny's older sister, Karen, who was two years older than Wayne. Although no one knew why, Wayne despised Karen. He made that much known. Maybe Karen, an attractive brunette, had turned him down.

Kenny listened to Valerie. But he wanted to forget. The aftermath of the hit that came when he landed at the airport was still weighing him down, a complete pressing of his torso, in no particular location, just everywhere a weight. What Valerie told him about Wayne seemed just as pathetic an explanation of his mother's murder as the fact that Wayne knew where the gun was hidden. So what? It was too easy to suspect Wayne.

Kenny wanted to get away from all the friends and relatives who had gathered together after the funeral to sing hymns. His father had become withdrawn. Now Kenny wanted to get out. He drove Valerie home. Then he went to a friend's house where they drank beer. Dale Nickelson was there. And Wayne showed up, and they all sat around together, talking around the big issue of Kenny's mother's murder. Kenny was keeping a close eye on Wayne, watching for any indication, looking directly at Wayne at times. He wanted to catch Wayne looking away quickly, at some brief telling moment, or to get any kind of sign that would enable him to say "Yes, he possibly did it," because he knew where the gun was, because of what he was saying at Sentinel.

Wayne gave him no such sign.

The whole problem was a lack of anything concrete that pointed inescapably at Wayne or at Harvey. The polygraph examinations of the two suspects had failed to focus the investigation. When Harvey was hooked up to the electromechanical device that measured his cardiovascular and respiratory response, and his galvanic skin reflex while he was asked questions about his wife's murder, the chart produced by his answers told investigators that nothing could be concluded about whether he was lying or telling the truth.

Wayne's chart indicated he was telling the truth.

An even bigger problem was the physical evidence. The ropes had led the investigation to every hardware store in town, but to no avail. The pubic hair they had hoped to match was now a mere hypothetical: It was simply gone, misplaced by the pathologist who shouldn't have done the autopsy in the first place. Dusty Deschamps took the blame for not spending the money to send the body to Great Falls, to Dr. Pfaff, the forensic pathologist. When the FBI in Washington finally weighed in, at least they knew that the blood on Wayne's underpants was human, but it couldn't be typed because of the good washing the pants had been given by Wayne's mother. The FBI was unable to find any fingerprints on the single amber rubber glove.

By late May, all there was to the Donna Pounds murder case was misty circumstantial theorizing, and that told Deschamps that no warrant would be issued for the arrest of anyone. No matter how desperately Sheriff Moe and Deputy Sheriff Phil Nobis wanted Harvey Pounds, they couldn't have him. He had returned to work at Yandt's, abandoning the dream he had shared with Donna to move south to Stevensville. Wayne never did hire an attorney, and a few days after graduation, on June 19, 1974, he joined the Navy to see the world—and to get out of town.

Chapter 10

The Grand Jury

Verna Joy Kvale was not the kind of person to be late for anything. But where was she? It was now after one in the afternoon. She was late for Easter dinner.

Verna's mother and her uncle were expecting Verna for a family dinner at her mother's home in Ronan, a small town near Flathead Lake, north of Missoula. They had called Verna's home in Missoula, and when they got no answer they just figured she was on her way, taking more time than usual to drive the fifty-six miles north.

Single, shy, pretty, blonde and blue-eyed, about five-foot-four, Verna Kvale was not the kind of daughter to pop any surprises on her mother. Even as a young girl, she was the responsible one. Everything about her life as a special education teacher in the Missoula school system and as a member of the women's Toastmistress Club was more or less an open book, and it told anyone who knew her that this thirty-seven-year-old schoolteacher was a straightforward, solid citizen. If her friends at Toastmistress puzzled over anything about

Verna, it was her apparent lack of social life outside of school. The question came up mostly among her married friends, who wondered why such an attractive, hard-working woman had remained single so long.

As she stood by the window, looking for Verna's car to pull up any minute, Velma Kvale looked down at her watch. It was now 1:30, and she knew something was wrong. If Verna had left at 10:00 A.M., she would have been here at eleven. They had called every half hour, so she would have been at home until 12:30, if she had waited that long to leave. If so, why didn't she call?

It was 1:33 P.M. Three more minutes had passed, and no Verna. Maybe she had just missed her, she thought, feeling the grain of false hope. No. Something was wrong. She was going to call the Missoula police department.

The sergeant on duty listened as the woman told him that her daughter was late for Easter dinner, and that there was no answer at her daughter's home at 632 Cleveland Street.

"Could you send someone over there? My daughter's a teacher. She's never late for anything. I'm afraid . . ."

"We'll send someone over to take a look."

The patrol officer who made the spot check of the house, located in an older, established neighborhood just south of Missoula's downtown district, first knocked on the front door and then determined that it was locked. He walked to the back of the house. Still no answer, and that door was also locked.

He could hear a dog barking inside, but that didn't seem out of the ordinary. Nor did anything else about the house. And when he peered through the windows, everything inside seemed to be in order.

He radioed the desk with his report. Velma Kvale was told to wait a little longer. Maybe her daughter had gone somewhere else first, somehow forgotten to tell her mother.

After waiting two more anxious hours, Velma Kvale had still not seen or heard from her daughter. She called the Missoula police again. Again, they told her that the check of the house hadn't turned up anything to be alarmed about. It was now 4:15 P.M. The distraught mother waited some more, until by 6:30, as the day's twilight was beginning to move in, she was certain that something was gravely wrong. Velma Kvale decided to call a family friend, Bill Phillips, who was also coincidentally Sheriff Phillips, head of Lake County law enforcement.

"Something terrible has happened, I know, Bill," she said over the phone, explaining that they had waited hours for Verna, had called the Missoula police, had been forced to postpone Easter dinner, which she couldn't have eaten anyway.

"I think we should go down there, don't you?"

"Well, that would be . . ."

"I don't have a key to Verna's, but I just think we have to go. Will you come along?"

"Sure."

The hour's drive down seemed surreal to Velma Kvale. She had so looked forward to the Easter celebration with Verna. Now, instead, she was riding in a sheriff's car south to Missoula. It was dark out now, and her mind could do little but replay the various worrisome scenarios that had shadowed her thoughts all day long.

When they arrived at the city police station, Velma Kvale learned that Sheriff Phillips already had called ahead. It was a protocol thing, letting the Missoula police know that the Lake County sheriff was coming, and that he would appreciate their assistance. Police Lieutenant Dale Kidder was waiting to accompany them to the Cleveland Street house.

As they came to a stop at the curb, Velma could see that the lights were out. And her heart wasn't comforted, either, when they discovered that the doors were still locked. With her permission, the two law officers said they would break a basement window.

"Please, please, do it."

Kidder and Phillips called out as they ascended the stairs. But the dark house offered no sound in return.

Near the front door they found a pair of slippers. They were Verna's. They rested there in the doorway as if being kept at the ready to slip into.

The two law officers advised Velma to remain outside, then started to move through the house, calling out, flicking lights on as they went, eventually coming to the woman's bedroom, where they found Verna. It was a grisly sight.

There, naked on the bed, lay Verna Joy Kvale. The handle of a knife protruded from the flesh between her bare breasts. It appeared to be a large butcher knife, which someone had inserted to the hilt. The flesh, the two men were horrified and sickened to see, had been routed with the blade.

The date was April 18, 1976. Only two years had passed since the Siobhan McGuiness and Donna Pounds murders. They had been mind numbing, and this one was no less so. It too was a violent, sadistic sex murder, committed on an Easter Sunday.

When Dusty Deschamps arrived at the scene that night, as he looked at the body of Verna Kvale, he envisioned that the handle of the knife in her chest was attached to a large butcher knife. In fact, it turned out to be a kitchen steak knife. Deschamps would make no mistakes with this one. He would get a coroner's jury in to view the body, then have it shipped to Great Falls for a forensic examination. It was clear there was severe trauma to the head, and it didn't take a specialist to surmise that the dime-sized whitish blob on Verna's thigh was semen.

A police reconstruction of the crime assumed that whoever killed Verna Kvale had known her quite well. She apparently had opened the door and died at the door, or at least her death began there. She apparently was knocked right out of her slippers. The autopsy showed that she had been struck about the head with a blunt instrument and that her death was caused by the brutal knife wound to the chest. She had been raped. There were no fingerprints. Blood typing from the semen would provide the only physical evidence.

Just as in the Pounds case, police were close mouthed about the particulars, hoping to preserve salient details for use against a suspect who might know something he shouldn't. Police blotter reports of the initial visit to the Kvale residence were sanitized and not made available to reporters either on Monday or Tuesday. The initial reports of the murder were withheld from the press for a full twelve hours. There was no report of it in the Monday papers. By the time news of the murder surfaced, it was treated as a page-one story in the *Missoulian* on Tuesday. The headline—"Local Teacher Slain in Home"—carried a smaller kicker headline that reminded readers that this was the second killing in two months, as the story recalled the still-fresh and unsolved Gil Wooten homicide.

Less than two months earlier, on February 22, 1976, city police were called to a South End residence at 1815 Arlington Drive, the home of Robert J. Grafft. Slumped on the couch in a living room, they found the body of fifty-eight-year-old Gille V. Wooten, a local attorney, who had been staying at Grafft's home. Wooten had been shot once in the head. Officers who arrived on the scene first thought they were looking at a suicide.

But when they opened the curtains, they found blood and physical remains splattered across the window. Because there was no blood on the curtains, it was obvious that someone other than Wooten had fired the weapon, a bolt-action rifle, and then pulled the curtains closed afterward.

After investigators discovered that the rifle had been wiped clean, eliminating fingerprints, it became clear they were dealing with a homicide. An autopsy further pointed to murder because there was no evidence of powder burn, which would not be the case in a self-inflicted gunshot. The trajectory of the bullet indicated that it had been fired from eye level height from across the room.

Wooten was known in town as an irascible, eccentric loner. Everybody knew somebody who didn't like him, and that complicated the process of identifying possible suspects, because police received information about many people who were suspected of having a motive to kill him. The only hot suspect in the case, a man who was known to have had an argument with Wooten about land up in the Rattlesnake, a swank stretch of land north of town, had refused a polygraph. In the end, lacking any physical evidence, the case lingered.

For Dusty Deschamps and Sheriff Moe, the Kvale case was not merely the second unsolved murder in two months. It was the fourth unsolved homicide in just two years, and three of the cases were in the category of unsolved sexual murder. The headline in Thursday's *Missoulain* said it all: "4 Murders in 2 Years Stump Local Officials."

The Missoula Reward Fund had now upped the ante for any information that would lead to an arrest in the McGuinness, Pounds, or Kvale murders. The fund was offering $1,000 for information about the Kvale murder, $2,500 for information about the McGuinness murder, and $1,500 for information about Donna Pounds's killer.

In the days following the discovery of Verna Kvale's body, police interviewed numerous people, but no one emerged as a suspect. They hadn't forgotten about Wayne Nance, but when the semen found on Verna Kvale's leg was blood typed it didn't match. A check of Wayne's whereabouts further eliminated him as a suspect, because he was still in the Navy and was not on leave at the time. Harvey Pounds, the only other viable suspect in any such homicide in the past two years, was not even under suspicion in the Kvale case.

The sadness of Verna Joy Kvale's death was magnified by the local virtue that she embodied. A gradulate of St. Ignatius schools north of Missoula, she had been graduated from the University of Montana and had taken advanced studies at the University of Oregon and the University of Seattle. She had taught for several years in Missoula's public school system before becoming a special education teacher at Immanuel Lutheran Kindergarten, where she was teaching at the time of her death.

The house on Cleveland Street was emptied and put up for sale, and for all those who drove past, the longstanding "For Sale" sign was a reminder that no one was interested in living in a house where a murder had occurred. Eventually it was sold to a local policeman who wasn't troubled by any potential legacy of what had transpired there on April 18, 1976—another Easter killing.

For more than two years now, starting in the summer of 1974, Missoula's law-enforcement community had kept a vigilant eye over its shoulder, looking for the unseen element that might surface, the missed lead that might suggest itself. One unwanted result of this new extra willingness to check out every report of odd or suspicious behavior was a constant flow of new material—no matter how specious—to frame ever more interpretations of the devil-cult rumor.

A few months after Donna Pounds was killed, a woman in hysterics called police to report that her next-door neighbor was a devil worshipper and was, she believed, involved in the murder. She said that she knew that her neighbor was in the cult because he had been sacrificing dogs in his backyard. Sheriff's deputies checked it out. The man was a coyote hunter. The skins draped over his back fence were simply hung there to dry.

When early in 1975 a University of Montana student disappeared, a rumor spread that he had been sacrificed by the cult. It turned out he had taken an unannounced trip to California. A few weeks after that, a woman had jumped to her death from a bridge. The story floating around town was that she was trying to escape the cult. The truth was she had committed suicide as a result of severe personal problems. In the same year, when two high school students were found dead and their two companions found unconscious in a parked car in Pattee Canyon, the rumor mill laid responsibility for the incident to Pattee Canyon's incipient devil worshippers. The fact was the two teenagers had died as a result of an overdose of wood alcohol.

Each time there was a plausible explanation, but it didn't seem to matter. The lingering, unsolved murders were laminating themselves onto the public consciousness. Front doors that used to be left unlocked during the day—or even at night—were now being secured. Hardware stores sold more locks. Gun counters at Missoula's all-purpose department stores found more new customers. Police stepped up patrols southeast of the city in the neighborhood of Pattee Canyon, where young lovers, seeking seclusion, now in growing numbers reported seeing spooks—men in white robes.

At its peak, the public's raw tension fed a rumor machine that in the end produced a textbook case of mass hysteria, which itself captured the imagination of a University of Montana sociology professor and a graduate student. Professor Robert W. Balch and graduate student Margaret Gilliam would train their academic eyes on the origin of the rumors, in a sense putting the entire community under the microscope of sociology.

Professor Balch, a logic-minded, inquisitive man whose every hand gesture seems to beckon for more information, more fuel for the conversation, was teaching a course in collective behavior in the fall of 1974. The course dealt with rumor construction and dissemination, and because the class project focused on devil worship, he was particularly intrigued by the so-called episode of rumor formulation right under his nose.

The word that Donna Pounds had been sacrificed by devil worshippers started to spread through the town within only a few days of her murder. The rumors spread mostly by word of mouth between friends and acquaintances. The *Missoulian* even carried a front-page story that articulated the rumor in detail and made reference to other cult slayings around the country.

A typo in the text, however, rendered a lot more local significance than was intended: The *r* in "country" had been dropped, so the sentence appeared as "around the county."

What surprised Balch and Gilliam was that a full seven months after Donna Pounds was killed, the murder was not only still on the minds of many people in Missoula, but new rumors about it were continuing to pop up. In fact there seemed to be so many more stories and so much more community concern that Gilliam decided it was a worthy topic for her master's thesis. Professor Balch and Gilliam coauthored a paper entitled "Devil Worship in Western Montana: A Case Study of Rumor Construction." In it, they describe a case of consensual validation: An idea develops its validity simply because everybody seems to believe it, despite the absence of hard facts. The two academics themselves didn't for a minute believe any of the stuff about satanic cults, witchcraft, and devil worship. But the more they heard varying stories from many different people, who by all other measures were, they believed, credible, who would say, "Well, my son's a good friend of so-and-so in the Pounds family, you know," the more curious they got. Always there was a connection made to a prospectively credible source to validate the claim.

Balch and Gilliam interviewed reporters, lawmen, teachers, and ministers, as well as others who were supposed members of Missoula's occult community. They also sent a 13-page questionnaire to 219 students in Missoula's Hellgate High and Sentinel High and to 266 sociology students at the university. Gilliam also mailed

300 questionnaires to Missoulians selected at random in the telephone book.

They were pleased that the results of their questionnaire were in line with the information they were gathering on the street. They had an extraordinarily clear picture of how all the rumors started and why they weren't dying out. They weren't in any way connected to a man who turned up in the interview process who was an active practitioner of ritual magic. Then in his fifties, he had ended up in a state mental hospital for getting his daughter involved in a sex–magic thing. The man showed Balch and Gilliam a large box that contained his treasure of potions, bloodstained ropes, and daggers. And the rumors weren't connected to the nerdy boy at Hellgate, a bright but effeminate student who spoke French and Latin fluently and who claimed to have a coven of girls. He confessed, once they got to know him better, that he was merely capitalizing on the mystique of Pattee Canyon, that it was a setup. He staged scary events for the girls. The phony magic empowered him with Svengali-like control, and it was no secret that other kids at Hellgate were afraid of his supposed black magic.

"The interesting thing about this was that every time we were able to trace one of these rumors back to what appeared to be the source," Balch recalls today, "it turned out to be false. Or there turned out to be alternative explanations that people were either unaware of, or they were unwilling to consider."

Steve Shirley, a reporter at the *Missoulian*, had told them about altars in Pattee Canyon that had become the object of wild speculation

about sacrificial rites. It turned out the altars
had been built back in the 1920s and 1930s by
a semisecret student forestry society at the university. They called themselves the Druids,
after the ancient Celtic priesthood. The original
Druids were diviners, men of magic and priests
who supposedly met annually to feast on two
white bulls that were sacrificed for the Druids'
conference, which was occasioned by the growth
of mistletoe on an oak tree. The modern-day,
University of Montana Druids are said to still
be on campus. Gilliam's husband, a forestry
major, told the researchers that the Druids used
the altars for initiations. Dressed in white robes
just as their ancient counterparts were, they
would march their pledge classes out into the
woods to perform secret, but decidedly more
tame, initiation rites.

The results of the questionnaire provided
ample evidence that the rumor alleging that
Donna Pounds was killed by devil worshippers
was widespread. Sixty percent of the respon-
dents had heard that story. Of those 60 percent,
31 percent claimed they believed the story and
only 8 percent said they didn't believe it. The
rest—among those who had heard the rumor—
didn't know what to believe.

Balch himself had become so acutely involved
in the research that he found his own academic
armor wearing thin. Without any new objective
information that led them to a source, he too
was starting to get spooked. Pretty soon, he too
was locking his doors. For the first time, he
kept a loaded handgun in the drawer next to
his bed. He was being swept up in this hysteria—just like those people who wouldn't an-

swer the door for him when he canvased, thinking he might be a member of the cult. After his visit to the Christian Book Store to talk to Donna Pounds's coworkers, they had called the police to report that they believed somebody from the cult had been there.

Balch and Gilliam hypothesized that the questionnaires would suggest the most likely place of origin of the rumor attributing Donna Pounds's murder to a satanic cult. The answer would be limited by the scope of their sampling at Sentinel, Hellgate, the University, and Missoula at large, but whichever of those subgroups contained the most number of people who had heard the rumor would most likely be the place where it all started. That place turned out to be Sentinel High School.

"Now I got Kvale dead," Dusty Deschamps told District Judge Brownlee, "and this satanism stuff still cooking."

By early 1976, the rumors about satanic involvement in the 1974 homicides had actually started to die down. They had run their course, made their sense of the inexplicable. Now, just as the air seemed to finally be clearing, Deschamps didn't want to run the risk of a replay of that wild-goose chase after devil-cult killers. Seeing that the two-week-old Kvale murder was going nowhere, he knew he had only one course left: to summon a grand jury.

Dusty was sitting in Judge Brownlee's chambers, making his case.

"We've gone as far as we can go," he said, shaking his head. "In some of these cases I don't have any idea who committed the crime.

In one of them, I have probable cause, enough evidence to try to file a homicide charge, but not as much as I would like."

The judge listened, thinking about what Deschamps was asking. It would be the first grand jury ever called in Missoula County. Under Montana statute, a grand jury is empaneled to look into "all public matters in the courthouse," a broad mandate that also seemed to be an open invitation to a public soap opera. For that reason, judges were loathe to convene them. In fact, it had only happened once in the history of Montana, when the attorney general was investigating a state worker's compensation division scandal.

"I don't think I've got enough to charge anybody," Deschamps continued, "and I don't want to do a coroner's inquest, because I don't want this to be a public proceeding. The only solution I can see is maybe we can do a grand jury, and perhaps compel some of these suspects to come in and testify."

Judge Brownlee signed the order. On May 19, 1976, eleven grand jurors—seven women and four men—were selected from a group of twenty candidates. What was striking about the selection process was that the group had been hand picked so that each and every one of the jurors was familiar with, or knew, someone who was involved. In a sense, Deschamps had effectively deputized eleven people to play the inquisition role. His hope was that someone who might know something, who may have been hesitant to talk to an officer in uniform, would be less reluctant to talk to a group of citizens, some of whom they knew quite well.

The jury would subpoena witnesses, compel testimony from them, and demand documentary evidence, but its deliberations would be shrouded in secrecy, which would protect anyone's reputation from unfounded accusations.

Deschamps planned to personally handle the questioning of witnesses called to testify about the McGuinness, Pounds, and Kvale murders. He relegated the Wooten case, which he viewed primarily as an unrelated murder, to an assistant. In fact, Deschamps also saw the Kvale case separately from the McGuinness and Pounds cases, and he was ready to spend most of the jury's time delving into the Donna Pounds murder.

More than 100 witnesses were called. Among them were friends of the deceased; relatives, teachers, friends, and acquaintances of the prime suspects; and the prime suspects themselves: Wayne Nance and Harvey Pounds. The county paid to fly Wayne in from San Diego, where he was in training as a ship's electrician on the USS *Robison*.

The last time Wayne had seen anyone from home was in February of the previous year. His senior counselor at Sentinel, Darlene Smith, was on a teacher's holiday in San Diego, touring the Naval base. She spotted Wayne among the technicians at work as her tour group strode through the room. There he was, sitting in a booth, working away on electronics gear, and she went right up to him.

"Wayne."

He looked up, startled.

"I had no idea you were here."

"Mrs. Smith."

Wayne greeted her warmly and after a brief visit at his work station, they parted. Wayne conveyed the impression that it was good to see someone from home, and Darlene Smith was pleased to catch up with an old student.

The next time Wayne would be surprised by someone from home was June of 1976. He was served with a subpoena to appear in the small courtroom on the second floor of the Missoula County Courthouse. There he would see more of his Sentinel teachers, who would be called as witnesses.

Bill Van Canagan was surprised and also annoyed when he came home from Stanford for the summer. There, waiting for him, was a subpoena. A grand jury that was investigating four homicides requested his presence. Hoping to put the spring of 1974 behind him, and relieved to know that his high school classmate who had transformed into his nemesis, who should have been no more than an innocuous acquaintance, was somewhere far away in the Navy, Bill was looking forward to a summer that would be free of anxieties. After all, Wayne, he was certain, was somewhere far away, serving out his commitment.

On the appointed day, Bill came practically unglued. The court officers showed him where he was to wait. It was a small room just off the hearing room. They pointed to a door and Bill walked through it. Inside, to his horror, were the two people he most wanted never to see again, Wayne Nance and Nick Nickelson. There was no one else, either. Just the three of them, and no one said anything for what felt to Bill like a very long time. Then Wayne spoke.

"What are you doing here?" His tone was menacing.

After thinking about it, not forgetting the pledge that Wayne had made to kill a friend who betrayed him, and realizing, too, that he was now in a position to obviously meet that requirement to the maximum, Bill thought of an answer.

"I don't know, Wayne," trying to sound sarcastic, "apparently they connect you with Pounds and they want to ask me about your character. Maybe they think you know something."

Nickelson stood up. He paced back and forth, finally stopping behind a row of chairs, glaring down at Bill.

"Wayne didn't do it," Nickelson said, glowering.

Bill said nothing. He just sat, looking out a window, waiting until finally he was called into the jury room, where he served as a pretty reluctant witness. It was not due to an unwillingness to do his duty. It was because for the entire time he sat in the chair, Wayne's face was plastered against the small glass window that peered into the courtroom. He was looking directly at Bill. All Bill could think was that Wayne was trying to read his lips. It was a nightmare.

When it was over, Bill reentered the waiting room, and it was Wayne's turn. Bill watched through the same little window. Wayne was questioned for hours, and Bill could hear some of it.

"Have you ever seen this before?" Deschamps said loudly, thrusting an open file into Wayne's face. Bill didn't know what it was that Deschamps was showing Wayne, but whatever it was failed to elicit any reaction. Wayne's face was stone cold. He betrayed no response, just a cool glance at the evidence and pat answers in return.

Deschamps knew he wasn't the world's most skilled cross-examiner. He tried to rattle the boy, but nothing worked. He thought Wayne could be moved by the sight of the crime-scene photographs. One by one, he held up the images of the bloody body, fallen into a crouch on the basement floor, naked, shot five times in the back of the head, her hands and legs bound. He brought out the pictures of the Pounds bedroom, where Wayne could see the bloodstain dead center on the sheet, the stray shoe resting on the floor by the bedpost, the Kotex, the gun holster on the bed cover, the ropes again.

Wayne didn't flinch at any of it.

"Have you ever seen this?"

Wayne answered in the negative.

"This?"

Again, the same oblique shake of the head.

"This?"

"No," came the icy answer.

"Where were you on the afternoon of April 11, 1974?"

"Home."

"You weren't in school?"

"No."

"Why weren't you in school?"

"I stayed home to work on a project."

"So you were playing hooky?"

"Yeah, but I worked on a school project."

"What kind of project?"

"It was for a class."

"Tell me more."

Wayne explained to Deschamps and the jury that he had skipped school that day so he could work on a class project, which was to make a tomahawk. He said he had been outside, wandering the West Riverside neighborhood searching for rocks and sticks that he would need.

"And who was your teacher?"

"Mr. Cooper."

Deschamps excused Wayne, and told him that he should be ready to be called back for more questioning. In the meantime, Deschamps planned to find out more about Wayne from Mike Cooper, a teacher at Sentinel who had taught a unit in anthropology back in 1974. They were studying ancient weapons systems, Cooper told Deschamps, and because Cooper liked hands-on experience, the students were assigned to create their own arrowheads or spears or tomahawks. Cooper was impressed by the care that Wayne employed in fashioning his own versions of these early weapons. He once remarked to a colleague that Wayne's effort in the class was above and beyond the call of duty. That explained why Wayne received an A for his magnificent tomahawk, the teacher said. But it didn't, in fact, clarify why Wayne would be stalking the West Riverside neighborhood on that snowy April day, the teacher told Deschamps. The weapons class had been taught during the previous fall semester, Cooper explained.

"You're a liar!" Deschamps fired back at

Wayne when he brought him back before the grand jury.

No response. No wince. No falling back in his seat. No shifting of the body. No movement, just a steady stare that further unsteadied Deschamps.

"Do you hear what I'm saying?"

Wayne nodded, but it meant nothing to him.

It was clear to Deschamps that Wayne understood everything about this proceeding. He was able to speak in normal tones, providing answers to mundane questions and responding in unequivocal ways to provocative ones. He was always unflappable, and seemingly unconcerned that his alibi had just been destroyed.

Wayne was dressed as a civilian for his three appearances on the stand, which added up to a total of seven hours. His father, George, never showed up. During most of the time Wayne was testifying, his mother, Charlene, waited anxiously in the outer hall. She was not permitted in the jury room, and when Deschamps either came or went from the room, Charlene lunged at him, accusing him of picking on her son for no reason. Deschamps would never forget running the gauntlet of Charlene's fury each time he came or went, and the shrieks from this slight, dark-haired mother filled the cavernous hallways of the courthouse, filtering upstairs, echoing the hostile, wild happening on the floors below.

One of the women jurors who worked with Charlene was among the minority on the panel who were beginning to believe, along with Deschamps, that Wayne had killed Donna Pounds. She was distressed to see how the teachers from Sentinel, who were called to testify, appeared to be seriously afraid of Wayne.

The jury spent almost a full month on the Pounds case, and Harvey was the prime focus. He spent more time on the stand than Wayne, and he was just as unflappable. There were times when, as he studied Wayne's detached presence, Deschamps could at least detect that Wayne seemed occasionally bothered by the whole proceeding. But Harvey wasn't fazed a bit that people were suspecting him of killing his wife.

"I didn't do it," he said flat out when asked by Deschamps.

"I don't know, Harvey, if I were an innocent man, being falsely accused and being suspected of these horrible things, you know, I would be pissed off. I wouldn't just take it very calmly, as you seem to be."

There were many more issues to explore with Harvey than with Wayne, but foremost was his relationship with the alleged other woman, who also was called to testify. Tragedy had visited her again in the two years since the murder. Her husband had been killed in a plane crash.

Deschamps spent less time on the McGuinness case and less so on the Kvale and Wooten cases. It was October by the time the grand jury had exhausted its resources and prepared to vote whether or not there was sufficient evidence to bring an indictment against anyone. The jury knew that eight of eleven of them had to agree on who that might be. They fell short of indicting Harvey by two votes. The disparity was even greater when they considered whether

Wayne was culpable. By the time the jury was finished, Deschamps knew that he would have been hard pressed to obtain a conviction against Wayne if the grand jury had decided to indict him. So, he figured, the jurors had done him a favor. Deschamps was certain that Wayne would have been found not guilty due to a lack of direct evidence.

Had the jury indicted Harvey, Deschamps would have had a full-blown disaster on his hands, because he would have been prosecuting a father and husband, whose reputation had only been recently rubbed the wrong way by this very investigation, and all Deschamps would have at his disposal was a bag full of conjectural evidence out of which he would have had to have pulled the proverbial but tired charge: "The husband did it."

"I'm sad we didn't have any indictments," Deschamps told reporters as the grand jury adjourned. "I was in hopes, but I agree with the jury's decision not to indict anybody."

For the community, there was at least a sense of relief. It seemed as if there had been a thorough investigation, and as the months passed and winter came and went, without the repeat of another seemingly random Eastertime killing, everyday life in Missoula was restored to a degree of normalcy.

Harvey Pounds, who returned to selling shoes at Yandt's, eventually faced heart surgery again, and after he got out of the hospital this time, he wasn't invited back to work at Yandt's. He moved back to his native Washington state, to Spokane. In time he would remarry, and also would sink more deeply into his religion—and to further intolerance of his own family. The congenital heart problem would recur, sending him to Veteran's Hospital in Seattle several times over, and by the time he would reach age fifty-five, it would kill him.

Wayne, who had served about two years of his tour, returned to the USS *Robison*. While he had maintained a spotless Navy record for more than a year following his enlistment, by the time he was summoned back to Missoula for the grand jury, things had already begun to sour. On November 5, 1975, just two days after he arrived at nuclear prototype school in Idaho Falls, Idaho, Wayne fell into some trouble. He was booted from the school and his record was stamped "demonstrated unreliability." Wayne was soon transferred to the *Robison*, his base of operation for nearly two years, until he was suddenly cashiered.

This time, the offenses were spelled out. On September 13, 1977, Wayne was caught in possession of marijuana. He forfeited two hundred dollars in pay, was reduced in rank and was restricted for fourteen days. The reduction in rank was suspended for six months, and had he stayed out of trouble it would have been restored to him. But he didn't. On September 29, just two days after his fourteen-day restricted punishment had lapsed, Wayne was found in possession of more marijuana. He also had on his person a quantity of LSD, two illegal butterfly knives, and a pair of stolen Navy binoculars. His commanding officer further reduced him in rank, fined him another three hundred dollars, restricted him for thirty days, and added thirty days of duty to his timesheet. The second drug offense meant almost immediate ouster from the Navy, which was soon to come.

On November 29, 1977, Wayne was given a "general discharge by reason of misconduct." An honorable discharge was out of the question here. Wayne's commanding officer wrote the following: "In accordance with the provisions under which this recommendation is made, it is considered by this command that ICFN [interior communications fireman] Nance be separated immediately from the Naval service by reason of repeated drug abuse offenses."

Wayne came home, secreting a stolen Navy telescope in his duffel and bringing somewhat less than honorable discharge papers.

"You know, his discharge was a mutual agreement. It was an honorable discharge. He decided he didn't like the Navy, and that's the way they operate these days," was how Wayne's father, George, explained his son's abrupt return home.

Wayne again took up residence with his parents, in their trailer at Tamarack where the multifarious remnants of his childhood were still stacked in hodgepodge assortment in his room. His *Weekly Readers* were there. His collection of knives. He was surrounded by all his stuff again, and it was time to carry on.

Chapter 11

A Mother's Suicide

George Nance was tired. He had been on the road for days. Now it was after midnight. He had just completed a long haul and it was time to go home. He could see it in his mind: an easy chair, a beer, and some television. He would be kicked back for awhile. But when he stepped through the door, though noticing that Charlene's car wasn't parked outside, he still wanted to believe that she was inside waiting for him.

But he was disappointed. Charlene wasn't there, and in the same moment he became certain of that fact his anger started to flare. He knew exactly where she was. She was at the Cabin, and he turned right around and headed back out the door. He climbed behind the wheel of his old, blue and white Dodge pickup and headed out to get her. The truck would barely have a chance to warm up in the mile or so drive on this early April night. But his temper would.

George had never wanted Charlene to work at the Cabin in the first place. Charlene worked as a barmaid, in addition to her waitressing job at Taber's Truck Stop across the highway. Del Tyler, the owner who had recruited her, allowed the women to drink whether they were on shift or not.

George pulled up, parked his truck, and headed inside, where he found his wife. The argument started immediately. George insisted that Charlene come home. She refused. She wouldn't have any of it. He accused her of being drunk. She spit the words back in his face, and the two of them commenced another drag-out fight, another page in their hard-bitten life. By the time George and Charlene had taken their argument outside into the parking lot, it became clear that Charlene was planning her own exit. She yelled and screamed her way over to her own car, a 1976 Chrysler Cordoba, and got behind the wheel. The roar of her engine told George it was time to get into his truck. Charlene was leaving. The argument was still alive, as far as he knew, and he doubted that Charlene was headed for home.

But by the time he got his truck into gear, Charlene was accelerating away at a high rate of speed. She was heading eastward, in the general direction of home, though George still didn't believe that's where she was headed. So he pursued. But Charlene's powerful Cordoba was too fast, and after George lost her in the night, he headed back home.

It was about an hour later when George heard the car pull up. He was waiting for her. Then he heard the knock on the door, and instead of Charlene, he found two sheriff's deputies standing outside. They were there to inform him of an accident.

Charlene had driven no more than a mile from the Cabin when she turned off onto the Speedway, a semi-oval switchback that makes the loop back along the Clark Fork River to the western side of East Missoula. A quarter of a mile along this road, she had turned left onto Deer Creek Road, crossing a bridge and continuing east on a gravel road that leads up to the ridges that become Hellgate Canyon. She reached a terrific speed in the short time she navigated a long, easy curve in the road. She hit the tree, a giant Ponderosa pine that stands just off the road shoulder at the terminus of the arc, head on.

The crash site was on a stretch of lowland known as Bandmann Flats. Charlene had died just two miles from East Missoula, and less distance than that from her own home at Tamarack in Pine Grove, diagonally just across the river. Sheriff's deputies could see that she should have been able to avoid the tree, given the path of her vehicle up to that point, but that she instead had hit it head-on, and there was no sign that she had tried to brake. The fierce impact of the crash had split her Cordoba in half. A single piece of sheet metal still remaining on the driver's side was all that held it together. She had died instantly. The date was April 4, 1980. Charlene was the fifty-fifth fatality on Montana highways that year. Her death was designated a suicide.

A few hours later, as the sun rose over the valley, George and his children, Desiree, twenty-seven, Wayne, twenty-five, Bill, twenty and Veta, eighteen, the younger three of whom still lived at home, would realize that they faced the rest of their lives without their mother, and the first thing they would have to do is think about funeral arrangements.

Charlene, who had married at sixteen on Missoula's North Side, would be laid to rest only five blocks from there in the city cemetery. She had lived forty-four years and thirty days, raised four children—changed their diapers, dressed them as infants, tied their toddler shoes, washed their faces, sent them off to school, and generally tried to keep them in line as best she knew how. During most of that time, she worked too, and earned an undying reputation among her coworkers at Ming's Restaurant and Paul's Pancakes and Taber's and the Cabin as a first-class waitress. She was fast, dependable, and honest. She had earned the professional respect of her peers. Charlene was salt of the earth. But now she was gone. There would be no more morning chatter over coffee, no more standing and arguing, no more screaming and hollering from Charlene.

George bought a double headstone for her grave, reserving a place for himself, with his name also carved in the granite next to hers. A month later to the day of Charlene's crash, George's father died, and the family was presented with their first opportunity to move out of the trailer and into a house of their own. George's father had left him a modest ranch house on Minnesota Avenue in East Missoula, no more than a stone's throw from the Cabin. So George decided to move in there with his children, to get away, he told them, from the many memories of Charlene still harbored in the trailer at Tamarack.

*   *   *

Wayne confided in his friends that no one really knew if his mother drove off the road on purpose, had accidentally veered too far off the shoulder, or had had too much to drink that night. One rumor spread that Charlene had a boyfriend who lived up Deer Creek Road, offering an explanation for the route she had taken. Whatever the case, it was once again the start of Easter season.

Wayne was twenty-five years old, living at home with his father in their new house on Minnesota Avenue, bouncing at the Cabin at night, and trying his hand at college at the University of Montana. Four years had passed since Wayne had been resurrected as a suspect in the McGuinness and Pounds murders. Unsolved murders number three, Gil Wooten, and number four, Verna Kvale, were now four years old and still unsolved. But the discovery of the remains of the young murdered girl whose body had been thrown down an embankment along I-90 on the eastern end of the county was only two months old. The corpse of the victim Captain Weatherman had dubbed Beavertail Hill Girl had been found in late January of 1980. Later, much later, Captain Weatherman would identify the body and also determine approximately when she had been so unceremoniously dumped along the interstate.

As if it had been mandated by some memorial clockwork, on March 1, 1978, a few months after Wayne's Navy discharge and his prodigal return to Missoula, the *Missoulian* resurrected the story of Missoula's unsolved murders. On an inside page, next to the movie ads for *Close*

Encounters of the Third Kind and *Looking for Mr. Goodbar*, playing at the Village Twin, and *2069*, a spacy skin flick at the Wilma Theatre, the un-bylined story marked the anniversaries of the springtime murders with an update on the Missoula Reward Fund. It reported that the fund's board of directors had decided to keep the more than five thousand dollars that it had amassed for another year, even though no one had collected any of it so far. Esther Fowler, the fund secretary, said police officials doubted that anyone would ever collect any of the money offered for information about the McGuinness and Pounds murders, thus explaining why the board had set a five-year limit on those cases.

It was an innocent enough decision for the board to make, as was its earmarking of two thousand dollars of the reward money for the Law Enforcement Youth Camp. It also was considering putting some of the money in a fund for rewards for information about other serious crimes in Missoula. But the story struck an exposed nerve at the sheriff's department, where Sheriff Moe was serving out the last year of his last term in office. He didn't want history to close out the possibility—not while he was still sheriff—that his department would someday solve the McGuinness and Pounds murders. He especially didn't want history to be thus carved in stone on the same day Charles "Ray" Doty, a retired Missoula policeman, filed as Democratic candidate for sheriff to run against Sheriff Moe's hand-picked successor, Robert Zaharko, the undersheriff, who was running on Sheriff Moe's Republican coattails.

The small notice of Doty's primary filing appeared in the *Missoulian*, however, on the very same page and right next to the story about the so-far fruitless McGuinness and Pounds investigations, and it thus tweaked a political nerve. In the next day's paper, the headline appeared in bigger type. It read: "Area's Unsolved Murders: 'Something May Turn Up.' " And Sheriff Moe had his say. He didn't dispute what Esther Fowler said. But he did insist there were good suspects in both murders. The problem was, he explained, insufficient evidence to charge and convict them.

"That doesn't mean to say," added city police captain Marvin D. Hamilton, hammering home the point, "that the two murders will never be solved. We always have hope that something will turn up."

In the past four years, the *Missoulian* had printed thirty-one stories about the McGuinness, Pounds, and Kvale murders. Sixteen of those stories had appeared on page one. Wayne was an avid reader of the *Missoulian*, and he regularly watched the local television news. The consecutive reports of the squabble over whether the reward would ever be paid out because someone might someday help solve the crime, and solving the crime without ever paying out a reward would no doubt have drawn his interest. It is doubtful that Wayne even raised an eyebrow at the wishful thinking connoted in the line, "Something May Turn Up." No one at the sheriff's department even knew that Wayne was back in town. What is certain is that in the late spring of 1978, as he was considering enrolling at the University in the fall, he left town again. Wayne wanted to spend some time with a former Navy buddy who was living in Seattle.

Devonna Nelson disappeared from the streets of Seattle without a trace. It was July of 1978. She was a slight fifteen-year-old, weighing no more than a hundred pounds. Her wavy strawberry-blonde hair fell neatly to her shoulders, cupping a sweet face. Her eyes were an innocent blue. And her parents were going through a messy divorce.

Devonna had been living with her father in Illinois and then in Louisiana, and most recently had been shuttled to Seattle to stay with her mother, Hazel Jones. When Devonna ran away, she was wearing a dark-colored dress, a pair of earrings, and some costume jewelry. Hazel Jones never saw or heard from her little girl again, and as the days turned into weeks and then months, then years, the Mother's Day card that Devonna had given her became ever more precious.

When the work train crew found the remains of the stabbed and dumped Beavertail Hill Girl, no one knew that it was Devonna Nelson, the Seattle runaway. Captain Weatherman had run a description of the Beavertail Hill skeleton through national police computer networks every six months since the discovery of her body. He had a hunch the girl might be from the Pacific Northwest, but it was just a hunch.

In time, Captain Weatherman would identify her but would never know what exactly had happened to Devonna after she failed to return to her mother's home, except that she had been transported hundreds of miles across two state lines and deposited—as if in last-minute haste—on a roadbank not fifteen miles from the Missoula city limits.

Weatherman would also eventually learn that Wayne Nance's visit to Seattle coincided with the girl's disappearance. The name Wayne Nance hadn't yet crossed his mind. There were, in fact, no suspects in the Beavertail Hill Girl case.

By the winter of 1980, Wayne was maintaining 3.53 cumulative average (out of a maximum possible 4.0) at the University, though he had gotten off to a poor start in the fall of 1978. He managed an A in a first-year studio art course, but earned F's in a modern fantasy English course and in a course entitled "Introduction to Woman." He dropped a course in logic and finished the term on "Academic Warning." The following semester, he applied himself and earned straight B's in four courses—an anthropology class in primitive technology, two art classes, and a history class in European civilization.

Though Wayne managed to maintain a strong academic profile, at times he would lighten his load considerably. In the spring 1979, for example, he took two art classes, a class in local flora, and a course in fresh food preparation. In later semesters, he would excel in a subject, such as earning an A in a five-credit biology course, only to turn around and fall down in it, pulling only a C in the next sequence. Still his overall grade-point average was impressive, and he racked up consecutive semesters of progress as an A and B student, taking some of the toughest courses the University had to offer.

But Wayne's academic career would be short lived. After his mother's death, Wayne didn't continue in summer school as he had in past summers. When September rolled around again, Wayne was back, enrolling in German, Spanish, and physics classes. But it was to be a perfunctory commitment. He pretty much had dropped the idea of college. He got F's in all three courses, and dropped out.

And during this summer of 1980, Captain Weatherman would investigate a bizarre incident—one involving ropes—that would cause him to once again vividly recall the Donna Pounds case.

Chapter 12

On the Prowl

It was a hot July night. Like anyone else would have in the summer of 1980 in Missoula, Montana, Denise Tate had left the windows open and the front door ajar so what little breeze there was could find its way inside and keep her trailer a little cooler. She was going out. When she got back, at least it wouldn't feel like an oven inside.

The date was July 3, a Thursday night, and later, when she arrived back home, she was pleased to discover that the place was comfortably cool. But she was upset, very upset, about what she found in her bedroom. She didn't notice that anything was wrong until she had started to get ready for bed, hoping for a good night's sleep.

What was that down at the corner of the bedpost? As she moved closer, she could see the ropes. Puzzled, scared, she looked up, then all around. She listened. Nothing. Then she walked around to the other side of the bed and saw that someone had tied ropes to the bedpost and frame on that side, too. She decided to undo the ropes, lock herself in and go to bed.

She was alarmed, but she was also tired. She would call the sheriff's department in the morning. This kind of thing, she thought, ought to be reported, even if it was a practical joke.

The next day, Captain Weatherman was dismayed to learn that she had casually disposed of the rope. He didn't doubt the woman's story for a minute. But he was sorry to once again be without physical evidence. He listened to her explain how she had found the bedposts tied. He asked her to describe exactly where the ropes had been placed.

On the bedposts, she told him, then looped around the frame. He understood, and it wasn't hard for him to envision what it had looked like, because he had seen ropes tied to a bed that exact same way. It was six years ago. That's how the murderer had done it in Donna Pounds's bedroom. The ropes had been tied to the posts and then laced around the bed frame itself.

The next image to fill his mind was the face of Wayne Nance. But then the picture of that fresh-faced high school senior, with the piercing eyes and the red curly hair, faded from the nether reaches almost as quickly as it had materialized. Weatherman had no idea where Wayne was these days. He wasn't on Weatherman's mind, really. He didn't pause to connect Wayne with this suspicious incident, nor did he think to connect him with the Beavertail Hill Girl. Weatherman was still wrestling with the paucity of means to identify the poor girl's bones. He was intrigued by this repeat of the ropes on the bed, but that was the end of it.

Dusty Deschamps would have had occasion

to at least wonder about Wayne in the first half of 1980, because Wayne's mother, whom he would never forget from the grand jury days, had just died in a newsworthy, violent crash not a mile from Deschamps's own home. Deschamps lived across the river from Bandmann Flats, between East Missoula and Pine Grove, high on a ridge overlooking the valley. Charlene's crash had for a while been the talk of the neighborhood. People even drove out to the Ponderosa pine that stood at the end of the long curve in the road, curious to inspect the massive gash made by the speeding Cordoba. Deer Creek Road was also a favorite for neighborhood joggers and walkers, who could see the damage each time they passed.

Stan Fullerton, the high school classmate who had listened to Wayne brag about being a suspect in the Pounds murder, was one of the deputies who responded to the accident call. Fullerton had joined the sheriff's department in 1977, after graduation from Spokane Community College. He hadn't seen Wayne since high school, but he hadn't forgotten the cryptic farewell that Wayne had drawn in his yearbook— the picture of Stan in the likeness of Julius Caesar with the hilt of a knife in his back. Now Fullerton was at the accident scene. Here was Wayne's mother, a dead woman wrapped around the wheel of an almost unidentifiable car.

From the highest level to the lowest, there were law-enforcement officials who knew Wayne to be strange, to have been a prime suspect in a sensational sex murder that involved binding with ligatures of clothesline rope, tied in a specific way. In the years since the grand jury had looked into Missoula's four unsolved homicides, the stabbed body of a young girl had been dumped within the county's borders, not five miles from the place where little Siobhan McGuinness had been found. Now, a woman had found ropes tied to her bedposts when she came home alone. But no one thought for very long about where Wayne Nance was hanging out in the summer of 1980. If anyone had asked, his father, George, would have told them that Wayne was bouncing at the Cabin, along with his younger brother, Bill.

Rick Davis told the story of what happened one terrible morning in 1968 to his Marine artillery squad, dug in on an unimportant hillside in the jungles of Vietnam.

"It was 4 A.M.," he began.

Wayne listened.

"We got overrun. It was four o'clock in the morning and all of a sudden all hell breaks loose. When it was over, there were a lot of dead guys lying around. There was this guy I shot, I mean I was eighteen years old."

Wayne listened. Rick had paused.

"I blew the top of his head off. His brains were splattered all over the gun pit. And I walked in 'em. We walked in 'em. They stuck to the Vibram soles. On my boots. We had twenty-five dead bodies on the hill, they were NVA."

"Viet Cong?"

"Yeah. North Vietnamese. And the guys started mutilating 'em."

Rick is a man of few words, and he hadn't

told the story to very many people since he
came home from the war. But he told Wayne,
even got into some detail about the mutilations, because Wayne had become someone
he thought he knew pretty well. Since they had
worked together as bouncers at the Cabin, they
had enjoyed an honest camaraderie. By telling
this piece of his past to Wayne, Rick was hoping to add another dimension to their friendship. Rick wanted Wayne to know what the
war had done to him, what posttraumatic stress
disorder was all about.

But Rick was disappointed. In fact, he didn't
know what to make of Wayne's reaction. Most
people would be stunned, and some would try
to comprehend and be solemn about it. But
Wayne got into it. He laughed, titillated by the
gory detail. He wanted to know more.

Rick chalked it up as another example of
Wayne's otherness, that quotient of his character that set him apart, however obliquely, from
his peers. One day he was Old Reliable. The
next day he would be a fleeting enigma. On
Halloween, which he insisted was his birthday,
rather than October 18, Wayne turned into a
little kid. He put on makeup and dressed up in
elaborate costumes that he was able to just
throw together with convincing cleverness. He
had a knack for the dramatic moment, and it
pleased him immensely when nobody knew
who it was in disguise. The next day, he would
be Wayne, the Professional Bouncer.

Wayne was good at bouncing. He pressed to
the fore at the right moment, exerting just the
needed amount of force, avoiding a scuffle. On
three or four occasions, Wayne and Rick had

had their hands full. The incidents happened quickly, as they usually do. But they never found themselves dragged into a long fight, and that was the right way to do the job.

Wayne had always told Rick that he had a real fear of getting into it with somebody.

"I get real violent," he told Rick. "I don't want to lose my temper. So it would be better, since you're the better talker, so you get in first and try to talk the guys out of it. I'll cover you."

Wayne always did stand off in a corner, covering Rick, and while Wayne insinuated that he was a tough guy, he never said it outright to Rick. Yet for some reason Rick was aware that Wayne wanted him to think he was tough. It didn't matter. Wayne could handle himself well enough, except, it seemed to Rick, when it came to women.

Whenever Rick observed Wayne talking to women at the Cabin, it appeared just as it should: the gestures, the laughs, the trying to talk above the country-and-western crescendos. Some of Wayne's admirers were archetypically good looking, but he would invariably pass.

"What's wrong with him?" some of the girls would ask Rick. "Why doesn't he get the hint?"

Rick didn't know what was wrong with Wayne. In response, he would scoff at the remote possibility that they might not be Wayne's type.

Wayne liked petite blondes. But when he talked to Rick about a girl, there was never an occasion when he would simply say that he was attracted to her, or that he liked her, or that she was neat and he would like to get to know her. That was all verbal foreplay to Wayne.

"I really want to do it with her," Wayne would say, with the braggadocio of a twelve-year-old pumping up in front of his pals.

"Okay, Wayne, end of conversation," Rick would say, knowing where Wayne was coming from, not wanting to ply further.

Wayne made comments like that about a lot of women at the Cabin. He didn't, however, tell anyone, especially Rick, that he had been in some of their houses, even made detailed diagrams of the interior layouts. He had even been inside the houses of some of the women whom Rick knew personally. The proof of his illicit visitations were the secret hand-drawn floor plans he kept in his room at home.

Dory Schmid had just moved from the small town of Manhattan, Montana, into a one-bedroom apartment that was part of a three-unit building just off the road about a mile east of East Missoula, across from the Greenwood Trailer Park, and just west of Pinewood. In her late forties, she was living alone and at the time was between jobs. She and her husband, Bill, had been having problems. Much of the trouble had to do with his drinking, which was one reason he was staying with his parents in Lolo, just a few miles south of Missoula. The other problem was that his father was dying of pancreatic cancer. Bill and Dory's daughters were young women now, out on their own, and Dory's son from her first marriage lived just down the road from her new apartment.

For three full days, Dory had thrown herself

into cleaning the new apartment. And she was doing a terrific job, because she was a commercial-trade cleaning woman by profession. She knew how to bring up a shine on heavily waxed floors, and how to sing along as she worked, shaking out rugs and polishing tabletops, because as Dory Modey or Dory Barnes, Dory Schmid was also an aspiring country-western vocalist and song writer. Those were the stage names for this older, but still attractive, slender, blonde live-wire.

On the third night she was there, she got a call from her mother-in-law.

"Please come down, Dory. Take Bill home. Just for one night," she asked her daughter-in-law. There were some things she wanted to talk over with his father, and she wanted the privacy of being there alone with him.

"It's just for one night," she repeated.

Dory understood. She also understood that her mother-in-law's son was a handful. But she would do it. So she drove the fifteen miles south and got him, wondering how it would go. On the way back, she began to find out. One of the first things Bill insisted upon was that they stop for a six-pack. Dory complied. She didn't want to get into it. This was a one-night deal.

Dory also didn't show any reaction when Bill threw an open can of beer on her newly scrubbed and waxed kitchen floor. She didn't say or do anything when, at seven o'clock, Bill fell asleep on the floor. Maybe it was because of the dream she'd had the night before, a nightmare that had run around in her head all day. Somebody was beating Bill on the head with a club and she was trying to cover him up with a pillow. All day she had tried to figure what it meant. Now she would be patient.

By the time she got into bed, she had to crawl over Bill, who had taken the outside half. She was jammed up against the wall, but it was okay, and she had no trouble falling off to sleep, listening to her soused husband's heavy breathing.

It was past midnight when she awoke, hearing Bill cussing.

"You sonovabitch, what are you doing in this apartment?"

"What do you mean, what am I doing in this apartment?" Dory answered him, trying to rouse him from his delirium. "Wake up. Wake up." She elbowed him. "This is my apartment."

Then, as she sat up, she saw the man standing in the arched doorway of the bedroom, the man her husband was yelling at. In the dim bedroom light, all she could make out was a silhouette, but she could see the clear outline of a wild head of hair, a lot of curly hair.

Bill was still railing.

"Me and my wife don't need you in this apartment."

"Oh, I got the wrong place," answered the voice of the intruder, who had walked through Dory's unlocked front door.

"Get the Sam Hill out of here," Bill shouted.

The intruder started to turn, staggering a little. Bill didn't move off the bed. Dory stayed put, too, listening with sharpened ears as the footsteps retreated down the hall, past the kitchen, and into the living room. She didn't hear the door close, but she lay back down. Bill dozed off. Dory stared up at the ceiling, panicked, very happy that Bill lay beside her, her ears pricked for the slightest sound. Just as she began to relax with the thought that they had gotten rid of this character, she heard the sound of the couch as it struck the wall. It had rolled back on its casters.

"Bill," she whispered. "He didn't leave."

Bill had had enough of this. He was mad now, and he lifted his six-foot frame off the bed, pulled on his boots, and headed out of the room.

"Well, he will this time."

Dory was scared. In a flash, she remembered the dream from the night before, and she slipped across the bed and followed Bill out. She headed for the kitchen and grabbed a knife. Just in case, she thought.

Bill towered over the intruder, who was lounged, half-asleep, on the couch. With one hand he yanked him up.

"You sonovabitch, I said out, and when I said out, I meant out."

The intruder mumbled something.

Bill had him by one arm and was opening the front door with the other, and out he went.

"What in the Sam? Who was it?" Dory asked Bill.

"Oh, some fuzzy-haired character with glasses," Bill muttered, falling back into bed. "Some kid. He's probably drunk, and probably got the wrong apartment."

The next morning, as Dory's eyes glanced out the bedroom window, the intruder they didn't know lay huddled on the ground below, wrapped in a jacket. Dory never saw his face, but she could now see the mop of curly red hair that had been silhouetted in the doorway. Dory's unwanted guest, they would later learn, was Wayne Nance.

"For God's sake, Bill, what is that? Is that the guy out there?"

"He's just sleeping one off."

Dory felt a chill. She knew she had been alone in the apartment for three nights. Maybe Bill's presence surprised this guy. It was God's answer, she decided.

Rick stayed in touch after he left the Cabin in September of 1981 to take a job at Conlin's Furniture, where he worked in the warehouse and made local deliveries. On two occasions, when Rick and his wife, Laura, were moving, Wayne helped them out.

What Laura, a computer programmer at the U.S. Forest Service, could make of Wayne, based on having heard Rick talk about him and from seeing him in person occasionally, could be boiled down to one observation: Wayne was too nice. He would always make flattering comments about what she was wearing or about something in the house, but he sort of overdid it. She thought he was one of the most polite people she ever had met. Rick respected Wayne for being so gracious and he also didn't think it was out of character when Wayne declined Laura's offer to fix dinner for all of them, or even stay for one beer after all the heavy lugging of furniture. He had spent many hours with this guy. He had been to Wayne's house, seen the outrageous inventory of crap in his room, knew that Wayne was Wayne, whatever that meant.

After a few months at Conlin's, in February of 1982, Rick mentioned to Wayne that a job was opening up. Maybe he should drop in and fill out an application.

An astute reading of Wayne's job application would show that he had no employment history for the past two years. He didn't list the Cabin among his former employers, and he left blank the years that he attended the University of Montana, where he had flunked himself out. To the question: Were you ever injured? Wayne answered yes. He wrote down five words: "right hand no after effects." Was that a veiled reference to the pentagram scar on his right forearm? The badge of courage not to be forgotten?

None of this mattered to Louise Lightener, Conlin's assistant manager. She was looking for someone to work in the warehouse. She knew nothing of the suspicion that had once surrounded Wayne, the teenager, who was now twenty-seven years old. All she saw was a young man who had gone to local schools, had been in the Navy, had attended the University for awhile, and who lived with his father. He came highly recommended by Rick Davis. Rick Mace, the warehouse boss, who had come to know Wayne through Wayne's brother Bill, also vouched for him. So Wayne was hired. It was a part-time position. He would be paid four dollars an hour and he would help unload the three semitractor trailers that arrived each month from Conlin's South Dakota warehouse. By summer's end, in September, when Rick Davis again moved on, this time taking a job

Left: Wayne Nance at 15 during his freshman year of high school. (1971 *Bitterroot*) *Right:* Eighteen-year-old Wayne Nance was a senior in high school when Donna Pounds was murdered. (1974 *Bitterroot*)

Left: Wayne Nance enjoying an outdoor concert in 1984. *Right:* Wayne Nance's driver's Montana license photo from 1985.

The East Missoula home Wayne Nance shared with his father, George.

The main road cutting through East Missoula and leading into Hellgate Canyon, where police found several unidentified murder victims. At right is The Cabin, the bar where his mother waitressed and which became Nance's favorite hangout.

Donna and Harvey Pounds celebrated their 22nd wedding anniversary less than two weeks before her murder on April 11, 1974.

Downtown Missoula.

Left: Robert L. "Dusty" Deschamps III, Missoula's County Attorney who refused to arrest Harvey Pounds for his wife's murder. *Right:* Missoula County Sheriff John C. Moe.

Robert W. Balch, Professor of Sociology at the University of Montana. He certified that the town was collectively suffering from a case of mass hysteria stemming from several murders which resembled satanic sacrifices and cult killings.

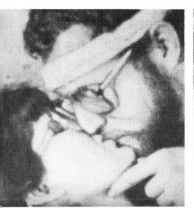

Wayne Nance and his girlfriend, known only as Robin, in a series of coin-booth photos from the summer of 1984. Robin was last seen in Missoula on September 28 of that year. If you recognize Robin, please call Undersheriff Larry Weatherman at the Missoula County Sheriff's Office, 406-201-5700.

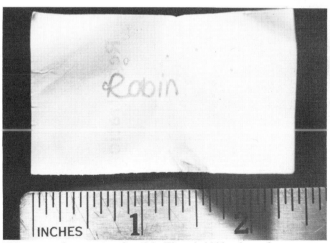

This scrap of paper was found in Wayne's hidden box of mementos. The writer of the note is unidentified.

Devonna Nelson at age 15. Her disappearance in July 1978 coincided with Wayne's visit to the city. Her remains were discovered east of Missoula in January 1980.

The Cobblestone Apartments, where Janet Wicker was attacked by an unidentified intruder who, it was later discovered, had hand-drawn maps of the complex.

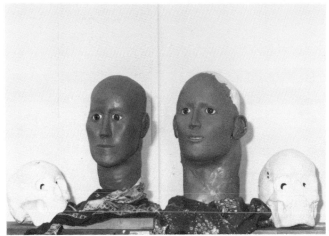

Anthropological constructions of the heads of the victims found east of Missoula in 1985, along with their bullet-holed skulls. Chryssie Crystal Creek is on the left, along with Debbie Deer Creek, who was later identified as Wayne's girlfriend, Robin.

Undersheriff Larry Weatherman of the Missoula County Sheriff's Department in his office. Chryssie Crystal Creek and Debbie Deer Creek are on his bookshelves in the rear.

Top: Conlin's Furniture. In his position as a deliveryman, Wayne Nance was so trusted by Missoula residents that often they would leave him the keys to their homes. *Center:* Wayne Nance with saleswoman Sheila Claxton at a Conlin's Christmas party in 1985. *Bottom:* Though fellow workers believed Wayne Nance to be harmless, this drawing (done on top of a note from a saleswoman) found after his death shows Nance's hidden nature.

Left: Kris Wells, Conlin's manager. By the time this shot was taken in December 1985, Wayne had already developed his deadly obsession for her. (Wayne Nance) *Right:* Another shot of Kris Wells. This one graced the first page of the photo album Wayne Nance had devoted to her. The signature at the bottom is taken from an insurance form.

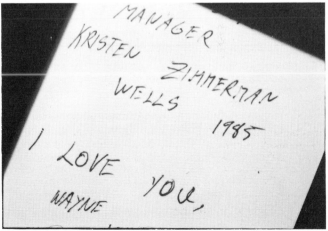

A note to Kris Wells written on the back of her photo was found in Nance's hidden box.

The Shook family. Mike and Teresa and their three children, Matt, 7, Megan, 2½, and Luke, 4 (from left).

The house that Mike and Teresa Shook built. Wayne Nance delivered a new couch to them only days before their murders on December 12, 1985.

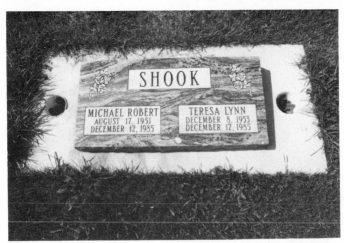

Mike and Teresa Shook's gravesite.

Bob and Georgia Shook, Mike's parents.

A sampling of the items found in the box Wayne Nance hid in a corner of Conlin's warehouse.

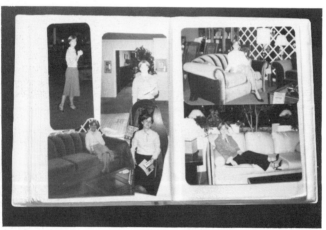

A spread of photos from Wayne Nance's album. Included were 35 photographs of Kris Wells.

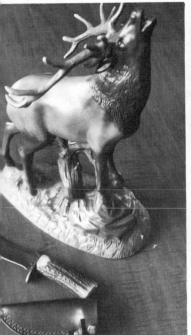

Left: The bugling elk and the knife Wayne Nance stole from the Shooks proved his presence inside their home. Less than two weeks later, Nance gave the elk to his father as a Christmas gift. *Right:* The kitchen cutlery knife that Wayne brought with him to Kris and Doug Wells's home on September 3, 1986.

The Ruger single-action six belonged to George Nance.

The basement pillar to which Wayne Nance tied Doug Wells as he had similarly trussed Kris Wells to her bed upstairs.

The Wells's bedroom, where the final battle between killer and would-be victims took place.

Left: Kris Wells in her bloodied nightclothes after the attack.

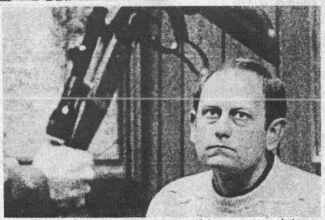

Doug Wells, on November 20, 1986, testifying at a coroner's inquest into the death of Wayne Nance. Robert "Dusty" Deschamps holds the broken stock of Wells's Savage 250 rifle which he used against Wayne Nance. (Dawn Feary/*The Missoulian*)

Doug and Kris Wells have provided invaluable insight into the mind of the serial killer and now are FBI experts. September 1990.

Wayne Nance's gravesite.

behind the counter at Rice's, one of Missoula's ubiquitous secondhand stores, Wayne took Rick's place. Now he was working full time in the warehouse and making local deliveries in one of Conlin's trucks. In time, Conlin's would mean more than just a paycheck to Wayne.

Five mornings a week he would get into his small brown pickup and head for work at Conlin's, leaving behind the dismal environ of Minnesota Street. Conlin's would give Wayne the socioeconomic leap his father and mother had failed to provide. Behind the wheel of a company truck, delivering to any of Missoula's middle-class neighborhoods, the view through his windshield was uncannily suggestive of a scene right out of a TV commercial for a bygone era. There, on Crestline Street or Strand or Beckwith, as if encased and preserved against time, was the proverbial American ideal. Elderly couples stroll along quiet sidewalks, the man sporting a pork-pie hat, the woman wearing a light sweater. The chick-a-chuck-a-chick of lawn sprinklers seems the only intrusion, and even that's somehow monotonously comforting. The yellow clapboard house is perfect. So is the white banister-railed porch, trimmed with hanging flowerpots and all around a freshly cut and edged, weedless lawn. Isn't this the way it's supposed to be? This American Gothic model of a place.

And the store would serve as a base of operations. What better way to gain entry to someone's home than as the furniture delivery man whom the delighted customer greets with a "Hello" and a "Come right in"? It wasn't uncommon for customers, if they knew the saleswoman well enough, to hand over the house keys, so the delivery could be made even if they weren't planning to be at home.

The Conlin's sinecure would open new doors for Wayne, but none of his coworkers would know it. To his newfound family, Wayne was the unbearably shy new guy in the warehouse who hardly made eye contact. He was the squarely built redhead with all the tattoos, which went on display when he doffed his shirt on hot days, wringing out the sweat after a big job. There was a spider, a snake, a bat, the grim reaper's scythe. His muscle-molded shoulder was imprinted with a dragon. To look at him, Wayne was a veritable Illustrated Man. But on the inside, he remained an unknown.

The guys in the warehouse and the women on the salesfloor would become direct objects of Wayne's obsessive attention. In ways, he would treat them as family, mixing love and hate together, as families sometimes do. The more he misled them with his guile, the more he was free to overindulge his estranged world view, living out—many, many times over—his anxious, recurring, and violent sexual fantasies.

It was April 27, 1983, a Wednesday night. Janet Wicker had come home from work to the Cobblestone Apartments, a new complex of townhouse-type dwellings nestled right in the bowel of Hellgate Canyon, just east of Missoula proper, bounded by the old Route 10 that paralls Interstate 90 and the Clark Fork River. As she parked her car and made for the front door, it was already getting dark. She looked forward to seeing her husband, who would be home soon.

She unlocked the front door, and as she was stepping inside, reaching for the inside light switch, she was grabbed by a hand that came out of the dark. The masked man who stood before her had been waiting inside. He had climbed to the balcony that was off the upstairs bedroom and gotten inside, and the first thing he said to her was that he wanted money.

Janet screamed.

"Shut up," he ordered. "I want money. I'll tie you up if you don't cooperate."

She screamed again.

And the man came at her.

"Shut up. Shut . . ." His words stopped and the fists came. He swung at her, knocking her to the floor.

She tried in vain to fight him off, kicking and screaming, trying to get away.

"Shut up!" he ordered one more time, this time from behind the shiny steel blade of a knife he had pulled from a sheath on his belt.

"Shut up. Or I'll stab you. Just shut up."

Frozen, Janet was quiet. She listened as the man told her all he wanted was money. That he was going to take her upstairs. That she should cooperate. All he wanted was money. He kept saying it as he led his frightened prey up the stairs at knifepoint.

Maybe that's all he wanted, Janet wanted to think, as she obeyed. But Janet Wicker never got the answer to that question. Just as the masked man had gotten her upstairs, they both heard the front door open. Her husband was home.

The man with the knife was gone in a flash, dashing across the second-floor balcony and over the railing. When he hit the ground, he ran for the riverbank, racing eastward in the direction of East Missoula, which was approximately one-half mile away.

Janet's husband called the police, but by the time they arrived, the suspect was long gone into the night. Janet had never seen the face of her attacker. Without a suspect, or a lead, there would be no arrest. Wayne, who had made a hand-drawn map of the Cobblestone Apartments, showing the floor plan of the Wicker's apartment and its proximity to other nearby apartments, had also carefully delineated an escape route in a series of tiny footprints that led down to the river. He saved it after the foiled attack, stuffing it into the treasure mound in his room in his father's house on Minnesota Avenue.

Though sheriff's deputies would not inquire at the time about it, they would later learn that many residents of the Cobblestone Apartments, including the Wickers, had ordered furniture from Conlin's and had had it delivered to their homes.

Chapter 13

A Split Personality

It was the early days of the new year, 1985, and being outside was like being in deep freeze. Julie Slocum and her new boyfriend, Kreg Brager, couldn't take it anymore. They had been working on Julie's car, which was parked at the curb in front of the apartment. But they decided that the minor repair could wait. It was too damn cold.

"Want some hot tea?" she asked, not waiting for his answer as she continued. "Let's go in."

Kreg moved into the living room and parked his chilled bones in front of the TV. Julie headed for the kitchen, where she swished out the tea kettle and filled it with cold water. She could hear the muffled wamp-wamp of a TV commercial as she ran her fingers across the stack of teabags, debating which it would be—orange pekoe or something light, the jasmine. Or chamomile. Between her momentary pauses of thought, she could tell that Kreg had tuned into something, because he had turned up the volume. The teakettle creaked quietly as the hot electric burner did its work, and Julie's delightful presence of mind was suddenly inter-

rupted. Her ears caught the broadcast. It was a
Crimestoppers Report, one of the ones put out
by the sheriff's department. This one was about
the Jane Doe whose body had been found on
Christmas Eve—only two weeks before—just
below Bonner Dam.

A creepy feeling seized her as she focused
her attention directly on what the announcer
was saying.

"White female. Five-five to five-eight. One
hundred twenty-five to one hundred-forty
pounds. Hair appears to have been permed and
dyed auburn. This victim had pierced ears.
Anyone who has . . ."

Julie didn't need to hear any more. She stood
rigid, her eyes fixed on the screen, holding a
bag of orange pekoe tea in hand. Then she
turned to Kreg.

"God, that's that girl," she said.

"What?"

"That's that girl, Robin. Robin," she said to
herself, the words coming in a whispering
shudder.

"Yeah, I think it might be," Kreg said.
"You're right."

As much as she loved Wayne, whose artwork
still graced the walls of her living room even
now that she had a boyfriend, she was not
ready to believe the words that had just come
out of her own mouth.

"Something weird's going on, man."

"Yeah, I know," a disbelieving Kreg chimed
in.

"I'm gonna call Crimestoppers. This is too
weird. It can't be."

As she dialed the number, there came a ris-

ing whistle in the kitchen, and she waved at
Kreg to get the kettle. Crimestoppers was a
local nonprofit tip line supported by a citizens
group that also pays rewards for information
that leads to the closing of a case. Crimestoppers calls are directly patched into the Missoula
city police or the county sheriff's office, de-
pending on the jurisdiction of a case, and the
caller speaks directly to a detective.

When the voice came on the line, Julie suddenly became reticent as she was asked for her
name. The decision to call Crimestoppers had
been made almost without thinking. After a
pause, she did give her name to the detective.
But she wasn't going to mention Wayne. She
didn't want to tell the detective anything about
Wayne. After all, she wasn't sure. Maybe her
mind was playing tricks.

Shadow boxing around some of the questions
the detective asked her, she threw back a lot of
questions at him. Exactly how tall was the girl?
Was she really heavy set? But she didn't get
any answers. It was clear that only a set
amount of facts about the girl who Captain
Weatherman called Debbie Deer Creek were
cleared for release. To Julie, it seemed that the
detective on the line was being evasive, not
helpful. Maybe he was trying to tell her it
wasn't who she thought it might be, and tiring
of the apparent lack of response to her call, she
let it go. Actually, she thought to herself as she
hung up, it was a relief.

"Great," she told Kreg. "Boy, am I glad. It's
a load off my mind. It's not Wayne."

Julie's mind then flashed back to the last time
she had seen the girl named Robin. It was her

birthday. There was a party right here in her new apartment. It had only been three months ago. And she remembered how Wayne avoided her after that, and it still bothered her, because they were supposed to be best friends, buddies who shared everything. In the long blink of an eye that Julie Slocum, Wayne's friend for six years, even suspected that the Jane Doe on the Crimestoppers report was Robin, and that Wayne had something to do with it, the air in the room seemed to have thinned, lost its oxygen. Was it a vision, a synthesis of all the information that she carried around with her on this particular January day, locked into focus by a television report? Or was her mind playing tricks?

Kreg had shared her suspicion at first, but he didn't know Wayne as well as she did, and he had met Robin only once, at the party in late September. At the time, Julie didn't want to admit to it, but she knew that her friend and cohort Wayne was two people, a split personality who carried on his relationships with friends as if nothing could be more transparent than the Wayne they knew and loved. But Julie knew some things about Wayne that most people didn't. Wayne had confided these things to her.

"Whenever he would stay out too late and his dad would be gone, and it would be later than his mother thought he should be out, she wouldn't confront him face to face. She'd catch him when he was trying to sneak into the house and she'd bonk him with a baseball bat. Here he's a grown-up person, had been in the Navy. That was her way of disciplining a young man that was tougher than she was. She cracked the whip, and George was none too easy on him."

It was what Wayne didn't say about his father that bothered Julie. She observed a perverse obsession on Wayne's part to please his father.

"Snapping to. There was something there that you wanted to ask about it, but you're afraid to. It was too much. Especially here he was about thirty years old and he was still doing it.

"I thought his dad ruined his social life. Wayne didn't have a whole lot of friends. He was real serious about his job. And when he did get out to a party he had such a good time.

"It irritated me at times. I think his dad was much too hard on him. When he would come back into town, man, Wayne would drop everything. He'd leave parties. He'd be home with his dad."

The tea had brewed. It was time to snuggle up with Kreg in the warm living room of her apartment. She had done the right thing. She had called, and even though she had been sure that the Jane Doe and Robin were one and the same, she wasn't sure anymore.

Chapter 14

The Bear Hunter

The orb-shaped fragment that lay among the rounded rocks was the top of a human skull. It rested at the bottom of a slope in the crease of a parched creek bed. Come spring, the clear mountain waters would return, running downhill to the Clark Fork River in the valley below. But now, on this Monday afternoon in September, the man who tramped uphill through this rugged mountain terrain was on dry ground. He was a bear hunter slowly ascending a logging road along a ridge that led up to the meager beginnings of this drainage called Crystal Creek. His eyes were peeled to the ground. He was scanning for any telltale sign that he was still on the trail of a wounded black bear.

He was looking for tracks, or a blood drop, a broken branch, and at whatever fell within his tight-grid vision, when he spotted the distinct rounded object that wasn't, he could tell, an ordinary, water-polished rock in the stream bed.

It was the Monday afternoon of September 9, 1985. Later that day, when sheriff's deputies, led by Captain Weatherman, would climb to the shoulder of the ridge, to a spot that marked the nearly imperceptible headwater of this mountain creek, they would find most of the rest of the skeleton. It belonged to a young woman. It appeared that she had been dumped on the side of the slope at least a year ago and maybe longer.

One large leg bone, the femur, was found nearby, as were numerous bits and pieces of bone. There was evidence of a lot of dental work, and that encouraged Captain Weatherman. The skull of this latest victim showed two bullet holes. She had been shot once in the back of the head and once in the temple. Two .32-caliber slugs were found at the site.

A forensic examination of the skeleton would eventually tell Weatherman that this victim was smaller than Debbie Deer Creek. She was between twenty and twenty-two years old. Her height was probably five feet to five-foot-two. Her weight was estimated at approximately a hundred pounds. She had light brown hair and may have been of partial Asian descent. Forensic determinations suggested she may have been right handed, and she was definitely a smoker. Ballistics examination of the slugs were fairly conclusive. They were Winchester/Western Silver Tip bullets, which could have been fired from any of the following gun makes: Ceska, Walther, Llama, Star, Savage, or Astra.

But Weatherman didn't have a weapon. All he had was another body of a murdered female. No clothing or personal items were found at the site. This woman had been shot, stripped, and left nude on the ground. Animals may have disturbed the body, and the force of water would have washed the rounded skull down the grade.

As the crow flies, this body was three miles southeast of the Bonner Dam, where Debbie Deer Creek had been found. What was more sobering to Weatherman was the relative proximity not only to Debbie Deer Creek, but also to Siobhan McGuinness and the Beavertail Hill Girl. This was the fourth young female body found slain—and the fourth unsolved homicide—in the fifteen-mile stretch east of Missoula to the county line.

Captain Weatherman had only recently retired the mystery of the Beavertail Hill case, disposing of the facial reconstruction that had so badly deteriorated anyway. His persistence had paid off. Twice a year, he would dig out the file and send the dead girl's description out across the national network of police computers. In early 1984, the had become aware of a massive effort in Washington State to track the so-called Green River killer, who was suspected of having killed more than forty women in a stabbing and strangulation spree that ran from July of 1982 to March of 1984. Most of the victims were prostitutes or runaways who would not be reported missing for weeks. In time, all but four of the Green River victims would be identified by the machinery of the Green River Task Force.

But more importantly to Weatherman, on February 6, 1985, he hit a match. Investigators in Washington didn't suspect that this Montana skeleton belonged to the Green River killer, but at least they knew who she was. Her name was

Devonna Nelson, a fifteen-year-old presumed runaway.

The long, slow process of making the identification had begun on March 9, 1984, almost a full year earlier, when someone on the street tipped a local Seattle policeman that Devonna might be among the crowd of missing persons being sought by the task force. On March 27, the task force harvested Devonna's dental records and entered her into the net. Ten months later, after they had issued a regional broadcast for records of unidentified skulls, Captain Weatherman sent the dental evidence from both of his Jane Doe bodies to William Haglund, chief investigator at the King County medical examiner's office in Tacoma. It was to be one of eleven positive identifications of unidentified bodies found in California, Idaho, and Montana made through the forensic screening process.

Now, as the fall of 1985 was upon him, Weatherman knew what his next move would be. He would call Dr. Charney in Fort Collins one more time, and ask him to work with this new bullet-holed skull to produce a likeness that he would place on his bookshelf in the company of Debbie Deer Creek. He would name this one Chryssie Crystal Creek.

The *Missoulian* didn't make much of the Crystal Creek skeleton. A six-paragraph story that appeared on page 9 of the September 17 edition was prepared by the Associated Press, not by a local staff reporter, even though the discovery of a single unidentified human skeleton was rare enough in Montana at the time. In the whole state, from 1981 to 1985, close to a dozen unidentified bodies in various stages of decomposition had been discovered. Only four remained unidentified and unsolved. One of those was found in Lewis and Clark County to the east. The remaining three were the ones found in Missoula County. After the Beavertail Hill girl was identified, two remained, and their plastic reconstructed heads emitted blank stares from the bookshelf in Captain Weatherman's office, as if looking over his shoulder as he labored in vain to put a real name to their faces.

The slight differences in M.O. notwithstanding—one victim was buried, the other dumped on the ground—Weatherman was certain that the same person had killed both Debbie and Chryssie, and he was beginning to see that the beautiful Clark Fork River valley had become someone's dumping ground.

Chapter 15

A Really Nice Guy

Wayne saw her coming. Was he dreaming, or
was that really Kris Wells getting out of the car,
coming into the Cabin? He wasn't dreaming.
Now he heard her voice.

"Aw c'mon," she was saying to the group
that was getting out of the car. And he certainly
recognized Kris's voice. He liked the friendly,
efficient upturn of it, just as he liked the precision cut of her hair, which she wore pixie style.
He was mesmerized by her clear, direct manner
with people. She was all business, just like him.
And she was the only petite, blue-eyed blonde
at Conlin's. Of all the women at the store, Kris
Wells was number one in Wayne's eyes. And
here she was, coming to the Cabin.

"Wayne!" she greeted him, leading her husband, Doug, and a handful of friends to the
door. Kris and her party were coming from a
wine-tasting party. It had been a little fancier
event than the run-of-the-mill wine-tasting parties that their group usually held. Kris was a
little tipsy, exuding camaraderie, perhaps more
than she typically would, because after all, Kris
was Wayne's boss.

She had started as a saleswoman in June of 1982, just a few months before Wayne went full time. Then, she'd been twenty-nine years old, and one of the first things he noticed was that she wore a wedding ring. Two years later, in the summer of 1984, she had been made sales manager. Now she was manager of the store, and it was no secret that Wayne was crazy about her.

"We thought we'd show our friends visiting from California a real cowboy bar," Kris said, igniting her words with a twinge of hometown pride. "So here we are!"

Wayne couldn't have been more gracious. There would be no cover charge.

"It's on me."

"Oh, Wayne, thank you."

"Hey, save a dance for me," he called to Kris as she began to melt into the crowd inside the door.

"Sure," she answered, disappearing.

The music was loud. The crowd was authentic. And before long, Kris and Doug and their friends were falling into the scene. The Cabin packed a pretty good reputation. Besides being a bona fide trucker, biker, and cowboy bar, it also attracted a voyeuristic, adventurous middle-class clientele. White-collar types looking for a thrill brought their wives and girlfriends to the Cabin for a little rough-edged fun. There were other cowboy bars in town, but this was the real thing. The Cabin didn't have a dignifying Western name, like the more studied Duelin' Dalton's, or any of the extraneous and phony, stylized Wild-West decor. It was a Friday night mecca for secretaries and dental hygienists and assistant store managers, who could go out as girls-en-masse to the Cabin and live to brag about it on Monday morning in the office, eliciting "oohs" from co-workers who would want to hear all about it.

"I'm gonna ask Wayne to dance," Kris said into Doug's ear, knowing that her husband wouldn't dance, because he never did. She also didn't think he would mind, because he never did mind when she danced with other men.

"I don't know if I would egg him on," Doug said.

What was this? It seemed he was scolding her.

"Aw c'mon. Just one dance."

"I wouldn't do it. I just wouldn't do it. Not this guy." Doug stood his ground. He really didn't mind when Kris danced with other men. If she wanted to dance, fine. But not with Wayne. Doug sensed that it would mean a lot more to Wayne than it would to his wife, and that was why he was displeased when Kris ignored his advice and went up to Wayne anyway.

The next day, Kris was sitting at her desk when Wayne asked if he could come in for a minute. In the few steps he took into the room, Doug's admonition flashed in her mind.

"I have something for you," Wayne said, holding a small card in his hand, which he then placed on her desk. It was a watercolor drawing done on a small paper card. Kris felt a tightening as she looked down at the mildly erotic image. Wayne had drawn a scantily clad woman, and he had posed her, in a not so sub-

tle way, legs up in a wine glass. The inscription
he wrote was: "First wine-tasting."

Kris was embarrassed and offended. She
didn't know how to react, but she knew she
would throw this thing away as soon as he left.
She knew Doug would say, "I told you so."

For the next three nights that Wayne worked
at the Cabin, he brought flowers with him, prepared to give them to the girl he had put in the
wine glass, the one he adored.

It was not hard for anyone to see how much
Wayne liked Kris. All they had to do was look
around the store, especially in the back warehouse, where Wayne had inscribed the walls in
giant script, making the initials *KZ*. That was
the way Kris signed off on orders.

Born Kristen Zimmerman on August 10, 1953,
in the small Illinois town of Moline, she was
the bright, blue-eyed apple of her father's eye.
By the time she entered high school and was
elected to the cheerleading squad at Riverdale
High in nearby Cordova, (population 900), this
baby of the family was well on her way to becoming the fully grown girl next door. An out-
sider would have found it hard to disagree with
her father that his daughter Kris, who didn't
drink, didn't use drugs, who loved football and
basketball games and sock hops and Sadie
Hawkins Day dances, was anything less than
the American ideal. After all, Harold Zimmerman read the newspapers. The year was 1968.
The streets of Chicago—no more than 160 miles
away—were filled with the obscene chants of
a generation that was laying siege to the 1968
Democratic national convention, and somehow

managing to catalyze a response that, through
its own police violence, succeeded in shaking
the very foundation of the Establishment.

Harold Zimmerman and his wife, Patricia
Coe Zimmerman, were, they had no doubt,
that Establishment. He was an engineer at
American Air Filter. She was a secretary for the
superintendent of schools. Their children, Wes,
the oldest, Kathie, and Kris, never had cause
to doubt what that meant. Nobody was making
a lot of money in Cordova. Nobody had a lot
of time to do anything much else but work in
this down-to-earth town.

Kris's parents hadn't gone to college, but it
was taken for granted that all three of their children would, and they did. Kris attended the
University of Iowa in Iowa City, an hour and a
half drive from home, and earned a bachelor's
degree in interior design and related arts. After
graduation she worked in the custom drapery
department of a local department store, then
moved on to a local supply house where she
tried her hand at kitchen design. Then, at odds
with her career, she became a stewardess for
Trans-World Airlines. Her TWA stint would
last only six months, because the man she was
getting serious about was in Montana. She had
known him since high school. His name was
Douglas Wells. He was a football player who
was two years her senior. Everybody called him
Doug.

He was a kind of quiet, down-to-earth type,
a plodder, whose ordinariness was a disguise
for the poetry in his simple approach. The dull-
thudding moments in his life were not to be

overlooked. They were like soundings off bed-rock. They always yielded an inspiration.

Born in Van Nuys, California, on September 27, 1951, to Warren and Lucille Wells, he was named Douglas because both his parents worked at Douglas Aircraft Company. Their son, with the obvious company name, was the second-oldest of five. Joanne came first. In the winter of 1953, the Wellses moved back to Illinois, where Dale, Dennis, and Peggy were born. The family settled in Hillsdale (population 395), and Warren Wells quickly set to work building a family logging business while Lucille raised the children.

From the time the boys could understand anything, Warren Wells lectured them about work. He always was brief and to the point.

"You work. That's what you do," he would say. "No summers off. You work."

In time, the logging business had grown up to include a respectable hardwood sawmill, plus there was the family farm. After the boys did the chores, they cut brush to keep pastures clear, or they mended fences.

The work ethic was infused in the father's sons just as thoroughly as a walnut grain is densely whorled, and Doug wasted no time when he graduated from Riverdale High in the spring of 1969 in getting down to business. He started a small trucking enterprise with a rattletrap pickup, hauling sawdust and splitting wood. Then, after a year of ups and downs, he decided to try college. In the fall of 1970 he enrolled at the University of Montana in Missoula as a forestry major.

The following summer, while home from college, he met the girl he had eyed from afar in high school. Then she had been the sophomore cheerleader. Now, just graduated, the two of them fell together. He was bound for Missoula in the fall, and she was due in Iowa City. At least they had the summer together.

Doug's career at the University of Montana was short lived. After the fall semester, he quit. But his love affair with Big Sky country was to endure. He returned briefly to Illinois, but then almost as quickly returned to the high valleys and even higher mountains that he missed. An avid outdoorsman, he seized upon the world-class hunting and fishing that is a treasured way of life for Montanans. Roadside billboards, paid for by local taxidermists, beckoned: "Preserve Your Hunting and Fishing Memories." For big game, there was elk, antelope, white-tail deer, muledeer, grizzly bear and black bear, Rocky Mountain Big Horn sheep, mountain goat, mountain lion, fox and coyote. There was ringneck pheasant, waterfowl of all kinds from teal to mallards, upland birds that included three species of grouse. Montana was and still is among the five states that give swan permits. Fishing in the clear lakes and streams was equally gratifying, due to abundant lake trout, cutthroat, largemouth, and, to a lesser degree, smallmouth bass, pike, and brown, rainbow, and bull trout.

Doug was a bachelor, living in a sportsman's paradise, driving a forklift in a warehouse for money. For awhile, he signed on with a logging crew cutting timber. It was a good life, but something was still missing. He didn't want to work for wages the rest of his life, and after he was witness to a tragic accident one day—his boss fell from a truck, broke his back, and died on the spot—Doug decided to go back to school. He applied to a gunsmith school in Denver, and returned home to Illinois to cut wood for his father and rekindle the romance with Kris. When the time came to leave for Denver, to enroll in the Colorado School of Trade, he knew he would hate the city-boy life. But it would only be for a year, and he would write to Kris. The letters she wrote back would make the separation a little easier.

After graduation, Doug returned to Illinois and opened a small gunsmith shop in Moline, but it was a false start. Montana still beckoned, and he was on his way. Back in Missoula, he returned to the back-braking jobs he had left, but he had plans this time, and he hoped Kris would soon join him. The wait wasn't long. In the fall of the year, Kris loaded her car and drove to Missoula, where she found work for awhile in a department store, and then as flooring, cabinet, and wallpaper saleswoman.

But after the winter came and went and spring was upon them, the two transplants found themselves taking stock of their lives. Doug was twenty-seven. He ostensibly had a trade, but he wasn't practicing it. Kris was twenty-five. She was a college graduate but was still sweating it out in sales. They were living together, but they weren't married. They wanted to stay in Missoula for all the same reasons that people had moved there in droves, but they also realized they would never make their fortune on the local pay scales. So once again they shuttled back to Illinois.

Doug gunsmithed and Kris took a job in the insurance department at John Deere in Moline, but it didn't take long for them to discover that they weren't happy. Doug, as was expected of him from his old-fashioned parents, lived on the farm. Kris had taken a small apartment in Port Byron, where Doug spent a lot of time. After almost a year of this in-between life, on April 14, 1979, in a courthouse ceremony in Rock Island, they made it official. Kris's father and sister, Kathie, were there, and so was Doug's brother, Dale. Afterward, there was a reception in the home where Kris had grown up. Within two weeks of the marriage, as if some invisible filament had once again exceeded its stretch point, destiny yanked them west again, back to Montana, where they had been the happiest, even if they were the poorer for it. Alone, in a fully packed car, Kris drove out first. She had a job lined up and was needed immediately. Two weeks later, having packed the rest of their belongings, Doug followed. This time it was for good.

Doug started Lock, Stock & Barrel, his own gunsmith business, and Kris went to work for Home Interiors, where she was perfectly willing to sell the store's carpets and cabinets until something better came along. The following June, when she joined Conlin's sales staff, she had found it.

Within two years, Kris was promoted to sales manager. Doug's gunsmithing business had taken hold, and in the short four years since their last return, though the Wellses were not making the fortune they had sought in Illinois's Quad Cities, they had made a solid beginning, and they were comfortable. Kris was able to begin furnishing a new home on Parker Court that they bought in a small tract development on Missoula's western periphery. Doug was independent enough as a businessman to arrange his life around the hunting and fishing calendar: The first Saturday of September begins bird season; antelope season starts on the first Sunday of October, followed by big game season on the third Sunday of the month. They had collected a set of friends, whom they socialized with over chicken barbecue dinners or at Grizzly football games at the University or over dinner at one of their old-standby restaurants.

The Wellses had aspirations, but only to a point. They worked harder than they played. They were hardly yuppie types, but if neither of them felt like making dinner, they might pop out for nachos and beers. And they could, at the drop of a hat, because there were no children in their life. Before work, or after work, whichever time suited her, Kris could slip into her nylon jogging shorts and go for a run on the quiet roads around her neighborhood. She would already allow herself to think ahead, to the day when they might even get a bigger house, a little farther out in the country, where they would have more land, where Doug could test-fire his guns without having to get in his truck and drive somewhere. She had no way of knowing that her free-associating, aerobic privacy was being invaded, that Wayne Nance was watching in the bushes, snapping pictures of KZ.

*   *   *

The man Louise Lightener had hired to work in Conlin's warehouse was not the run-of-the-mill local boy described in awkward, stiff pencil scrawl on the job application. Wayne Nance was a mercurial, seething psycho, who in due course would earn everyone's complete trust, especially when it came to the women at the store.

The female side of Conlin's was represented on the sales floor, the vast high-ceilinged showroom that appears to the wandering customer as an impassable maze of mauve-colored La-Z-Boys. A handful of saleswomen typically were on duty at any given time, and besides selling the customers, they arranged for deliveries and generally kept the public space of Conlin's stocked and ready. Their duties brought them into regular contact with the warehouse, a world surfaced in cardboard and plywood just feet away through a doorway. The men were the grunts who took the paperwork orders from the saleswomen. The saleswomen were half-apologetic when they inquired of the men about whether a delivery could be made on a certain day, maybe a day earlier than scheduled. Maintaining peace on the common ground of that doorway was crucial for Conlin's success.

Customers came in the front door and the furniture went out the back. It all had to go smoothly at this juncture, which on busy days became a stress point, where the men in blue jeans and work boots intersected with the women in moderately upscale casual business attire and costume jewelry. On hot days, the

warehouse ached of sweat. The showroom betrayed the wilt of perfume.

The sales force at Conlin's was a cross-section
of single, married, and divorced women. Some
of them absolutely needed a paycheck. Some of
them were biding time here while they fashioned modest entrepreneurial dreams. Some
were making careers here. Others just liked the
work, and were grateful to have such a good
job. Most of them were older than Wayne,
some old enough to be his mother. But he
found them fascinating, and they became the
objects of his affection.

They had grown accustomed to Wayne's outward weirdness as much as they had come to
appreciate his flattery. He remembered everyone's birthday every year, and would bring
them each a present. Often it was flowers or a
pair of inexpensive earrings or some other trin-
ket, which he frequently picked up at the Hall-
mark store in the mall where his sister, Veta,
worked. Wayne remembered wedding anniversaries. He did it up on Saint Patrick's Day,
bringing in green ice cream and shamrock-
trimmed cups and saucers.

The women tolerated his gift giving and listened to him complain that he couldn't get a
girlfriend. They assured their husbands and
one another that this was all harmless. This was
puppy love. They felt a little sorry for him and
they played along. Sure, he was different, but
the world is full of people who are different,
whose idiosyncracies might just as easily be ignored. Here was a sweet boy with a crush.

Cindy Bertsch, a pretty brunette, was twenty-
four when she joined the Conlin's office staff in

September 1982. Recently graduated from the University of South Dakota with a degree in criminal justice, she had been offered a position at the state penitentiary at Sioux Falls, but her previous experience as an intern with probation work ultimately dissuaded her from taking the job. Instead, she followed her sweetheart to Missoula, got married, and in time became the office manager at Conlin's. She was in charge of the books, payroll, servicing the work orders, and whatever else didn't fall into someone else's in-basket.

Cindy's husband, Carey, an insurance adjuster, thought it was definitely out of the ordinary when his wife came home one day with a new pink belt that a man at work—Wayne—had given to her as a present. It matched a pink sweater that she had worn the day before.

"Nice jacket," Wayne often said to Cindy as he passed her office en route from the warehouse to the showroom.

"Thank you, Wayne."

"Nice dress, you look great in that," he would say on another day, when Cindy was wearing one of the couple of outfits that caught Wayne's attention. It was always polite flattery, and it cemented the impression Cindy formed of Wayne as a really nice guy, a friend.

Once, when Wayne invited Cindy and her husband to join him at the Cabin for a night out, he tapped his old connection and got them in without a cover charge. Cindy and Carey felt a little special.

Without thinking twice about it, the women at Conlin's would hand Wayne the keys to their houses, so he could deliver something for them while they were at work. They trusted him completely.

Ruth Ann Rancourt, who worked with Cindy in the office, didn't for a second worry about giving Wayne her keys. She had bought a new mattress for her daughter Stacy, who was fourteen. It was ready to be delivered, but neither she nor her husband, Lee, would be home. So Wayne delivered it, putting the mattress in Stacy's room, as Ruth Ann had requested.

Later, when Wayne asked to see a picture of Stacy, leading Ruth Ann on with a tease about how he liked young girls, the woman played along.

"Oh, Wayne, she's too young for you," she teased back. Then, though still engaged in the lightness of the moment, she remembered that in Stacy's room, where Wayne had put the new mattress, there were photographs of her daughter, and they were right out for anyone to see.

"No, she's not too young. I like young girls. I'd like to see a picture of her," Wayne insisted.

"Her father says she can't date 'till she's thirty." Ruth Ann played along some more. "Anyway, if you had looked in the bedroom there were pictures of her there."

Wayne stopped.

"Oh, no," he said after a pause, pulling away from the conversation, heading for the warehouse, adopting a neutral, righteous tone now. "If I'm in a customer's home, I never look around. I don't do that."

They knew he was impossible. But they also knew they could count on him to do them a favor. He was such a nice guy.

Sheila Claxton, another Conlin's saleswoman

who started at the store during the same month Wayne did, found less reason to despair over Wayne's eccentricities and his peculiar definition of reality. An attractive, dark-haired divorcée in her late thirties, mother of two boys, she was a little wiser in the ways of the world, and being a child of the Sixties, her temperament was geared to letting Wayne be Wayne. They became good friends, and Sheila didn't hesitate to ask favors of him. On occasions when her aging Pinto was out of commission, Wayne was always ready to swing by her house and give her a lift to work. Once, she had asked Wayne if he could get a small tree for her sister Vicki, who wanted it for a window display at the store where she worked. There was no hurry.

"Whenever you're out in the woods again, you know, something about this high," she said, gesturing with her hands to show him how big the tree ought to be. Vicki wanted to drape handbags off the branches, Sheila explained.

The very next day, Wayne delivered the perfect tree to Vicki's store. Sheila was surprised that he did it so quickly, but not really. It wasn't out of character. Wayne really aimed to please.

In the next few days and weeks, when Vicki told her sister that she thought somebody was watching her house at night, Sheila never made the faintest connection to Wayne.

Nor did Joyce Halverson, another saleswoman, when she lost a regular customer after Wayne had gone to the woman's house to pick up a loveseat that needed repair. The customer complained to Joyce about obscene phone calls that she had started to receive after the Conlin's pickup. The woman swore to Joyce that she was sure it was the delivery man, Wayne, who was harassing her. She was furious about it, and after she had her telephone changed to an unlisted number, she never came back to Conlin's. Joyce was sorry to lose a customer, but she certainly didn't believe Wayne had anything to do with it.

Other customers of Conlin's had similar problems. They would get a delivery and then be haunted by obscene phone calls. One customer had to get her phone number changed twice. After she got the first new, unlisted number, the calls stopped for a while, but then the caller was at it again—after she had taken another delivery from Conlin's. The customer was sure now that calls had something to do with the deliveries from the store, so she had her phone number changed again to a second unlisted number, and refused to do any more business with Conlin's. The calls stopped.

Wayne told everyone at Conlin's that he didn't like to talk on the phone. If he and Sheila made arrangements for him to give her a ride to work the next day if she couldn't get her car started, she would offer to call him first.

"No, I'll call you," he would say. And then when he did call, he more than once pretended to be an obscene caller.

Ruth Ann once took a call for Wayne, and when she went into the warehouse to get him, he blew up at her.

"I told you I don't take phone calls!" he yelled. "Go back and tell whoever it is I don't take phone calls."

So Ruth Ann did. "I'm sorry," she told the party on the line, "he doesn't take phone calls."

"You go back and tell that sonuvabitch it's his dad," came the angry imperative.

When she returned to the warehouse the second time, repeating his father's words to him, Wayne sailed for the phone.

"You can tell anybody I won't take a phone call," he said. "But not my dad."

Wayne's family was known to the sales staff at Conlin's. His brothers and sisters bought furniture from the store. Bill Nance bought a dining-room table from Sheila shortly after he was married. Desirée and Veta, who were both married now, would come in and buy things and say hello to the staff, who knew them as Wayne's sisters.

It seemed everyone in Missoula, at one time or another, bought furniture from Conlin's. Most of the time, the arrival of Wayne Nance on a customer's doorstep was nothing more than an ordinary delivery made by an anonymous driver who came in, set the furniture in place, got a signature, and left. But after Deputy Sheriff Stanley Fullerton, Wayne's high school classmate, who had investigated the scene of his mother's suicidal crash, bought a sofa from Conlin's for his apartment up in the Rattlesnake Canyon, he was mighty surprised when Wayne showed up at his front door, delivery receipt in hand.

"Wow, Wayne, God, it's been years," he greeted him, now face-to-face with the acquaintance from his past who had stayed with him all these years like some recurring tailwind.

Since he had joined the sheriff's department, Fullerton had known that Wayne had been more than a routine suspect in the Donna Pounds murder, more than just a neighborhood boy who had been brought in for questioning. When any of his buddies would learn that he had gone to Sentinel with Wayne, they would find it intriguing, and they ribbed him about it: "Jeez, you knew Nance?"

The two 1974 alums talked a bit about old times as Wayne and his riding partner carried the new sofa into the living room. As they made conversation, Stan made what he considered to be a requisite but nevertheless empty promise to get together sometime for a beer. After Wayne was gone, Fullerton was uneasy, thinking to himself: *God, I really don't want this guy to know where I live.*

Missoula's resident FBI agent, Dale Willis, was a good customer at the store, and he and his wife, Rosalie, had a not-so-ordinary experience with Wayne, the delivery man.

Rosalie Willis had found a strange pair of sunglasses on the sink in an upstairs bathroom off the couple's master bedroom. Whose were they? How did they get there? The glasses, it turned out, belonged to Wayne. How he had managed to boldly sneak up to the second floor and poke around in the bedroom and bath was never figured out. Nothing was missing. Nobody made a federal case out of it.

After all, everybody knew that Wayne was the best worker in the warehouse. He was a really nice guy, too. They trusted him completely.

Chapter 16

A Delivery South

"I want to see it on the map." Wayne was adamant.

"I know where it is," Vern muttered under his breath, knowing that it was useless.

"The map."

"You know, turn right here." Vern started up. "Take a left on Stephens and there's a shortcut and we'll be in the 2000 block."

"I want to see it," Wayne said. He was sitting behind the wheel. The truck's engine was idling, and his eyes were fixed on the windshield.

Vern Willen had been here before, waiting to head out of Conlin's delivery dock at 1600 West North Avenue, or parked at the curb in the general vicinity of a delivery destination, with Wayne insistently demanding that he consult the map, even when they both knew exactly where to go.

Vern was himself a map aficionado. He had a big collection that was started when he was a boy in Europe, and he was still adding to it. This was too much, but he just put up with it, because there was a lot about Wayne that, in

Vern's eyes, redeemed an otherwise quirky, weird personality.

Sure, Wayne was constantly changing his appearance. He let his hair grow long and then would show up at work with a radical buzz cut. He would grow a mustache, then add a goatee, then turn it into a goofy Fu Manchu, then shave it all. He wore two different types of eyeglasses—wire-framed ones and a plastic pair with slightly tinted lenses—but sometimes he wore none at all.

Wayne wasn't handsome by most standards. His tightly curled red hair framed a rectangular face. His oddly white skin was punctuated by penetrating, blue-flecked hazel eyes. His thin mouthline was poorly distinguished. His lips were mere liver-colored slivers.

The guys in the warehouse would have no occasion to know that he had misrepresented himself on Conlin's job application. He stated that his hair was brown, although it was indisputably red, and he listed his eyes as being green. His height and weight were correctly filled in at five foot nine, 175 pounds. But his coworkers knew he wasn't above lying. When he went out drinking with Rick Mace, he would often make up a name for himself, operating in disguise because, he told Rick, he didn't want some "fat broad" to know his real name. That's what he always ended up with: overweight women, he would complain.

Wayne still dressed as the dirtball, although it was now less in the Jerry Rubin freedom-fighter mode and more the Seventies' post-revolutionary freedom-lover. He wore headbands, and certain pairs of his blue jeans displayed excessive flare at the leg bottom. He always wore a knife in a sheath on his belt, even though no one else in the warehouse found it necessary to port a five-inch blade all the time. Most of the guys carried a folding knife, often a Buck in a foldover belt sheath, which they used to open cartons and break down cardboard. Wayne would cut string with his knife, but he rarely dulled its edge on cardboard. That was sacrilegious.

Vern wasn't like the younger guys in the warehouse. He didn't go out drinking after work, didn't carouse at the Top Hat or the Elbow Room with the others, who would talk the next morning about the chicks they picked up. Wayne would hit the bars, sure, but he didn't talk about how fast his car was, and Vern was impressed by Wayne's all-business approach to the warehouse. Though Wayne didn't talk much, when he did say something it usually struck Vern as a positive, constructive contribution. Vern was a Montana native, but he hadn't grown up here. His youth was spent with his expatriot parents in the Canary Islands and in Spain. Though Vern was versed in three languages, he was still a laborer. For many years, he had worked in the oil fields, where he had encountered a few gung-ho types. But none of them were a match for Wayne. This guy, Vern could see, really pushed himself.

Wayne was always the first to punch in. He warmed up on a chinning bar in the back of the warehouse, or did a few curls for his biceps' sake with a heavy slag of metal that he stashed behind a table. Wayne was a physical culturist who brought imagination to the back-breaking warehouse work.

"There's a mattress truck," he would say. "Let's turn this into a workout."

Vern was a couple of inches taller than Wayne, but not as strong. The posters of Sylvester Stallone as *Rambo* and of Arnold Schwartzenegger as *Conan the Barbarian* that Wayne had tacked on the warehouse wall served as Wayne's inspirational heros.

"The body is an instrument," he would tell Vern while they were backlifting a sleeper-sofa off a semi. "Here, watch. You carry the weight on one side, and then shift and carry on the other. Try to work yourself both sides. The body is an instrument."

Wayne never walked slowly, and he rarely punched out for lunch at twelve-thirty. He worked straight through, when everyone else had left to either go home to eat or to run errands. When the others returned, they would see that Wayne had gotten a lot of work done, especially on Mondays, when the big truck arrived. He would have unwrapped several sofas and readied them for tagging. If there was a list of things to unpack on the floor, he would have already started. Every week, his paycheck would be bigger by four hours of overtime.

For his own lunch-on-the-run, Wayne always had a candy bar and a Coke from Conlin's canteen. Later in the evening, he would wolf down vitamins from his stockpile at home.

About the only thing Vern couldn't tolerate about his work companion was Wayne's attitude about women. Vern was a happily married man, but that wasn't it.

"Women are just an appliance," Wayne used to say to him, breaking into a hard, queer smile. "You put 'em on the bed and plug 'em in."

The young couple seemed to zero in on what they wanted: a Benchcraft sofa with matching loveseat, chair, and ottoman. The striped, light-colored fabric would probably survive the milk spills and banana smears of their three young children. Joyce Halverson, the Conlin's saleswoman, nodded in agreement.

For Joyce, it was a pleasure to wait on this young couple. You can categorize customers, she would always say, and these were nice people. They had been in the store a couple of times to look at living-room furniture. They each wanted something that was cushy, but they didn't want to spend a lot of money. Joyce was impressed because the husband seemed to take a genuine interest, and as a couple they agreed pretty much on what would be the right choice. Too often Joyce had faced the embarrassment of having to slink away as the husband started arguing with his wife right in front of her.

It's hard, Joyce understood, to make such a big purchase. This particular living-room set would cost more than sixteen hundred dollars, not including finance charges. That was more than Mike Shook made in a month. Teresa, his wife, was well aware of that, and she was good at stretching Mike's twelve hundred dollar monthly teacher's paycheck to meet all the family's bills. And they had gotten used to scrimping, because they were building their first home, mostly from scratch and almost entirely by themselves. The house would be ready to move into in a couple of months.

It was now the middle of August. Could they hold the furniture until November? Would they have to put anything down?

"No problem," Joyce said, assuring Mike and Teresa that Conlin's would hold the order, and they wouldn't have to make any payments until after it was delivered. The three of them sat down to do the paperwork.

As they filled out the credit application, Joyce learned the basic facts about this couple. Mike and Teresa Shook lived some fifty miles south of Missoula in the small city of Hamilton. Mike taught history at the high school in Stevensville. Teresa was a homemaker and mother of three—Matt, seven, Luke, four, and Megan, two-and-a-half. By the time November rolled around, they would no longer be living with Teresa's father. They would be in their own new home.

As they left the store, Joyce told Teresa to call when she was ready for the delivery, and to give her a couple of days leeway. Teresa thanked her, and as she and Mike walked out to the car, she couldn't wait to tell her mother-in-law, Georgia Shook, about the new furniture. Georgia had hopped a ride with them to Missoula, and while they were at Conlin's she had been visiting with her sister.

"Guess what?" Teresa said, before Georgia had even gotten into the car. "We bought some new furniture."

"Oh, tell me about it."

It was an hour's drive home, and Georgia,

sitting in the backseat of Mike's little red Ford, listened to an excited Teresa tell her about the new living-room set.

"I know all the kids will do is jump on it," Mike said to no one in particular, his voice carrying across the steering wheel.

Georgia smiled to herself. She knew her son was feeling a bit taller that day. His father used to say the same kind of thing. She knew it was an endorsement, and not even a reluctant one.

"Oh, am I ever getting tired of spending money," Teresa sighed, and Georgia understood that sentiment, too. She and her husband Bob had watched the young couple scrape together the means to build the house, and even helped them with some of the hammer-and-nail work. At every turn, it seemed more money was needed. But now they were close and it would all be worth it.

Teresa's mother had sold her a small plot of land just south of Hamilton, but it seemed too far from Stevensville, where Mike taught history in the high school. First they tried to sell the land so they could buy something in Stevensville, but having no luck, they decided to build on the land in Hamilton. Teresa would design the house, Mike would build it.

Their new house on McCarthy Loop would be simple and rustic, with an open-beamed ceiling in the living room. The three-bedroom, one-bath house would have only one extra feature, a small writing and sewing loft up above the living room. For now, the interior would be utilitarian.

They had labored on the project for three years. First they got help with the concrete foundation work, and they paid a carpenter to help them along. Then they had to get professional help with the roof. It was pay-as-you-go for awhile, but they eventually borrowed from a bank to finish the job. Still, they had personally built, along with friends and family, nearly 90 percent of the house. The couple's friends helped them paint the exterior. Mike's father came over at night to help paint inside walls.

The window mouldings weren't yet done, but the house had a roof and walls and doors and windows. They had water, and a wood stove to keep them warm. The particle-board floor was only the subfloor of something to come, but it had a fresh coat of paint. It would do.

Mike was determined to move in before the hard set of winter. They set the date for November 18, 1985, a Monday, in time for Thanksgiving. Their friends and family would again pitch in, and by nightfall on that day there was a gratifying semblance of order in the Shook household. Matt and Luke were ecstatic. They had their own room. Their little sister, Megan, didn't join in their horseplay, but she was excited. She would have her own room, too, in time. Now it was filled with construction equipment. Her father set her crib against a wall in the master bedroom. Mike and Teresa had plans to get new bedroom furniture for Megan, but it would have to wait.

By the time the house had taken shape, the floor plan, as designed by Teresa, translated itself into an exterior shell that was boxy and awkwardly proportioned. But the house still made a pretty picture, sitting as it did under a line of shade trees at the end of a long, two-lane dirt driveway that was off a gravel switch-back that led to Sleeping Child Road. They were 3.7 miles from the first stop light in Hamilton, but the wide-open space of it could just as well have been found a full day's drive from town. The confines of their rooms were cozy, but the breathtaking view that they owned was the best money could buy.

To the east, they looked out on two of the higher peaks of the Sapphire Range—Skalkaho Mountain and Fox Peak. Behind them, to the west, rose the even steeper crags of the Bit-terroot Range, the border with Idaho. It was their home in Bitterroot.

At the southernmost pan of this broad green valley near the Continental Divide stood Shook Mountain—7,561 feet in elevation and named after Mike's great-grandfather, who had home-steaded in this valley, too. And that was one more reason for Bob Shook to be proud. His oldest son was putting down roots right behind him.

Teresa had already called Joyce Halverson at Conlin's. The new living room furniture would be delivered on the coming Monday, in time for Thanksgiving.

Wayne drove and Mike Skillicorn rode shot-gun. They had two deliveries to make on this run. One was in Stevensville. The other was the Shooks in Hamilton.

Wayne frequently checked the map, and Mike more or less watched the scenery. To Mike, this was just another delivery. It would be an hour's drive south along Route 93 and an empty run back to the warehouse.

Teresa was home alone when the panel truck pulled up to the house. The open space of the living room was waiting for the striped couch, loveseat, chair, and ottoman. Ecstatic, she directed the delivery men as they brought her new furniture into her new house. She signed a delivery receipt and thanked them. Wayne clipped the receipt to his delivery board and climbed in with Mike. Again to Mike, the drive back was as uneventful as the drive out. By the time Wayne pulled into the loading dock at Conlin's, Mike could see that he was in a particularly foul mood. That in itself didn't strike him as even worth notice, because Wayne often got into a funk. Who knew why? But Sheila Claxton noticed this time, as she came through the warehouse and inquired about Wayne's day. Sheila knew the Shooks slightly. She herself had family down in Hamilton, where everybody knew almost everybody, and she wanted to ask about the delivery.

"How'd it go?" she inquired.

"That Mike Shook is an asshole!" Wayne sniped.

Sheila rolled her eyes a bit. She knew Wayne was capable of acting out like this.

"Why?"

"He's an asshole."

"Well," she said, her irritation showing a little, "why do you say that? Did he do something to you?"

"No." Wayne almost shut up, then continued. "You know I used to buy drugs from his brother, who is one of the biggest pushers in the Northwest. And his brother was killed by the Mafia."

Sheila was incredulous. She knew Mike and Teresa as customers, and she knew people in Hamilton, because her ex–mother-in-law still lived there, and she and her sons still stayed pretty close. Sheila knew that Mike Shook's brother wasn't dead, that Steve was a city police officer in Hamilton. What Wayne had said simply wasn't true. But she didn't go into it with him. Wayne may have been confused, because Teresa, not Mike, had experienced the death of a brother. Just six months ago, her older brother, Daniel Ray Schmitt, was found hanging from a barn door beam at the residence of a friend he had been staying with. He was thirty-three years old and the father of three children, all of whom lived in Washington State. He had been divorced for five years. Police theorized that he had committed suicide with the electrical extension cord that was found wrapped around his neck.

What Sheila didn't know, because neither Wayne nor anyone else would have occasion to tell her, was that Mike Shook wasn't even home when the delivery was made.

Later that week, Mike and Teresa invited Mike's mother and father over for coffee. Teresa wanted to show off the new furniture. They all sat around, admiring it, poking the cushions, trading opinions about how comfortable it was and how it would survive in a household with three young children. Bob Shook was pleased. There he sat in his son's new house on new furniture, with his own wife of thirty-seven years and his sweet daughter-in-law, as three more little Shooks scampered underfoot. It was one of those moments when all the hard work and struggle is not forgotten, but is now seen as the means to an end. Here, in this little house in the valley, at this particular family gathering, was the reward. He would never forget it.

PART III

Chapter 17

Twelve Days Before
Christmas

Mike lounged on his new Benchcraft sofa. He
had kicked his shoes off after dinner and
parked in front of the TV. It was his habit to
watch a little television or read for awhile during this transitional time in the evening, when
Teresa was usually steering the children toward
bed.

Matt, a second grader, was already in bed.
His mother now sent him off to bed by eight
or eight-thirty every night. It was a blessing,
they knew, because the two younger children
showed no such inclination. Luke, who was
still too young for kindergarten, was a night
owl, and Megan, who was two-and-a-half, was
still up on this Thursday night. They were preoccupied in play and supposedly helping their
mother, who was busy in the kitchen baking
cookie-dough ornaments.

Teresa planned to decorate the Christmas
tree, which they didn't have yet, with these
fancy sugar cookies. Tomorrow would be Friday the thirteenth—only twelve days before
Christmas. She was so excited about celebrating
the family's first Christmas in their own house.

The cookies had just been shoved into the oven when the knock came at the door. Mike started, and Teresa was just as puzzled.

"Did you see any lights?" she asked him from across the room.

"No," Mike said, leaning up. He hadn't seen any headlights either.

In the fleeting moment of time that both Mike and Teresa paused to wonder who could be at the door, little Luke made one of those quick four-year-old moves. He was already at the front door, and he was opening it.

A man pressed himself inside, standing at the threshold, wild-eyed behind his glasses.

"I'm Conan the Barbarian," the intruder announced.

Mike was too stunned to think. But he was up on his feet now.

"I want money. Stand back. I want money. Nobody'll get hurt. All I want is money."

Mike, who was closer to the man, could see that he had a gun and was wearing a knife in a sheath on his belt. What was this Conan stuff?

No one knows what was said next, or exactly how it happened, but Teresa was almost immediately shot in the leg near the ankle. The intruder may have only intended to fire into the floor to show that he meant business, but instead had accidentally shot Teresa. Did she recognize the face of the man who only two and a half weeks earlier had delivered her furniture? She held her balance on the kitchen counter, bleeding on the floor, directing Luke and Megan to get behind her.

Then the phone rang.

Teresa reached across the counter and answered it.

"Hello."

"Teresa, hi, Mary."

"Hi," Teresa said.

"I've been trying to call all week but you've been out."

"Yeah."

It was Mary Lakes, a friend, who was calling to find out if Teresa could babysit her son, Jesse, tomorrow. Mary immediately detected an odd hesitancy in Teresa's voice.

"Well, where have you been?"

Teresa didn't seem to want to talk, even though they hadn't visited for several days. Usually after they hadn't talked for that many days, Teresa would sit down and they would chat for a while.

"I'm baking some ornaments for the tree," Teresa said flatly.

"Well, are you gonna be home tomorrow?"

"I sure hope so," Teresa answered strangely.

"Can you babysit?"

"Sure, what time?

That was strange, too. Why would she have to ask. Eight o'clock was the usual time.

"Eight o'clock."

Before Teresa could give a one-word reply, Mary heard Megan scream in the background. Mary knew Megan was a pretty mellow child. She didn't scream much at all.

"It sounds like somebody needs you," Mary said.

"Yeah, gotta go. Bye."

Mary heard the disconnect before she could

say good-bye. She knew all too well the rigors of motherhood, and let it pass.

Wayne had come back, living out a fantasy, calling himself Conan the Barbarian. Most likely he tried to hold Mike at bay, trying to convince the leader of his hostage group that all he wanted was money, that he wouldn't harm anyone if they complied. That he had to tie them up. Whoever started it, whether Mike in his stocking feet grabbed the brass candleholder first or in self-defense, doesn't matter. There was some kind of struggle and it was clear that Wayne had prevailed. He managed to get Mike's arms and legs tied. Then he pulled his knife and stabbed his hostage in the chest. Mike fell into a sidelong heap, face down on the floor, dying.

Teresa may have gone for the first available weapon, a tennis racket, because it ended up with the candlestick on the floor next to Mike. Both Luke and Megan witnessed the scuffle between this crazed man and their mother, after they had watched as their father was tied up and stabbed. Matt was still fast asleep in his bedroom down the hall.

It isn't known whether Wayne tied Mike's arms and legs before or after he delivered a severe blow to Mike's head and then stabbed him. Had Wayne been able to convince Mike that he would keep his promise not to harm anyone if he got the money he wanted, Mike might have agreed to the restraints, but it's not likely. Wayne probably took him by surprise, clubbing him before using the knife.

As Mike lay in a spreading pool of blood, Wayne then turned to Teresa. He took her at gunpoint into the master bedroom. Luke was put in the bedroom where his brother lay asleep, and Megan was placed in her crib, which was still right next to her parents' bed.

Wayne then forced Teresa onto the bed, face up. He tied her arms and legs to its four corners, and, with Megan watching from the crib, proceeded to commit an atrocity of unspeakable magnitude. When Teresa would be found, a pillow would rest over her face. Her pants would be pulled up, but unzipped. She would be clothed above the waist in the tightly knit sweater she was wearing that night. A bathroom towel would have been placed over a large gash in her leg, near the ankle. Sheriff's deputies would find her bra and panties on the floor. They would show evidence of having been cut off her body with a sharp instrument in such a way as to allow their removal without undoing the ligatures on her wrists and ankles. She was fatally stabbed in the chest. An autopsy would later establish that she had been raped. The same forensic examination would reveal the nature of the gaping wound at her ankle. The perpetrator had fired a .22-caliber bullet into her leg, and then tried to recover the slug with a knife, creating a wedge-shaped hole as he routed the blade in the flesh and bone.

Investigators knew it was a .22 slug, because Wayne failed to retrieve the bullet. Maybe he began to grow anxious about how much time he was taking. What is believed is that it was about ten o'clock when he abruptly left the house. Mike and Teresa were dead. Matt and Luke were in their bedroom, and Megan was in her crib, in the same room with her dead mother.

A neighbor who had stepped outside to grab an armful of firewood about that time saw a pair of headlights leaving the Shooks' driveway. Later, possibly as much as two hours later, Wayne returned to the scene. Again, no one saw any headlights approach. Police theorized that Wayne had spent a great deal of time, after he had killed Mike and Teresa, rummaging through drawers, pilfering personal effects. He grabbed a twelve-inch plaster statue of a bugling elk, which he had found in the living-room loft. In the couple's bedroom he spotted something he couldn't resist—a handmade, stag-handled hunting knife with a tanned leather sheath. He took it, too. He found Mike's collection of silver dollars and he pocketed them.

Some time during his return visit, as Wayne zipped through the house, Luke ventured out of his room and watched from the hallway. He saw the man who called himself Conan, who said he wanted only money, move the wooden-legged, vinyl-upholstered kitchen bar stools under the stairwell in the living room. He saw him stuff magazines under the seats of the upturned chairs and light a match to them. Luke scrambled back to his room.

In all the fire-building frenzy, an electric clock in the kitchen had become unplugged. The stopped hands of the clock would later designate the presumed time of the start of the fire— approximately midnight.

As the lime-green and blue flames, colored so by the tint of the magazine ink, licked at the finished wood on the stair treads, Wayne was finally ready to leave. When he closed the front door behind him, he shut it tight. Mike and Teresa were dead, and as the foam and Naugahyde chairs burned, setting the house ablaze, Matt, Luke, and Megan would soon be dead. It is doubtful that Wayne realized that the fumes that emanated from his torch-murder job were lethal cyanide gas, enough to kill even without the flames. Without a doubt, he didn't realize that by shutting the door so tightly, he had cut off the air supply for his fire. The chairs smoldered most of the night but never ignited the house, because Mike had built the place to be virtually airtight.

Matt was a hard sleeper. He had slept through it all, including the single gunshot, but the high pitch of the smoke alarm woke him. Luke was there with him. Matt knew what he had to do. Remembering what the fireman told him in school, during a class demonstration about fire safety, Matt took charge. First he and Luke tried to open a window. After they couldn't budge it from the sill, Matt remembered that it was important to get down on the floor, because the smoke, being warmer, was rising. So he and Luke, now feeling tired, lay down on the bedroom floor. Megan was in her crib.

The fire on the stairs smoldered a while longer, then died out. The fire in the family's wood stove, the only source of heat, would in time burn out and the room temperature would begin to drop. The house filled with cyanide gas that could not escape. Outside, on this clear, starlit night, it was near zero. The children were falling into unconsciousness, and would be hypothermic soon. Megan, who was exposed to more of the toxic smoke, was falling into a coma.

The neighbor across the street who had seen lights leaving the Shooks' house wasn't sure if the vehicle was coming or going. He didn't know if it was a car or truck. But it was indeed a truck, a maroon 1984 Toyota Extra Cab four-by-four with a white camper top, Wayne's pride and joy. When he finally left the scene for good, heading along a snow-packed McCarthy Loop, turning left on Sleeping Child Road then onto Route 93, he headed north. In a couple of minutes he would encounter his first light, where the speed limit was a crawling 25 miles per hour, and in another few minutes he would come to the next light. At 5.1 miles from the Shooks' driveway, the third and final red signal light in Hamilton would come up. His speed would have picked up to 35 and he would be headed out of town. As his odometer clocked exactly 33.3 miles from Sleeping Child Road, he would be home free. That's when he crossed beyond the law-enforcement jurisdiction of the Ravalli County sheriff's department. He was back in Missoula County, and by close to 1:00 A.M., he would be driving through an empty downtown Missoula. The only people out on the street on this frigid night would be hurrying from their parked cars to the Elbow Room or the Board Room. He would cross the Clark Fork River, head east through Hellgate Canyon along Route 10-200, turn up the grade into East Missoula, then onto Minnesota Avenue to the little light-blue house, number 715. Door to door, it was 53.7 miles. But what he had done on this night drive south would never be measured so finitely. He was on the most ragged edge.

When he got a chance, he would slip his father's .22-caliber Ruger revolver back where it belonged. There would be plenty of time. Maybe he would do it in the morning. He had the whole day off.

It was a clear cold Friday morning when Greg Lakes said good-bye to his wife Mary and put Jesse on the chilled seat of his red sixty-seven Chevy pickup. Jesse was four years old, the same age as Luke Shook. The engine turned, and Greg headed out the winding dirt driveway to Lost Horse Road, where he would find Route 93 North.

The heater warmed their shins and Greg, nodding as his son talked about nothing in particular, kept an ear tuned to the hum of the old motor. The long straightaway up ahead was perfect for listening to the smooth, even drill of the pistons. They were bound for Mike and Teresa's, where Jesse would spend the day in familiar play with Luke. Greg himself had a busy day planned. As the Ravalli County reporter for the *Missoulian*, today he would escort his new boss around town. He was supposed to meet her at eight-thirty for breakfast. Mary had arranged for Jesse to come at eight, but he knew it wouldn't be a problem if he arrived a little early.

The Shooks and the Lakes were good friends, in many ways because their lifestyles were parallel. Like Mike, Greg was the principal breadwinner. Like Teresa, Mary was principally a homemaker, and on days when she taught school, Teresa babysat for Jesse. The two women were closer than the two men. Teresa and Mary had been friends for about three years. They first met at an Eckankar group meeting, when Teresa walked up and introduced herself, and soon a friendship was born.

Eckankar was a little too much for Greg to swallow, and he hadn't joined his wife at the meetings. Neither had Mike Shook. They didn't see any reason to mind that their wives had joined this New Age faith, described by its modern-day progenitor as neither religion nor philosophy, but as a path to God. While it relied on Tibetan and Indian philosophies, and revered certain Himalayan holy men, its self-help orientation seemed pretty down-to-earth and harmless.

Greg considered Mike a friend, but had never gone fishing or hunting with him. Both couples had children, and had been struggling to build their own homes for the first time on shoestring budgets. So they always had lots to talk about.

It was a little after seven-thirty when Greg completed the seven-mile trip to McCarthy Loop, and he was surprised to see Mike's car. It was a Friday; Mike should have left for school by now. Unless he had a long weekend. Maybe it was a teacher conference day, he thought to himself.

Greg and Jesse stepped out of the truck and walked up to the front door, knocking twice, anticipating it would open any second. But after no one answered, Greg figured they hadn't heard him. He knocked again, this time a little harder. He noticed that the lights were on inside.

When there was again no answer, he wondered if he actually had come too early. Maybe they were all sleeping in. He looked at his watch again. There was time to drive into town and treat Jesse to a muffin, drive back, and still be on time to meet this new assistant city editor. When they got back, the family would undoubtedly be up, he told his son.

"Matt has school," he said. "They would have to get up. Right? How 'bout a muffin?" he offered, knowing what the answer would be.

At eight-ten, Greg and Jesse were back. They retraced their steps to the front door, knocked, and waited. But there was still no answer. Greg decided to try the side door, and led Jesse around the house. He could hear the snow crunch under their footsteps. It was only ten above zero. A cold snap had come on the heels of a warm spell, turning the fresh-fallen snow into an icy glaze.

He knocked again, sure this time that either Teresa or Luke or someone would be up. Still there was no answer. He tried the door. It was unlocked.

Smoke caught him in the face. He could see the lights were on, all of them. He sniffed at the queer, acrid air inside, and poked his head in the doorway. He was planning to call out to someone, but the words never came, because his eyes found Mike first, lying on the floor next to a chair near the door.

"Shit," Greg said to himself, his mind racing to one conclusion, "we got big problems here."

With shock-horror clarity, he turned to Jesse, who stood right beside him.

"Jesse, I don't know what's inside. Just stand right here. Don't come in. Just stand here."

Jesse nodded, and Greg went in. He saw Mike lying on his chest, face down, arms off to the side. Greg didn't bother to take his pulse, or look to see if he was breathing. He just knew Mike was dead.

Jesse, he hadn't forgotten, was still standing just outside. Greg went out again and hurriedly put the boy back into the pickup.

"Look, I think we've got a big problem here," he told him. "I want you to wait here," he said, knowing that the truck was still warm. "There's gonna be sirens. I just want you to wait here."

Jesse broke into a big smile. Sirens!

Greg's adrenaline flow was clipping his words, but his voice summoned a firm, fatherly command.

"You stay put, now," he ordered, and then he walked the few feet back to the house. Inside, he dialed the sheriff. The number was at his fingertips. He called it every day.

"There's been a fire," he ordered into the phone, giving the basics to the dispatcher, then hanging up and walking to the back bedroom where he found the two boys, Matthew and Luke, on the floor. He picked them both up at the same time and carried them to the couch in the living room. Vomit covered their clothing. They were both unconscious, but he could see that they were still breathing. He opened the front door and the side door, trying to set up a crosswind.

Then he went into the other bedroom, where he found Teresa lying on her back in the bed, fully clothed and her face covered with a pillow. He saw the gash in her leg. It registered a grisly note, but he didn't know what to think. It crossed his mind that the family's new dog, which usually spent the night outside, had somehow done this to Teresa's ankle. But there was no time to waste.

Megan lay unconscious, but breathing, in her crib next to her mother. Greg carried her to the living room and placed her next to her brothers, and then called the sheriff again.

"There's two dead adults. There's three kids that are alive. I don't know what to do. Get out here!"

He hung up. Then he called right back.

"Tell me what to do with these kids," he asked. The dispatcher told him to take them outside.

"Jeez, it's ten degrees outside."

"Wrap 'em up. But get 'em outside," the dispatcher told him.

Greg grabbed some clothes from the closets, bundled the children, and moved them outside, where he laid them out in a row. The first deputy to arrive was Sergeant Jay Printz, who had gone to the wrong house on McCarthy Loop. He had stopped at Teresa's father's house, thinking the couple was still living there, not knowing they had moved into their new home just three weeks before. So when Sergeant Printz arrived, Teresa's father was with him, and Greg's heart sank further. Highway Patrolman Phil Meese arrived, responding to the fire call, because he was also a volunteer fireman.

"Are you okay?" Sergeant Printz asked Greg.

"I guess." The answer was a mumble, a shiver-filled utterance.

The officers lifted the three limp bodies into Printz's patrol car and raced out the drive. In less than a mile they met the oncoming ambulance at the turn onto Sleeping Child Road, and transferred the children, who were taken to Marcus Daly Hospital in Hamilton.

Greg stood there trying to put it together. It seemed that there had been a fire. Mike had almost made it outside. It was time to get Jesse out of here, so he took him to a friend's house, and then had to keep the appointment with the new boss. He was forty-five minutes late, but she was still sitting there drinking coffee when he showed up.

Sergeant Printz had told him to come by the office later, which Greg had planned to do anyway as part of the day's tour. When he stopped at the office the first time, Sergeant Printz wasn't there. He was still at the Shook house. When Greg stopped by an hour later, he was told the same thing. The third time, after another hour had passed and all the upper echelon of the office were still out on McCarthy Loop, Greg was growing impatient.

"Jeez, how long does it take?" he wondered to his new boss, who by now was ready to head back to Missoula, but he wasn't thinking straight, and hadn't been all day. He went home about three o'clock. After a while, he got a call. It was Sheriff Dale Dye.

"What the hell are you guys doin' out there?" Greg asked him. "That's a long time for a fire."

"Yeah, but it's not for a double homicide," Dye answered back.

Greg had gotten the second big shock of the day, and it would be his job to tell Mary that

Teresa and Mike hadn't died in a tragic fire, but instead had been murdered.

Megan nearly died en route to the hospital. Her lungs had collapsed. Matt and Luke, who were in the same room with her, were faring a little better.

At nine in the morning, Bob Shook was at work. His son and daughter-in-law were dead, and his three grandchildren were near death in the hospital, but he knew nothing about it until a fellow worker walked up to him.

"I think you better get to the hospital. I heard something on the scanner about Mike," he said. "I don't know if it was an accident or a fire or what."

Bob was out the door. When he got to the hospital, his son Steve, a local policeman, was arriving, and they both headed inside. Someone told Steve to go get his mother, Georgia, and that's when the people at the hospital told Bob about Mike and Teresa.

"They didn't make it. I'm sorry, Bob."

The tragic news, conveyed as it always is with solemn brevity, seemed unreal to him. When it hit, he was overcome. Out of the blank grief, all he could imagine was that Mike and Teresa were trying to save the children, but were overcome. He took it for granted, and so did Georgia, when he told her they were both dead, that they had died in the fire.

Bob and Georgia stayed there most of the day. When they saw the children, who were not improving much, it seemed that Matt had for a moment recognized his grandfather. But Luke and Megan certainly didn't. After hours

of standing around, they went home, deciding
to come back that evening. At five o'clock that
afternoon, Sheriff Dye was at their door, and
when they invited him in, they supposed he
would tell them about the fire. What they had
learned. How it had started. But the words
were different, and they were just as solemnly
blunt.

"Mike and Teresa were stabbed to death,"
Sheriff Dye told them. He was sympathetic.

The sorrow had been supplanted by something greater. There were no words for it. Georgia collapsed.

"It was bad enough the other way," Bob
said. "But this . . ." He broke up.

After Sheriff Dye left, the two gray-haired
survivors pulled themselves together and did
what had to be done, returning to the hospital.
When they arrived, they found Teresa's parents, Alvin and Marie Schmitt, holding forth.
They didn't know, either, that their daughter
and son-in-law had been murdered, so Bob had
to tell them. Hard as it was to believe, Mike
and Teresa had been stabbed to death.

Late that night, all three of the children were
taken by ambulance to Missoula, where they
were airlifted to Denver's Porter Memorial Hospital's burn unit. Matthew and Luke were admitted in stable condition. Megan was in critical
condition. Because there was ample reason to
suspect a further threat to their lives, they were
put under guard. Sheriff's Detective Scott Leete
was dispatched by Sheriff Dye to be their
sentry.

The house on McCarthy Loop was secured.
Sheriff's deputies drained the water pipes to

prevent the plumbing from freezing and bursting, and they turned on all the lights. They would be left burning round the clock. They set up an alarm around the perimeter outside. A trip wire would sound a siren placed inside the house.

They found the burned cookie ornaments in the oven—a tray of scorched dough pieces shaped as little Christmas trees. Everything in the house was covered with the gray-black residue of the burned Naugahyde covers and foam stuffing of the kitchen chairs—everything, they saw, except a patch of bedsheet in the crib where Megan had lain. There was the clear outline of a child, the imprint of this tragedy.

Chapter 18

A Christmas Present

Wayne had wrapped the present with care. He had put it under the tree. Now, it was Christmas morning. The time had come for his father to unwrap his gift, and Wayne sat nervously on the sofa across from George, who was in his favorite easy chair, as his dad held the pretty package in his hand.

The beloved son had loaded his Kodak Instamatic disc camera with film. He was ready for the moment, and as George undid the ribbon and clawed through the bright wrapping paper, he couldn't imagine what his son had gotten him for Christmas. It was heavy to hold.

As he pulled the paper away, he held in his hands a statue of a bugling elk. It was a handsome object, approximately a foot high. A bull elk, depicted as it would be in the wild, posed as it also would be sounding its deep, sonorous call. George held it in his hands. He was pleased, and Wayne, happy too that his father liked the present, raised his camera and took the picture.

Though George gushed over the present, Wayne was self-effacing, telling his father that

228

it wasn't anything really special, that there were probably 40,000 of them just like it. But he was glad George liked it, just the same.

Still, his father could see that it appeared to be very carefully made, and that it was artfully painted. Even the joined pedestal was nicely done. Wayne didn't know, and there was no way for George to know, that Mike Shook's sister-in-law, Karlene Shook, who was now divorced from his younger brother, Steve, had cast this bugling elk by hand. She had given it to Mike and Teresa. It was one of a kind.

Wayne had no way of knowing whether the elk, or the stag-handled hunting knife he had pilfered, or the stack of silver dollars he grabbed were among items listed as missing by family members. So it was a bold, or just plain reckless, move on Wayne's part to give his father a piece of the loot from his night of murderous butchery. In the twelve days since the murders, the Ravalli County sheriff had kept a tight lip about the case. But that didn't rule out the possibility that Sheriff Dye knew these things were missing from the Shook house, and that he was actively searching for them. For whatever reason, Wayne just couldn't resist putting this plaster-of-paris treasure under the tree for his father. He had even shown the statue and the knife around at work.

"You think my dad will like it for Christmas?" he asked Rick Mace, gesturing to the elk that he held up in his hand.

"Sure," Rick said, not much interested.

"I think he'll like it," Wayne said.

Rick also didn't make much of the knife that Wayne showed him. It was a bone-handled af-

fair with a broad, snub-curved blade. Rick
didn't look close enough to see that it was a
Kelgin, signifying that it had been custom
made. The knife had been a Christmas present
to Mike from his father the year before. Bob
Shook had given each of his sons and his son-
in-law a knife that year.

No one missed the statue or the knife or the
silver dollars Mike had collected, because Sheriff Dye had not yet allowed the families into the
house, except for an initial brief visit to get the
children's clothing and take out the beds they
would need when they returned from the hospital in Denver. As a result, while the investigation was officially and publicly ruling out any
hypothesis of robbery, there was actually no
way for sheriff's detectives to know if anything
was missing or not.

No one at Conlin's noticed anything different
about Wayne on the Saturday when he returned from his day off, rested from his Thursday night in Hamilton. Later they would recall
that he had made himself scarce for a few days,
but at the time of the tragedy, Wayne didn't
strike them as different in any way. When they
found out about the Shook murders, the saleswomen couldn't believe it. But there it was on
the front page of the Saturday edition of the
Missoulian. Joyce was grief stricken as she remembered the day in August when Mike and
Teresa had come into the store. It was a vivid
memory: the three of them sitting down, doing
the paperwork. It crossed her mind that they
hadn't even had the furniture in their house
long enough to make a single payment on it.

Sheila Claxton couldn't believe it either. She

called her former mother-in-law in Hamilton, trying to learn more, hoping to somehow get a better grasp of the horrible news. Sheila remembered the day, not four weeks earlier, when Wayne had returned from the delivery south. She hadn't forgotten his tirade about Mike Shook, but it never crossed her mind to make even the slightest connection between Wayne's outburst and the Shook murders. After all, Wayne was Wayne. He was subject to fits like that. He was a weird guy. That certainly didn't trip any neurons in her brain to suspect that he had anything to do with it.

Not Wayne, who would be expected to come, as he always had, to her Christmas cookie party this year. It was becoming a tradition. Every year, she threw a cookie party, and everybody was supposed to bake a dozen of the same kind of cookies. Then they would swap, and everybody would end up with a dozen assorted cookies. It was great fun for the eight women who had become regulars. As far as she knew, Wayne loved it, too. He was the only man who came. In fact, he usually was the first to arrive, and often the last to leave. And everyone was delighted that he belonged, because he baked the most delicious chocolate-chip cookies.

It was no different this year at the Christmas 1985 cookie party. Wayne came early, so early in fact that Sheila wasn't ready for him. She had just gotten out of the shower. *Why did he arrive so early*, she asked herself. He knew when the party was supposed to start. It was just Wayne, being himself. Just Wayne, carrying a dozen chocolate chip cookies under foil wrap on a dinner plate. Just as they did every year, everyone had a good time and Wayne was among the last to leave.

Three years before, when Wayne entered the ordinary, workday lives of the women at Conlin's, none of them knew he had been a prime suspect, as a teenager, in the horrifying sex murder of Donna Pounds, a case that still came up occasionally in conversations. The year before, on Christmas Eve in 1984, when Debbie Deer Creek was found, nobody at Conlin's suspected it was Robin, Wayne's late-summer fling. Nor did anyone draw a link between Wayne and the murdered girl found only three months before along Crystal Creek east of East Missoula, where Wayne lived. Yet something new had crept into almost everyone's perception of Wayne, and it wasn't so much because Wayne had changed. He was still the same old Wayne. It was more the result of his co-workers having becoming weary of his stupid attentions. For reasons they found difficult to pinpoint, they were now a little afraid of him. When Wayne showed up so early for the cookie party, Sheila was uncomfortable about it because she was only in her bathrobe as she opened the door for him. She made note of it. In the past, if something like that had happened she might have dismissed it or laughed it off, but for reasons she didn't quite understand, it irritated her. He knew when the party was supposed to start.

Kris Wells, as manager of the store, was noticing more hints about Wayne's temperament than she had seen before. Whenever he had one of his little fits, it seemed to be more extreme. Although he wouldn't holler and scream or in any way become violent, she detected an ominous undertone, and glimpsed a side of him that quite possibly could be violent. There seemed to be a deep rage within him that wasn't so hidden anymore.

That was the only reason she didn't fire Wayne, which she had wanted to do for a while now. Wayne was the very best worker in the warehouse, but she was tired of catering to his moods and displeased that he was drawing pictures all over the boxes in the warehouse. She finally had to tell him to stop. He had also filled an entire four-pane window with the silhouette of a large black spider. He had drawn a likeness of the hideously deformed protagonist in the film *The Elephant Man* on a large pillar, and there were the posters of Conan the Barbarian and Rambo. His four-by-four–foot plywood storage cubicle, unlike the personal areas of the other guys, was plastered with pinups of nude women. He was overtaking the warehouse with his own postpubescent, Edward Gorey touch, and it was an affront to Kris's sensibilities.

She was walking on eggs every time she dealt with him, and managing Wayne was especially hard when he was experiencing one of his prolonged bitchy spells, which seemed to cycle up once a month. The women used to joke about his menstrual moods, when Wayne would be on edge or particularly and unmercifully demanding, even though he was just a four-dollar-an-hour warehouse grunt, acting as if he were Lord God Almighty.

Kris became self-conscious about the special treatment Wayne seemed to demand. With the other guys in the warehouse, she could simply ask "Hey, would you do this?" But not with Wayne. To avoid setting him off, or initiating one of his moods, she found herself asking him as nicely as she could. When even that didn't work, it was wise just to avoid him.

So she didn't fire him. She wasn't directly concerned about herself so much, because though she was the manager, if Wayne were to be terminated, Rick Mace, as his direct supervisor in the warehouse, would have to do it. And Kris was concerned that Rick would bear the consequences, whatever they might be. She didn't dare find out.

Chapter 19

The Orphans

Main Street was bumper to bumper with police cars on the Saturday morning the hometown buried their own Mike and Teresa Shook. The onlookers in shop windows and on streetcorners had never seen anything like it. Every Hamilton police officer, every highway patrolman, and all the deputies from the sheriff's department provided a squad-car escort for the mourning family. There were cruisers ahead and cruisers behind, escorting them first to the Dowling Funeral Home on Second Street South, and then again along Hamilton's Main Street, past the eight short blocks of two-story, brick-faced storefronts. The vehicles made a somber, slow-moving line all the way up to Riverview Cemetery.

Mike and Teresa were buried together on a treeless plot of land that abuts the Bitterroot River. The Reverend Muriel Gooder, who had been Teresa's best friend in Sunday school and with joy in her heart had married the couple six years before in the tiny Grantsdale Community Church, now officiated at this final ceremony. A teacher at Mike's school, Susan Dolezal, who

235

spoke fondly of her colleague during a tearful memorial assembly at the school three days before, said everyone should take one message from this tragedy: "Let it be a reminder to us that we need to treasure our friends."

The show of sympathy and respect from the police community overwhelmed the family members, and it also provided them their first sense of security in a week. Sheriff Dye's deputies stood by, videotaping the funeral, hoping to identify any suspects who might show up.

Matt and Luke had come home two days before. They had been immediately whisked out of Ravalli County and were in the temporary, secret custody of Bob Shook's sister, who lived across the state line in Salmon, Idaho. Megan was still hospitalized in Denver, where her grandmother, Marie Schmitt, kept vigil. When Megan did come home, the day after Christmas, one of the highway patrolmen stayed with her overnight at her grandparents' house, doing it on his own time. The next night, a Hamilton policeman did the same, because the family had become paralyzed by a fear that whoever had done this would come back to finish the job, eliminating the only witnesses, the children.

Detective Leete, who had guarded the children while they were in the burn ward at Porter Memorial, had tried to gently coax information from Luke, who held the most promise as a witness. When Luke came home, he was again interviewed. It was a tender process, and though Luke had yet to offer them anything useful, they didn't give up. Even as their direct efforts seemed to fail, Sergeant

Printz was quietly trying another approach. He frequently stopped by to visit the boy, aiming to befriend him, hoping to win his confidence. While all the children were interviewed, Luke was the key. He had opened the door for the killer.

Megan, at two-and-a-half, was just too young to correlate the facts of the night of the attack. Matt, the oldest, had slept through most of it.

The last time Sergeant Printz tried to get Luke to remember what he could about the awful night, he made a tape of the conversation. That single, last recording told Sheriff Dye how the entire crime was committed, from beginning to end, but it still fell short in important ways. When they asked Luke if he knew the man, and what the man had called himself, the boy couldn't give them what they wanted.

"Did you know this man?"

"Yes, we visited him," was all Luke could reconstruct. He couldn't relate where or when. It was a puzzle.

"Did you know his name?"

The detectives went over and over Luke's response to that question.

What came out of Luke's mouth was incomprehensible to them. For one thing, the boy didn't talk as clearly as they needed him to. Was it unintelligible? Was it mumbled? Was it because Luke was in posttraumatic shock? Was it a foreign-sounding name?

Eventually, Sheriff Dye gave up trying to figure out what Luke was saying. While it was a high priority, he also faced pressure from a community that was growing uneasy. At Coast to Coast Hardware, a new stream of customers was requesting doorlocks, security lights, and related hardware, mentioning the Shook murders as the reason for the purchases. The Angler's Roost, a sporting goods emporium south of Hamilton, sold four or five handguns that it wouldn't have sold otherwise. Rumors were spreading that it was a cult killing, that the bodies had been mutilated. The mood of the community was further unnerved on more than one clear, chilly night, when wandering deer, possibly drawn by the blaze of lights emanating from the empty house on McCarthy Loop, tripped Sheriff Dye's alarm wires. Up and down the Bitterroot, the siren could be heard for miles, a scream in the night, a grim reminder of the events of December 12, 1985.

"Not a thing is new," Sheriff Dye said to reporters, dismissing a rumor that the slayings had anything to do with drugs or cults. "We found nothing to indicate that the Shooks were involved in any way with drugs." Indeed, the testimonials were still pouring forth on the letters to the editor page from agonized friends and colleagues, like Anthony Tognetti, the superintendent of the Stevensville school district. "You will not be forgotten," he wrote at the end of a tribute to Mike Shook printed under the headline: "A Truly Fine Man."

After the children were reunited in the early weeks of the new year, having been led to understand, as best as the family could say it, that their mother and father had gone to heaven and weren't coming back, they stayed with Mike's sister. She and her husband, who had their own children, were living in a trailer court at the time, and their neighbors, aware that the children still were perceived to be at risk, set up a phone-tag network to alert one another to any suspicious traffic.

The fears that fed the rumors found amplification in the common knowledge around town: Sheriff Dye had absolutely no idea where to start looking for suspects. Everyone knew it. It could be anyone in town, he suspected, which is just what confirmed the community's dread.

Sheriff Dye had a handful of physical evidence: semen recovered from Teresa's body, a stray red hair, and a .22-caliber bullet. He didn't have the gun, or the knife that killed Mike and Teresa. There was nothing missing from the house as far as he could tell, though it was too early to rule out any motive. Sheriff Dye's deputies checked on everyone who had been around the house in the recent past, especially the workers who had been hired to help with the last details of construction.

The autopsy concluded that the knife wounds to the chest had killed Mike and Teresa, and indicated that the couple died sometime around eight o'clock. The food in their full stomachs had hardly begun to be digested. The evidence of ligature marks on the arms and legs of both victims, indicating they had been tied, was kept secret, as was the gash on Teresa's leg and the evidentiary slug. Sheriff Dye's closed-mouth approach to the press during the investigation of a sensational murder was certainly precedented and partly warranted. Whole chapters in law-enforcement textbooks are devoted to the practical and otherwise harmful aspects of sharing information with the public, who then shares it with all viable suspects, including the guilty one. Had the sheriff elected, though, to share more information about the case—especially the use of ropes to restrain a rape-murder victim on a bed—it would have set off a battery of klieg lights in Captain Larry Weatherman's mind. It was just like the Donna Pounds case.

Within days of the murder, *Missoulian* reporter Larry Howell dug out the fact that ropes were involved, which he wrote about in a page-three story under the headline: "Double Murder Victims Had Been Tied, Says Official." The story was not officially sourced to Sheriff Dye, but it was nevertheless a true account. The law-enforcement official who spoke with anonymity asserted that the couple had been tied at one point during the attack and gave more details about how Teresa was found, such as how her bra had been cut off and her pants unzipped. Though the anonymous official source stopped short of saying she had been raped, it was easy enough to read between the lines.

But Captain Weatherman, sitting in his office fifty miles to the north, didn't make a connection. As chief of detectives in Missoula County, it wasn't in the cards for him to be privy to the casework in Ravalli County. The killings were also trademarked by the murder of a man as well as a woman, so it didn't appear to him to be related to his growing list of unsolved female homicides. And there was no precedent for him to pick up the phone and chat with Dale Dye about the case. Sheriff Dye watched his border. Jealous of his prerogative and protective of the power and authority of his office, Dye was an old-fashioned Western lawman. He was known to require Missoula County deputy sheriffs, if they were planning to even drive through Ravalli County on the way to Idaho, or were to drive through the county on official business for any reason at all, to call into Dye's headquarters to advise the desk of their presence. It was like asking permission to merely step on his turf, and you had to do it every time.

He wasn't about to share the signature of this killer with anyone outside his department, but it was there: the ropes, the knife, the sadistic, murderous rape.

It never occurred to Sheriff Dye to check on the recent delivery of furniture from Conlin's, even though he covered his bases by questioning other workmen who had been around. The insurance agent who processed the fire-damage claim for Bob Shook had made a call to Conlin's. It was routine procedure to establish the value of the furniture, which for claim purposes was still considered to be brand new, and to obtain a photocopy of the original sales receipt and check the delivery receipt. When he did, he found everything was in order. There was the sales receipt, and the delivery receipt. The goods had been delivered and signed for. There would be no problem, Bob Shook was told.

Chapter 20

A Company Man

Vern Willen knew how possessive Wayne was about his knife, the long blade that he always wore on his belt. Wayne had made it clear to everyone that he didn't lend it out, even for the smallest purpose. It was sacred.

But in the few months that Vern had worked now, side by side with Wayne, he had grown respectfully fond of Wayne. And on one particularly memorable day, as Vern and Wayne labored with a load of cardboard-wrapped furniture, Vern reached for his own folding knife, which he carried in his pocket. It wasn't there. He remembered that he had left it somewhere else.

Thinking to himself, looking at Wayne's knife, snug in its sheath, and knowing what the answer would be, he decided to go ahead and ask Wayne anyway. Could he use the knife. Just this once. To cut some string.

"Mine's not handy," Vern explained. "Hey, can I borrow your knife?" He came right out with it.

Wayne didn't look up.

"No, you got your own knife," he said point blank.

Vern shrugged it off. It was just another case of Wayne being Wayne. He didn't like him any less for it. But there was such a definitive quality in Wayne's response, such adamance, that Vern wouldn't forget it, even if it didn't really matter very much that Vern had to go retrieve his own knife to cut the string ties that day.

Months later, in the early part of 1986, Vern had a second occasion to ask the impossible: to borrow the knife. Wayne was behind the wheel and they were crossing town, heading back to the warehouse after making a delivery. Vern sat on the passenger side of the cab, prying with his fingernails at a wood sliver that had become deeply embedded in his palm. Just like the last time, Vern didn't have his knife handy.

"Can I borrow your knife?" he said, holding out his hand. "To dig this out." Vern may have colored his request with a pitiful tinge. Or maybe it was the sight of blood on his broad palm.

"Sure." Wayne didn't hesitate. He dropped his right hand to his side and pulled out the knife. "Watch it, though. The point is very sharp."

Vern didn't say anything as he dug away. He got the sliver and the bleeding seemed too profuse for what it had entailed. He wiped the blade and handed it back.

"Thanks," he said.

"Sure."

It was a simple human kindness, not worth recording to memory, but Vern did, because he knew how much it must have meant to

Wayne, the knife fancier. He had collected dozens of them. In his room at home he hung his favorite ones on the walls, along with swords and daggers he had either bought or made. He kept drawers full of them, and he added to his collection whenever he found one he couldn't resist. In between deliveries for Conlin's, when Wayne and Rick Mace were teamed up, they would often stop at Rice's, where his friend Rick Davis now worked, to look at the second-hand knives. Wayne bought half a dozen knives from Rice's, mostly junk-grade stuff, such as a serpentine blade affair of Japanese manufacture that was much like the one he already owned and had named "Hook"—the one he had flashed around at Taco John's years before. Wayne already owned a pair of brass knuckles from his days at the Cabin, and at Rice's he acquired a more lethal pair, the kind that when fitted on a closed fist have a two-inch blade protruding between the second and third finger.

While the simple acquisition of a knife, even an eight- or twelve-dollar knife from Rice's, where the price was scrawled in felt pen on the blade, gave him pleasure, it didn't give him ultimate satisfaction. What Wayne really wanted was a Ruana. Something like a 12A Ruana Sticker with standard sheath, described in the catalogue as an "all-around knife for any use—carpentering, fishing, hunting. A favorite with servicemen."

The 12A with five-inch blade was priced at eighty dollars, and Wayne's coworkers will never forget the day he got it. They recognized the name, because Ruana had been big in western Montana since any of them were old enough to remember. The Ruana Knife Works, Inc. got its start in the late Thirties. The local outfit traced its beginnings to Rudolph Ruana, who first started making knives as a farrier in the U.S. Army Cavalry in the early 1920s. When he eventually settled in tiny Bonner, Montana, in 1937, he started a business that has survived until today, with customers all over the world. Matt Hangas, grandson of the legendary knifemaker, was a classmate of Wayne's at Bonner Elementary. Now he worked in the family business, making knives in the family tradition.

When he started, "Rudy" Ruana priced the average-sized, five-inch working man's knife at what a Bonner mill worker made in a day. Today, the average knife ranges between $65 and $75, still about a day's pay for a mill laborer in Bonner. While Wayne, as a warehouse worker and delivery man, was making less than that—about $40 a day—he would have the knife anyway. Its blade was hammer-forged, heat-treated high-carbon sprung steel. Its aluminum handle was cast directly on the tang. Its grip was native Montana elk horn, beveled and riveted. Its hand-tooled sheath was made of heavy, naturally tanned leather, stitched with seven-ply harness thread and secured at the blade's tip with copper nails. This was a work of craftsman's art. It was the granddaddy of his collection, an exemplar of the sword that had slain the Jabberwock:

One, Two! One Two! And through and
    through

The vorpal blade went snicker-snack!

Wednesday was payday at Conlin's, and it was also the day that the bulk of local deliveries were scheduled. If Wayne were out in the truck with Vern, and happened to be near Vern's bank and they weren't in a bind for time, Vern would typically ask if they could stop so he could cash his check. The answer was always the same. Wayne, the company man, would lecture him about doing personal business on company time.

But Vern persisted. After all, he had just recently been honored by Wayne's permission to let him use the Ruana to extract a splinter from his hand. He thought he had seen a softer side of Wayne's otherwise dogmatic personality, and besides, Christ, the bank was right there.

"It'll take ten minutes tops. Why don't you cash yours?"

"You don't do that on company time." Wayne bore down, driving on.

"Yeah, yeah, yeah," Vern shrugged. How could he have presumed otherwise? This was the guy who had even refined a methodology for segregating the big plastic covers that they used in the warehouse from the smaller ones.

"These we use for sofas, loveseats, chairs. The small plastic we keep over here, for smaller stuff," Wayne would say.

"Yeah," Vern responded. "Yeah."

Chapter 21

Best Friends

When Sheriff Dye arrived at their front door, Greg and Mary Lakes invited him in. He had called beforehand, and they weren't surprised that he wanted to talk. Greg had found the bodies. Mary was Teresa's best friend. Naturally, Dale Dye wanted to talk. There was also the problem of dealing with Greg, who was not only the only eyewitness to the crime scene but also the only Ravalli County reporter the *Missoulian* had in Hamilton. This was easily the biggest story of the year, and Dye wanted to keep it under his control, not someone else's.

Greg showed the sheriff to the living room, where they would sit. Mary offered him a cup of her delicious, stout black coffee, and they got down to business.

"You're part of the investigation," Sheriff Dye explained, looking at Greg. "You know what that means? I want your help. I need it on this one. I'm bringing you in."

It was hard enough for Greg to deal with what had been thrown at him already. First he had found the Shooks dead from a fire that almost had killed the children. Then he learned

that they had been murdered. He had to tell
Mary about Teresa. Then they had to tell Jesse.
He didn't even want to talk about it. How could
he possibly cover it as a story?

That's what he had told his editor in Missoula,
where the first story was written on the desk.
Someone else would have to cover this one.

Both Greg and Mary wanted Mike and Teresa's killer stopped as much as Sheriff Dye
wanted their help. So they pledged it to him.

"One hundred percent," Greg said.

"Yeah," Mary chimed in.

"You can ask us anything you want," they
told him. "We'll answer the questions."

And he did. His questions were answered
with unhesitating candor. But as the sheriff
proceeded through his line of thought, both
Greg and Mary could see where he was headed.
There was something in the sheriff's tone. It
didn't bother Greg as much as it did Mary, but
they both honored the pledge, even as they
could now clearly see that the answers they
gave were leading Sheriff Dye expressly where
he wanted to go. They could tell he already
suspected someone. It was a man who had
been Teresa's closest male friend, who had actually called her on the day she was murdered,
Dye explained. Greg wasn't sure what to think
but Mary was certain Dale Dye was barking up
the wrong tree. She knew this man well. He
was her friend, too, and she told the sheriff
repeatedly that he was on the wrong track.

"Well, how do you know?" he repeatedly
asked back.

"I just know," she said again and again. "I
just know."

Mary was also troubled to see that Sheriff Dye was forging a connection that, in a different way, tied her into it. He seemed to be fixating on Eckankar, the "strange" new religion that had brought Teresa Shook and Mary Lakes together in the first place. The man whom he obviously suspected, who was Teresa's very close friend, was also an "Eckie."

His name was David Davis. He lived in Missoula, where he owned and operated a commercial auto body repair shop under the name Spraycraft.

It was not uncommon to see Dave, as everybody called him, around Hamilton, often in Teresa's company. Dave occasionally visited Teresa at times when Mike wasn't home. It didn't surprise Mary that Dave had called Teresa on the afternoon of the day she was murdered. Nor did it surprise her that Mike's parents would readily accept Dave's status as a suspect. They weren't particularly supportive of Teresa's interest in Eckankar. They didn't really understand what she was into. And as the saying goes—"born and raised in the Bitterroot and don't wanna know nothin' else"—they really didn't want to know. It was enough to see that when there were out-of-town Eck meetings, Teresa and Mary would take off and leave the children with their husbands. The husbands didn't mind. Nor did they mind when their wives took the children on Eck campouts.

It was also hard to swallow the fact that Teresa had a close relationship—friendship, not romance—with another man, who was married but not living with his wife, whose name was Merilee.

The circumstance of the Davis's unconventional marriage also defied Sheriff Dye's understanding, almost as much as Eckankar did. It seemed that when it was all put together, Dave Davis, a private, sincere man who minded his own business, also happened to be practicing the wrong New Age religion at the wrong time.

To the uninitiated, Eckankar could easily appear to be daunting and far-out. While its stated, simple goal is to give its practitioners a solid spiritual footing on which to base their lives, other, more ethereal aspects, such as astral projection, play a big role. Soul journeys on the Eck, or cosmic current, allow its followers to make out-of-body trips to higher spiritual realms. At bilocation workshops, Eckies learn how to slip in and out of their physical bodies. One can be in two places at the same time, and distance is immaterial—it can be within a single room or around the globe, or beyond.

Two weeks after the murders, Sheriff Dye announced that he had taken a crash course in this strange New Age religion in an attempt to better understand Teresa Shook's personality, adding that he had concluded that it was not the basis for the crime.

Few people in town knew that Dye was zeroing in on Davis, but Greg and Mary knew, and Mary still maintained that it was the wrong tack. It was also frustrating, because though she never wavered in her view, her husband wasn't so confident, and as the heads of the household, they both had been put on guard. Even more than most everyone else in town, they had been living in fear since day one. It didn't help that they failed to see eye to eye on the course of Dye's investigation.

Two days after the murder, Sheriff Day had showed up at their front door.

"Come out and sit in my car," he insisted to Greg.

Greg stepped outside and the two of them walked over to the sheriff's car. After they were inside, Dye turned to him. He seemed to assume the pose of a father figure. He wanted to talk to Greg man to man. Greg could convey the message to Mary, however he chose.

"I don't want to scare you. I don't want to make things bigger than they are," Dye said slowly, "but if anything happened to you guys, I'd never forgive myself."

The words sank in.

"Okay, Dale." Greg got the message.

"Be real careful."

"Yeah, I . . . we will."

"Cover your butt."

That was the end of the conversation, and it was the beginning of an emotional seige laid on the Lakes household that would last for months. The very next day, Greg bought a handgun. It was a .357 Magnum, big enough to stop a bear. He bought a holster for it so he could wear it around the house. He and Mary shot it and shot it and shot it until they mastered the weapon in their hands.

But it still didn't allow them to sleep at night. Or stop them from getting spooked on snowy nights when they had to walk from the main road up their long, snow-blocked driveway, prepared for someone to jump out of the woods at any moment.

Chapter 22

The Shutterbug

Wayne didn't always work through his lunch hour, even though he didn't punch out on the clock. Sometimes he would climb into an overhead crawl space between the warehouse side of Conlin's and the sales floor. In the space between these two worlds, where the office canteen was located, right next to the women's bathroom, he would quietly perch, gazing down through a ceiling vent over the bathroom stalls.

From his confined aerie, he watched the women come and go. They had no idea that the sweet boy who couldn't get a girlfriend, who swapped cookies with them at Christmas and always remembered their birthdays, who so often flattered them on their attire, watched as they undressed. After he tired of this overhead view, Wayne fashioned another peephole that offered a more eye-level view.

Later, perhaps concerned that the jig might be up, it was the Peeping Tom himself who reported the hole in the wall of the women's room.

But he assumed a much too righteous posture for Kris to believe that he had nothing to do with it.

"It's one of the warehousemen," he told her.

"Who?" She pushed him. "Who is it, Wayne?"

He wouldn't give a name.

"Okay." Kris let it go. "Thanks for telling me."

As soon as Wayne left her office, Kris investigated and found the peephole. It was right where Wayne said it would be. Then she called Rick Mace into the office.

"Look into this, Rick. And fix the wall."

When Rick confronted Wayne, he got an answer. It was the other guys. Wayne fingered Mike Skillicorn, Todd Zander, and Barry Eiseman.

"No way," they insisted. "Wayne was the one that showed us."

That afternoon, Rick patched the hole in the wall and blocked off the overhead crawl space, and though Wayne still maintained that he had nothing to do with it—if he had, why would he have reported it?—Rick knew better. He had every reason to believe the other men, not Wayne. Nothing would come of it. It was chalked up as another incident. Besides, Wayne seemed to have a new obsession.

Wayne had acquired a camera, a cheap Kodak disc model, and he was fast becoming a pest with it. At first the women didn't mind. As they turned quickly when he called their name, they would be briefly blinded by the flash.

"Hey, Cindy," came the tease.

"What?" She turned.

Click. Flash.

"Oh, Wayne, come on."

Wayne didn't take many pictures of the men, but he was taking roll after roll of the women. Cindy behind her desk. Sheila sitting on a La-Z-Boy. Joyce on a sofa. Close-ups. Overviews. Nearly all the time his technique employed the element of surprise, the ambush shot.

"Oh, I have to get one of you for my dad," he said to Joyce, bringing up his aim.

"Wayne, go take pictures of those young chicks. Quit doing this."

"No, my dad says that you're the best-looking one here. He always wants to see your picture," Wayne pleaded.

"Who cares?" Joyce gave up.

Click.

"Sheila, don't cover up your face. I just want a picture."

Click.

Wayne rarely showed his pictures off, and he never showed Sheila the photographs of her and Sandy McManus, another saleswoman at the store, that were taken during one of their frequent twilight strolls near the University.

Cindy finally became sick of it and got short with him.

"Knock it off, Wayne," she griped, leveling her voice at him.

He did, but by then he had amassed stacks and stacks of snapshots of the women of Conlin's. They were generally of poor quality, and the expressions on the women's faces reflected a definite lack of enthusiasm for the maniacal shutterbug who was taking their picture yet one more time. They were ill posed, parked as they might be on occasion sunk into a floral-patterned deep-line sofa. The flash lighting was harsh. They possibly wouldn't ever see the picture anyway. What was the point?

By the time Kris had grown just as weary of Wayne's picture taking as the other women, her complaining slowed him down. Then, after the other women complained to her, she finally had to tell him flat out that he didn't have permission to do it anymore.

Wayne's countless pictures of the other women were kept in a box at home, but he had done something special with his even bigger collection of Kris photographs. They were edited, cropped, and archived in a small white album. The first page featured a head-and-shoulders picture of a smiling Kris, bordered by a white oval mat. At the bottom, pasted below the mat, Wayne had placed Kris's signature, which he had scissored from the bottom line of a Conlin's insurance form. Page after page of photographs showed her sitting officiously at a desk; sinking into the plush of a showroom sofa; lounged legs-up on another; entering a doorway; standing on the loading dock; perched demurely on the arm of a stuffed chair, hands in lap, legs crossed.

The album pictures had been carefully cropped to eliminate extraneous subject matter. Wayne had meticulously cut off the corners on most all of them, leaving rounded edges. He had jammed up to four pictures on a page. When he didn't like the smallness of the image, he had blow-ups made. Besides the fifteen 3½ by 4½-inch pictures he got from one roll of disc film, Wayne often ordered enlargements, sometimes up to six per roll. There were requests for

5 by 7 and 8 by 10 prints from the same negative, giving him extra latitude when he made decisions about cropping down to show only Kris's face. The enlargements made from his snapshot camera were especially grainy, and the washed colors of Kris's skirts and blouses lack true-life vibrancy, but the notes Wayne scribbled on the backs of some pictures revealed in grainless, stark clarity the powerful nature of his obsession.

"Kris Zimmerman Wells—I love you, Wayne."

"Kris Zimmerman Wells—I'm crazy 'bout KZ."

"Kris, I want you to live with me and my La-Z-Boy. Wayne."

Wayne also carried Kris's picture in his wallet. He had snipped her handwritten work-order messages into word bits—taking the word "love" from loveseat and "boy" from La-Z-Boy—and pasted together a new message, "I love you, Big Boy," which he kept in his locked toolbox.

And it didn't stop there. In a far corner of the warehouse, Wayne had kept another stash, which was a more chaotic but equally telling testament to his desire for Kris. In what once had been a Hickory Farms sampler box, Wayne kept the other odds and ends, the not yet distilled evidence of his monomania. No bigger than a large dictionary, the box contained more than thirty-five additional pictures of Kris, some of them framed. There she was eating a banana, or standing near a mattress. It contained dime-store "Sweetheart" stickers, dozens of Conlin's red tags that had been trimmed down to leave only her signed initials—KZ. Newspaper and magazine clippings: a TV Guide feature on Benny Goodman; a movie ad for *Falling in Love*, starring Meryl Streep and Robert DeNiro; Wayne's business card; Kris's business card; a large color advertisement of a woman in a yellow Liz Claiborne dress holding a handbag, her head ripped off in jagged abandon; an ad for Victory Chapel, a wedding emporium; a routine office communication from Kris to Rick Mace, saying "Come Find Me."

Rick knew Wayne fantasized about taking Kris away from Doug. Wayne had told him so. And everybody knew that Wayne bristled whenever Doug came into the store. As a couple, Doug and Kris weren't inseparable, but Doug did stop in at Conlin's on a regular basis. They frequently spent the lunch hour together, or if Kris couldn't leave the store, Doug might bring her a deli sandwich. As the boss, Kris could be one of the gang at Conlin's, but less so one of the girls. She didn't go to the Christmas cookie-swap parties or go out after work for drinks, unless the party crowd was big enough to accommodate Doug. Conversational references to "Kris and Doug" were as commonplace as the mention of Kris's name alone. Their work lives were, it seemed, always intersecting, and that was a problem for Wayne, who had made it known he didn't like Doug.

When Doug would enter the front door of the showroom and head toward the back to find Kris, Wayne, if he happened to be out front, could be seen clenching his fists. Everyone else at Conlin's liked Doug. They had learned not to expect much chatter from him.

He was quiet—they knew that. But he fit in in every other way. Doug shared the same equivocal view of Wayne that the other husbands had. The fake gold necklaces and stick pins and junky doodads that Wayne had given his wife were no different from those he had given Carey's wife, Cindy or George's wife, Joyce.

Doug didn't know at the time, but he would find out later, that Wayne's interest in his wife was quite different. For one thing, he would learn that someone had been compelled—for whatever reason—to enter his house, search out Kris's teal-green silk wedding dress, which was hung deep in a closet inside a zippered plastic garment bag, and streak blood around the collar line, along the sleeve, and down the skirt. Whoever had done this had carefully put the dress back in its liner, leaving no outward sign of disturbance. Kris wouldn't discover this macabre handiwork until years later. But it would be clear that whoever had done this must have had a key to the front door.

"This'll have to be cleaned in mineral oil, ma'am," her dry cleaner told her. "It'll change the color a little, but it's the only way."

"What do you think it is?" Kris asked.

"Blood."

Chapter 23

A Dead End

It was a case of hitting one dry hole after another. The focus was still on Dale Dye's Number-1 suspect, Dave Davis, but it was getting nowhere. The diehard crew of detectives assigned to the investigation were meeting again this morning, just as they had met every single morning for four months now.

Dale Dye led the session, as he always did, relentlessly talking over the case, poring over the details, reconstructing M.O.s, never veering from his hypothesis that whoever had done this had known the Shooks. Because he had been enlisted from the start, Greg Lakes was there, too, but unlike most of the others he was reaching a different conclusion. He no longer saw any reason to suspect that Dye's prime target had anything to do with the murders. It wasn't because his wife had brought him around to her thinking. It was a combination of things, including the realization that if Dye had tried this hard on this one line of thought, how come he had nothing to show for it?

Greg had chugged coffee with these guys day in and day out. Now it was well into March and, with the morning seances still going nowhere, Greg's contribution to the brainstorming amounted to a new effort to talk Dye out of his prime suspect. Now two months had passed since the sheriff had gone public with his suspect, but he wasn't even close to making an arrest.

On February 26, 1986, Sheriff Dye told the world that he had a suspect. While disclosing nothing more than that, except to catalogue all the things he wasn't going to disclose, including the possibility that he would seek a "gag order" to further restrict the press and the public, Sheriff Dye asserted that the suspect met the test of his hypothesis that the killer knew the Shooks. He wouldn't speculate about when his office could make an arrest, but he knew well enough that the clock already had started on the Ravalli's County Sheriff's Department's duty to stop the unknown sociopath who was still menacing this idyllic, small Western town.

Dye was determined to get his man and he didn't want help from anybody. When District Judge James Wheelis issued the search warrant enabling Sheriff Dye to search Davis's home in Missoula, the judge also sealed the affidavit. That guaranteed that Dye would not be compelled later, after the search was done, to disclose any information about what he found or hoped to find. The judge and the Ravalli County attorney's office were very secretive. At first they wouldn't divulge that a warrant even existed. Eventually they relented, and a few days later, the *Missoulian* reported that the warrant had been executed.

The headline over the short story on page

eleven read: "Sheriff Keeps Lid on Investigation into Shook Double Murder." As expected, Sheriff Dye would not say what it was he had been looking for. Only the sheriff and the detectives on the case knew he was searching for rope, any kind of rope. As a result, yet another account of the Shook homicides was published without mention of the ligature marks on the victims, who had been restrained before they were stabbed—the murderous signature that remained etched in Captain Weatherman's memory of the Donna Pounds case. Only Sheriff Dye also knew, along with the tight circle of detectives, that he was looking for a .22-caliber firearm. Because the gunshot wound was still confidential to Dye's own department. And without that knowledge, Captain Weatherman could make no parallel with the murders Debbie Deer Creek and Chryssie Crystal Creek, both of whom had been shot in the head.

Dye didn't have a shred of physical evidence that tied Dave Davis into this thing, and the three times that Davis was interviewed by the sheriff, Dye had come away empty handed. The meetings took place in a small room at the Missoula County Courthouse. At their first encounter, the sheriff simply interviewed Davis. Dye wanted to find out about Dave's relationship with Teresa. He wanted to establish if this man, who talked freely about his close friendship with Teresa Shook, was a viable suspect. Afterward, Dye wasn't sure. He asked Davis if he would meet again, if the sheriff had more questions. Davis saw no problem with that.

But when that second meeting took place, Davis started to see where the sheriff was headed. Dye was trying to get him to incriminate himself. This was an interrogation, not an interview. So when Sheriff Dye requested to see Davis a third time in the small room in the courthouse, Davis brought along an attorney. This time, Dye's prime suspect refused to cooperate any further.

Sheriff Dye lacked any physical tie-in with Davis. So he had no evidence to use as a pry bar against Davis's alibi, which was simply that he had been at home alone on the night of December 12, 1985. His wife was out of state at the time. That was his alibi.

Sheriff Dye never tried to go for a lie-detector test, but that didn't mean he had given up on Davis, or on any other possibility, however remote. In late April, after a Missoula radio station reported that Sheriff Dye was investigating a link between the Shook murders and the slayings of a couple and their eleven-year-old son in a Billings, Montana, motel room, the sheriff was forced to conclude that there was no tie-in. Authorities in Billings had a suspect in custody. The couple had been killed by lethal injection. Their son had been forced to drink water laced with a drug. The only similarity was the multiple deaths.

"No progress to report," he told the *Missoulian*. "I will have nothing to say until I have something positive to report."

By late springtime, the investigation had been reduced to a virtual nonentity. The morning seances were now history. Greg Lakes still popped in to see Dye every morning, sometimes just sticking his head in the door as he passed.

"Anything new?" Greg asked.

"Nope," came the answer.

After all the intelligence had been exhausted and every investigative lead had tapped out, Sheriff Dye admitted he was stumped. His prime suspect had even left the state, which he was free to do. Dye was ready to try anything, even psychic power if it would help.

Through a network of law-enforcement colleagues, he located a woman who had worked with several police agencies on the East Coast, and she agreed to come out to help him in return for transportation costs. It was a good deal. He got a psychic on the case and he wasn't blowing his budget in the process.

When the woman arrived, she was driven to Greg and Mary's home, where she stood in the corner of the Lakes's kitchen. She made three connections.

First, she said, the individual who murdered Mike and Teresa has had an injury to his hip or leg. Second, she said, this individual works with wood, some type of wood furniture, or in a lumber mill. (Of course, Sheriff Dye knew, that wasn't too uncommon an occupation in the Bitterroot or anywhere in western Montana.) Thirdly, she issued a prophecy. She told the sheriff that he wouldn't solve the crime until September. That intrigued him.

Later, because Dye briefed her on case, she asked to talk to Merilee Davis, the suspect's wife. Merilee was a tidy, slight brunette, whose co-workers thought harbored a preoccupation with her state of health. For example, when her allergies acted up, she would explain that she cleansed them from her body by fasting. And those who knew her didn't necessarily share Merilee's ideas about links between astrology and health.

The psychic's interest in Merilee was casual. The two women sat and talked about jobs, friends, and her relationship with her husband. (It was a marriage that was not meant to last.)

When the subject of work was discussed, Merilee told the woman that she worked at a furniture store in Missoula—Conlin's Furniture, to be exact. She was a saleswoman who had been employed there for more than three years.

And when there seemed to be nothing more to say, the woman thanked Merilee for taking the time to talk.

It wasn't until more than six months had passed that Sheriff Dye ran out of reasons to keep the Shook murder scene under wraps, and he let the families into the house on McCarthy Loop. The grandparents on both sides had run out of patience long before. Here it was now June, and they still hadn't been allowed to go into the house. They didn't want to be sticking their nose in where it didn't belong, because more than anyone else they wanted the killer caught. If doing things Dye's way was necessary to that end, they would certainly go along. But still, six months seemed an eternity, and they weren't the only people in town who had begun to talk about the way Dye was handling the case. The topic of conversation in the cafes and roadhouses and at suppertime in Ravalli County dwelled on how Sheriff Dye had bungled the case. It was too bad. After all, he didn't *not* want to solve it, they all knew that.

Teresa's parents went in first to get her things. Then Bob Shook took over the rest. Mike's mother, Georgia, couldn't bring herself to ever go back to the house. It was Bob who became the family representative. He already had started dealing with the finance company in Denver that carried the installment loan on the furniture, and with the insurance agent who had written the homeowner's policy. There was a lot of smoke damage. Every surface in the house was covered with a dusting of black powder. The white porcelain bathtub was gray. The new furniture was smoke damaged and there was some of Mike's blood on the underside of a front fabric flap on the sofa.

Later that summer, Bob would sell the sofa, loveseat, chair, and ottoman at auction for three hundred dollars. The agent readily offered to pay the difference from the original cost.

Friends of the Shooks organized an auction to benefit the children, and placed fruit jars for donations on store countertops in Hamilton and Missoula. In all, some twenty thousand dollars was raised by the community and set aside for the children. Every bit of legal work was done free of charge. Mike had life insurance, too, and the children would collect Social Security. The house would be cleaned up and sold, the proceeds earmarked for the children's education.

When he started removing Mike's guns and fishing gear, and his personal effects, Bob Shook remembered what Karlene, Mike's former sister-in-law, had mentioned about the statue of the bugling elk.

"You guys might just as well take that statue," she said to him.

But where was it? It was no big deal, just another detail, but when he couldn't find it, he noticed too that the knife he had given Mike was missing, and that the silver dollars weren't in the top dresser drawer where Mike always kept them.

What was he going to do? Ask Teresa's parents if they had taken the things? After all these months of difficult feelings, which had escalated over arguments between the in-laws over who would get custody of the children, finally it was decided they would live with Mike's sister and brother-in-law, who already had four of their own children. The matter almost ended up in court. But it didn't, and now it was settled. The orphans would live with their cousins as brothers and sisters.

Bob would tell his wife that the things were missing, but that was to be the end of it. At this late date, he wasn't going to go out of his way to tell Sheriff Dye about it. What good would it do? Both Bob and Georgia Shook had become more than a little hardened on the subject of Dale Dye. They knew that his investigation was well intentioned, but they also had figured out that he had a severe case of tunnel vision, which had taken him nowhere. But the most bitter part of it for them was the way he had shut them out. Sheriff Dye hadn't even told them that Teresa, their own daughter-in-law, had been shot. They didn't learn about it until weeks after the funeral, and they had to find out the hard way.

Soon after Megan had returned from Denver,

Georgia and her sister were driving the two-and-a-half-year-old back to Georgia's daughter's home. As they drove south from Hamilton along Route 93, Georgia mentioned to her sister that they were getting near the newly built home of a couple who had been mutual friends of Mike's and Teresa's, and she began to wonder aloud.

"I wonder if Mike and Teresa had seen the new house," she said, trying to remember.

"No," Megan piped from the back seat. "Mom is dead. She got shot in the leg."

As her grandmother and great aunt wheeled around in horror, looking at Megan, the little girl had placed a hand on her ankle. She was showing them where. The car fell silent.

Chapter 24

Born to Kill

"Don't you have the kids this weekend?" Wayne asked.

Sheila Claxton didn't have to think about it.

"No, they're with their father."

"So, do you want me to bring over those boxes?"

Sheila thought about it for a second. She remembered that Wayne had offered to bring some boxes over to her house. She had said something about needing them, and he promptly offered, as was his nature, to do the favor. And she thought for a second about the way he asked her about the boys. He already knew she didn't have them this weekend. That fact had casually surfaced in an earlier conversation. But it was typical of Wayne to elicit information this way, pretending not to know something, triggering the answer. He wasn't just inquisitive. He was playfully devious.

"Sure," Sheila responded. "Yeah, Saturday night after work. Sure."

Perhaps more than any of the other saleswomen at Conlin's, Sheila was tuned into Wayne's peculiarities. It wasn't because she shared them. Sheila just had spent more time with him than anyone else. She didn't try to mother him the way some of the others did, but Sheila, who was half a generation older than Wayne, wasn't going to be his date, either.

Louise Lightener, who had hired Wayne, used to encourage it.

"He's so nice. You guys should get together."

"No, thanks," she would always answer. Sheila would have nothing of romance with this complicated screwball. When one of her co-workers suggested that she and Wayne could be dates at a Conlin's-sponsored barbecue, she just shook her head. She drove to the event herself, and when she pulled up to park, to her chagrin she could see Wayne running over to her car. In his hand was a single long-stemmed red rose, which he presented to her. She didn't want to offend him, but something told her to be direct and specific.

"I don't want to be with you, Wayne. I like you, but I don't want to be your date, okay?"

Wayne pulled back, smiled, said he understood. "No problem. No problem."

All during the picnic, Sheila tried to avoid him, but he just kept popping up, getting her drinks, offering her something to eat.

Over the months that followed, Sheila succeeded in crippling whatever amorous intentions Wayne may have had toward her, and she became a chum. On a few occasions, she went out for beers after work with Wayne and Rick Mace. They were congenial times. The conversation often dwelled on work. Sheila and Rick bitched more than Wayne did about Conlin's. Invariably, just as the good times started to roll,

Wayne would bolt the party. He always left before anyone else, and he claimed he had to be in the house by nine o'clock. Everyone who had heard about this supposed curfew racked it up as another of Wayne's oddities.

Among his coworkers at Conlin's, only Sheila knew the inside story of how Wayne rationalized his social handicap. She learned it from Wayne himself on the night he brought over the boxes she was going to use for storage.

After he carried the bound stacks of collapsed, folded cardboard into the house, Sheila thanked him profusely, then offered him a beer.

"I don't have Miller. How 'bout a Bud?"

"Sure."

They sat down at the kitchen table and fell into a long conversation about people and work and just about anything tangentially connected.

"I wish Kris liked me," Wayne said, turning sullen.

Sheila had heard this before, and she knew that Kris walked a different tightrope with Wayne. As a co-worker, it was easier for Sheila to tell Wayne in the flattest of terms that she didn't seek a romantic relationship with him. For Kris, being the boss and not wanting to encourage Wayne in the first place, it was more a matter of steering clear—politely acknowledging Wayne's gifts while simultaneously preparing to throw them out at the first opportunity.

Once, at a farewell party held at Kris's for another Conlin's employee, Kris had to confront the fact that Wayne now knew what she had done with the many things he had given her. Wayne dropped in at the party, and as he entered the house and stepped up into the living room, Kris shuddered. There, behind an easy chair in the corner, scattered on her dog Sundance's bed, was the proof. She had given the trinkets from Wayne to her dog.

Kris watched Wayne as he said his hellos around the room, and she saw that his eyes then fell on the wicker dog basket. He could see that among the gnaw bones and dog paraphernalia Kris had tossed his gifts to her. He had bought them, it was now plain to see, for this golden retriever, the same dog he had befriended at an earlier Conlin's barbecue by feeding it hunks of steak. Kris had told him to stop, but he did it anyway.

After Wayne left, Kris went up to Sheila and told her that Wayne had seen the stuff in Sundance's bed.

"I feel bad about it," Kris said. "But I don't know what to do."

"Yeah, I know," Sheila puzzled. "Don't worry about it. Wayne should know better, you know."

"I just feel bad."

On this night, as Sheila offered Wayne a second beer, she chose her words carefully as she responded to Wayne's moaning about why Kris didn't seem to like him as much as he liked her.

"Well, Kris has a pretty hard job to do, with all of our personalities," she told him, stringing the thoughts tightly together, hoping to form a convincing, but not depressing answer. "I think she really likes her work. It doesn't mean she doesn't like you, Wayne. She just has a lot of responsibility."

"I can't stand Doug," Wayne said, his voice hardening.

"Aw c'mon, Wayne."

"I can't stand him."

"Why not?"

"He's conceited."

"No, Doug's not conceited. He's very quiet. The only time Doug talks a lot is when he has been drinking, you know."

"If he ever did anything to hurt Kris, I'd kill him."

"Oh, Wayne, Doug's really a nice guy."

Sheila didn't take him seriously. It was an empty threat, as far as she was concerned, and being the kind of talker who can keep a conversation alive, and heading toward positive territory, she led the conversation away from the topic. They drank some more beer, and as Wayne opened up more, becoming almost confessional, they found themselves talking about God. But they got on the subject only because Wayne had been complaining in general about how hard it was for him to get along with others in social situations. Somehow, in his mind, the two were connected.

"I don't believe in God," he said, swilling a mouthful. "I believe in past lives."

"You mean, like reincarnation?"

"Yeah. I think the reason I have such a hard time dealing with people and being in crowds is that I haven't been allowed to come back for all these past lives."

"What do you mean?" Sheila wasn't exactly disbelieving, but she wasn't going to be taken in by any fantastic joke. "Not allowed to come back? C'mon Wayne."

"No, I mean it. I mean, I was held up. I wasn't allowed to have another life like everyone else. I wasn't allowed to come back for all of the lifetimes that everyone else has had. To learn all of the lessons that everyone else had."

Sheila had never heard this stuff before. She wasn't buying it, but she listened.

"Why, Wayne?"

"I believe that in one of my first lifetimes, I did something bad, like kill the last extinct animal, and I'm being punished. I wasn't allowed to come back."

Sheila laughed. Was Wayne getting silly or what?

"I'm totally serious. I have this big gap. I missed out on many reincarnations. I was allowed to come back in 1955."

It wasn't funny anymore. Sheila could see this wasn't Wayne's garden-variety bullshit. He was dead serious, and he certainly wasn't drunk. She felt a queer shiver. It was getting late, and suddenly the mood was wrong.

"Wayne, I have to work tomorrow and you have to leave now." She could hear the abruptness in her words, and she was relieved when Wayne took the hint.

"Thanks for the beers," he called to her from his truck as he backed out of the drive.

Sheila set her alarm and went to bed, but she couldn't shake the new, creepy feeling. It wasn't so much what Wayne had said, or that she had been alone with him in the house into the wee hours. What had gotten to her was a new insight: Wayne actually believed the stuff he had told her. There was no doubt about that, or that she had just gotten a glimpse of another facet of a very complicated Wayne, and had felt something cold come into the room.

Just two weeks after the Shook murders, Sheila threw a small New Year's Eve party. She had recently moved to a duplex apartment, and she had borrowed Wayne's muscle power to help her move. He was invited to the party, and he came, but she soon was sorry that he did.

Sheila's two sons each had invited a friend to stay over, and after the four boys had gone off to bed, most of the other guests left. It wasn't midnight yet, but a sudden heavy snowstorm had cut the evening short. When all but Wayne and Sheila and another man, a friend of hers but not a boyfriend, had left, the three of them sat down around the dining-room table to play Trivial Pursuit.

It was the kind of game Wayne was good at, and they played for hours. But Sheila wasn't very quick with the rapid-fire recall of past trivia, and after a while she grew tired of it. By the time five in the morning rolled around, she was not only tired of the game, she was quite ready for both of her guests to leave. But she didn't want her friend to leave before Wayne.

At an opportune moment, as her friend left the table to get another drink, Sheila followed him into the kitchen.

"Don't leave until Wayne leaves, please," she whispered.

He shook his head.

"I just don't want to be here alone with him. Just stick around till he goes."

Again, he nodded in the affirmative.

Back in the dining room, Sheila joined in the game again, and they played a little longer. Sheila and her friend appeared resolute, until finally, Wayne, who was becoming slowly but visibly agitated, got up from the table.

"Well, I'm outta here," he said.

After Wayne left, Sheila's friend said good night, too. That would be the end of it until two days later at work, when Rick Mace brought up the subject of her New Year's Eve party.

"Wayne was asking about you," Rick said. It was a teasing approach.

"What was he asking you?" Sheila wasn't that amused.

"He asked if that guy was your boyfriend. He said he was at your party the other night."

"No, he's not my boyfriend. Wayne knows that."

"Well, he said he was getting real pissed because the guy wouldn't leave."

Chapter 25

A Strong Suspect in Mind

As the summer months passed, it couldn't have been more clear to Wayne that the Hamilton authorities were barking up the wrong tree. Everyone at Conlin's knew that Dave Davis was under suspicion. They all knew Merilee, his wife, had been interviewed because she was the suspect's wife. They knew that his home had been searched and that he had been interrogated, but by now the Shook double homicide case was fading into memory. Because they worked with Merilee, they all knew that Dave had left Montana. If Sheriff Dye had a strong case against him, would he have allowed him to skip?

This inside knowledge undoubtedly would have comforted Wayne, until he read the news item in the August 3 *Missoulian*. It was only a brief account, but its content was explosively big. None of the previous seventeen stories ever had mentioned anything about a gunshot wound or the bullet Wayne knew he had left in Teresa's ankle, and this story didn't, either, but it presented a problem just the same. The story quoted Sheriff Dye saying he had received the results of an analysis of evidence submitted to the state crime lab. Wayne had no way of knowing exactly what evidence the sheriff had. He was pretty sure—and he was right—that Dye didn't have fingerprints. Wayne had worn gloves. A ballistics review of the bullet wouldn't match anything, except his father's gun, which wasn't going anywhere. Still, what could Sheriff Dye now have that would prompt a public comment almost eight months later?

"We have a very strong suspect in mind," Sheriff Dye was quoted further. That was a more troubling puzzle. Was this the same suspect he had in February? The story didn't say.

"We're still doing some background interviewing and hope to gather additional evidence to submit to the lab," the sheriff said in conclusion. What additional evidence? Wayne would have wondered.

It would be the last ever news story in the *Missoulian* in which Sheriff Dye would strut out his tired assertions. Greg Lakes knew he had nothing, because he was on the inside of the sheriff's investigation. But Wayne wasn't. He had gotten away with murder many times before, but if he believed that there was the slightest chance that someone was beginning to focus on him, the stress on his state of mind would have started to build, uncontrollably so, to a staggering point.

Robert R. Hazelwood, supervisory special agent at the Federal Bureau of Investigation's Behavior Science Unit in Quantico, Virgina, would later theorize that such a scenario probably began to unfold the moment Wayne began to feel unsure about the new course that Sheriff Dye may be taking.

"There's only one way to relieve that stress," Hazelwood said. "There's no question that Wayne was paranoid about the Shook investigation. Serial offenders generally commit their crimes as stress is building on them. That stress level reaches a peak, and that's when they make the kill. It's like a weight being lifted off their shoulders. That's what they [the killers] say. It's a cathartic experience."

The timing of this unsettling new development couldn't have been worse for Wayne, because he was busy preparing for an all-important event, the celebration of Kris's birthday. It was only a week away.

Chapter 26

Only Time Will Tell

Kris pretended to be excited, and pleased with the paperweight, a little ceramic turtle that she was supposed to put on her desk. Wayne watched as she opened the card he had included with the gift, and Kris tried to appear tickled by the card. She succeeded in keeping up the polite front until she actually began to read what he had written inside.

"Since you didn't seem to enjoy the jewelry that I gave you, maybe you'll appreciate a piece of artwork. I may be slow and cold-blooded, but only time will tell."

As everyone else lined up for a piece of birthday cake, which was busily being cut into thick slices with the store's own personalized, "Wayne Nance"-engraved cake knife that he had donated after several other large cutting knives had mysteriously disappeared, Kris began to shiver. She had thanked Wayne after she opened the paperweight gift, but she said nothing now.

She let her hand, which held the card, drop to her side. She didn't show it to anybody. At

the first opportunity, she would throw it and
the turtle paperweight in the trash.

The date was August 10, 1986. She was thirty-three years old. And like all the other
women at Conlin's, she was no longer some kid
who would be amused by this kind of haunting
humor. She was a mature adult woman who
had tried, but apparently failed, to navigate a
wide course around Wayne. It would be Cindy's turn next. Her birthday was coming up on
September 4. How would Cindy handle it?
What did Wayne have planned for Cindy's
birthday?

Neither Kris nor anyone else would get the
answer to those two questions. In the days
that followed the celebration of Kris's birthday,
Wayne would come unglued. Whether it had
been the news stories, or the building pressure
of his unrequited obsession with Kris, Wayne
again was getting cranked up. Sometime during
the middle of the month, while delivering a
chair to an old high school acquaintance,
Wayne's preoccupations were becoming noticeable. He was losing his ability to operate under
total cover.

Mark Lyman, who had been an underclassman at Sentinel, immediately recognized Todd
Zander, the other delivery man, because he recently had sold him a car at Bitterroot Ford,
where Mark was a salesman. Mark also then
put a name to Wayne's face. He remembered
the fearsome upperclassman who carried a
knife to school, who had jabbed another student with a hypodermic needle, who was a suspect in the Donna Pounds murder.

But that was then and this was now. Mark

was glad to see Wayne again, and it was like old-home week. The three men talked about Todd's new car, and about the good old days at Sentinel as Mark pointed the way to the master bedroom, where the new chair was to be placed. Mark's wife and children were stationed in the bedroom, looking on, studying the new furniture addition. As the three then left the room and headed back to the front of the house, again Mark led the way, talking away as he walked through the hallway to the living room.

Looking over his shoulder, to reinforce whatever collegial sentiment he was expressing to Wayne by making a momentary bit of eye contact, Mark was surprised to see that Wayne didn't appear to be listening at all. Wayne, in that flash of a second that Mark looked back, appeared instead to be casing the house. Though his head was pretty much oriented straight ahead, Wayne's eyes were in a scanning mode. Mark didn't know what to make of it. It made him feel uneasy, but he really didn't know why. Suddenly, though, he was glad that Wayne was gone.

It had been more than eleven years since Wayne had corrupted Bill Van Canagan's peace of mind with his incessant, gory fantasizing and his menacing threats. Bill never forgot Wayne's enigmatic confession: "It's been done." He would never let go of the memory that those words were tantamount to a death sentence on anyone who repeated them with the intent to turn Wayne in for the murder of Donna Pounds, because Wayne also needed, he had coolly and not so fortuitiously explained, to kill a friend who betrayed him. That would be his ticket to warlockdom.

Wayne had actually crossed Bill's mind only last winter, only a few weeks after the Shook murders. Bill was now a practicing attorney in the Missoula law firm of Datsopoulos MacDonald & Lind, where the same Ronald MacDonald who had encountered Wayne during the Donna Pounds investigation still practiced. Bill and a friend, John Wagner, were on their way down to Sleeping Child Hot Springs, a resort in the Bitterroot just north of Hamilton. It was a place that offered cross-country skiing, hot tubs, saunas, food and drink, and conviviality for anyone seeking relaxation along with leisurely exercise.

As Bill and John turned off Route 93 onto Sleeping Child Road, the conversation turned to the Shook murders, only because they passed no more than eight-tenths of a mile from the Shook house. What triggered a remembrance of Wayne was John's mention of the fire that had been set. Bill knew about the murders, but he wasn't aware that the killer had also set a fire. When John mentioned this fact, Bill immediately thought of Wayne. It was odd, but it was because he still held a strong memory of Wayne's torching of the Sentinel homecoming floats, a make-believe reenactment of a Viking burial at sea. It came blazing back at him now, and he and John talked about Wayne for a few miles. But as easily as the connection was made, it was dropped. For all they knew, Wayne was still in the Navy. He could be any-where in the Pacific.

In May, Bill bought a home up in the Rattlesnake, an upscale part of town that many
viewed as the ultimate station in life for Missoulians. Over the summer, he had thrown
quite a few parties in his new house, and a lot
of people, especially the young trendsetters in
town, knew that he had moved up there and
that he lived alone. It had been a hot summer,
and Bill got used to leaving the doors open at
night to cool the place down. With the garage
door open, and the adjoining inside kitchen
door open, whatever night breeze there was
could find its way into the house. While it
meant that the house was wide open, Bill had
no reason to fear an intruder, until one particularly hot night in late August.

On this night, as he lay in bed, drifting to
sleep, he was jogged awake by a noise. As he
pricked up his ears to listen, he could tell that
it was definitely something. It was the sound
of feet on the kitchen floor. Someone was in his
kitchen. He could tell by the familiar squeaking
sound of the floor in there. Whoever it was was
moving around. He sat up. He could hear his
heart pounding, and he tried to block it out so
he could hear more.

It was suddenly quiet. The entire house
seemed to envelop him in shadowy silence for
what seemed the longest time. It might have
been only a minute or two before he heard the
footsteps. They were coming down the hallway, heading for his bedroom.

Panicking, he thought of his golf clubs. He
kept them next to the bed. It was a quick but
sound decision, he thought to himself in the
allotted second of time, to grab his nine iron.

This would do some damage, he knew, as he slipped his feet to the floor, standing in his underwear near the doorway, gripped with terror, but ready. After a second or two, sensing that someone was just outside the doorway, waiting to make a move, he decided to go first. He flung open the door and yelled.

"Hey! Hey you!"

All he saw was the outline of a man bolting down the hall, running out through the kitchen, through the garage, and out into the night.

Chapter 27

A Day to Remember

It was September 2, 1986, a Tuesday. But more importantly, it was two days before Cindy's birthday. The women at Conlin's had to decide what kind of cake they would get for the party. Someone remembered that Cindy liked cherry cheesecake. So it was settled.

Sheila Claxton had been listening in on the conversation, wondering if she would even be at work on Thursday. Her mind was elsewhere, because the guy she was going with had invited her to his cabin on Flathead Lake, an hour and a half drive north. He wanted her to come up on Thursday, but she couldn't decide. Missing Cindy's party had nothing to do with her indecision. Sheila had driven up to the lake at the drop of a hat before, but this time, though she didn't have a clear reason why, she was hesitating.

That night, as she flopped onto the sofa after work, still debating whether to go or not, half-watching the six o'clock local news, her waffling was interrupted by what came on the screen. It was a Crimestoppers update, a TV spot generated by the sheriff's department.

Captain Weatherman still was trying to identify the bodies that had been found in the hills east of Missoula. The unreal plastic likenesses of Debbie Deer Creek and Chryssie Crystal Creek stared out from the screen. The voice-over appealed for anyone who had any information about these unidentified women to call the Crimestoppers' line.

Lounging there, alone in her apartment, Sheila got spooked. She suddenly felt goosebumps. Her mind was made up. She was going to the lake, and she immediately started to pack so she could leave right after work the next day.

By the end of that following workday, a Wednesday, after putting in her eight hours at Conlin's, Sheila was very happy to bolt out the front door and get away. It had been one hell of a day, mostly because of Wayne, who was in a miserable mood. For Sheila, it all started with a simple mistake. She had forgotten to post a delivery order. It was a special-order chair for Mike Sunderland, a local police officer who, along with his wife was a friend of Sheila's. She had promised them delivery on Wednesday, but had mistakenly posted it for Thursday.

Sheila knew she had no choice but to approach Wayne and ask him nicely. But it wasn't going to be easy. All morning long, Wayne had been sending out negative signals. He had worked like crazy right through his lunch hour, building up more than his usual amount of sweat, and he was glaring at everyone. When, for example, Vern had finished his own brown-bag lunch and was sitting back, enjoying a cigarette, Wayne seemed to get angrier. Here he had worked through lunch. Vern, who had stopped to eat, was now extending his break.

It had already been a hectic week. Because of the Labor Day holiday on Monday, when the store was closed, the men in the warehouse had had one less day to load the semi for the out-of-town deliveries and then prepare for the local deliveries, most of which were scheduled to be made today, Wednesday.

It was a quarter past noon when Sheila started to explain to Wayne that she had hung up a delivery for Thursday when it really had to be made today.

"Oh, Wayne, I screwed up. I hung Sunderland's chair up for tomorrow instead of today. Is there any way you can take it?" she asked in sugary lilt.

"Don't even talk to me," he screamed back, his voice carrying through the showroom. "I can't talk to you right now."

Sheila was mortified. Kris was sitting nearby.

"Okay, I'll call 'em," Sheila whimpered.

"I can't even answer a question. Don't talk to me!"

He wouldn't let up. Detecting a certain fragility under the bellowing, freakish rage, Sheila decided to go over to him.

"I'll call Mike and Linda and I'll tell them," she said, catering to him.

Kris had had enough of this. She got up from her chair and walked over to take command of the situation.

"Please take the chair, Wayne," she asked him firmly but nicely. "We've got to get this done."

Wayne was already steamed at Kris because she had given him two long lists of things to move from the warehouse stock out into the showroom. Normally there would be a single list, but she was trying to compress a five-day work load into the shortened week. In the end, Wayne did as she asked. He made the delivery.

All day long, Wayne played center stage. At times, he kept everyone at bay with his intolerable, foul mood. Then he would become the self-pitying, unappreciated zealot, who had made the warehouse what it was. In yet another role, he stepped completely out of character, playing the eager host to someone everyone knew he thoroughly despised.

When Doug stopped in to see Kris that day, he did what he always did: came through the front door, walked a straight line through the showroom, and found his wife somewhere in the vicinity of the office. But this time, Wayne intercepted him, and surprised everyone by greeting Doug as he passed by the canteen. He even offered to get Doug a cup of coffee. Here was a first.

"How do you take it?" he asked.

"Little creamer, thanks."

"Sure."

Had Wayne snapped? Later that afternoon, as they made their delivery rounds, Vern Willen was certain that something was different, quite different, about Wayne.

"Did you cash your check yet?" Wayne asked from the driver's seat.

"No."

"Well, we'll swing by the bank."

This was new. Where was the righteous Boy

Scout who had lectured about why it was wrong to conduct personal business on company time?

As they cruised out along Mullin Road on the west side of town, where they had a delivery to make, Vern mentioned that he lived in the vicinity. His trailer was back a ways. He wondered if someday Wayne, whom he knew to be a gardening buff, would stop by and look at some shrubs that Vern wanted to replant. Wayne was, in fact, a fairly accomplished gardener, and he often stayed up late into the night tending to the flowering plants he kept in his father's backyard. Once, on a strange whim, he created a small flower garden right in the middle of his father's driveway. Bordered by railroad ties, it effectively blocked any parking.

Vern didn't know whether his shrubs should be put in the sun or in a shady spot.

"Oh, yeah, we should have stopped," Wayne said cheerily.

Vern was nonplussed. He said nothing. He didn't know what to say.

"Oh, we'll stop on the way back," Wayne continued.

"That's another run way out Mullin," Vern said, realizing it was also a breach of Wayne's efficiency code to double-back across town on a personal mission.

"It's not that far out of our way."

When they arrived at Vern's trailer, Wayne seemed relaxed as they inspected the shrubbery.

"*Juniperus*," he said.

"Junipers, right," Vern was impressed that Wayne used the Latin name.

"Cyprus family," Wayne said, then offering advice about where they might do well.

Wayne seemed to be in no hurry, so Vern invited him inside, showing him the whole trailer. They paused for awhile to look at the houseplants, then Wayne was ready to leave.

"Well, we better go."

Vern figured Wayne must have had something on his mind, because on the drive back to Conlin's, Wayne talked like he never had talked before.

"I'm just getting tired. I'm just getting tired," he repeated. "This place has been my second home. This store has been my second home. Sometimes I care more about what goes on here than I do at home. That's really my second home.

"And nobody cares. It doesn't make a difference. You work your ass off, and it just doesn't seem like it makes any difference," Wayne said, his words curving downward.

He told Vern it bothered him that Rick Mace got all the glory for all the work he, Wayne, actually did, and that Kris didn't seem to realize how much he did, because Rick always took the credit. Vern knew it was true: Wayne made the warehouse, not Rick. Vern listened, offering little more than an understanding ear. It was not Vern's place to do anything more than sit and visit with his buddy, and nod when it seemed right.

"I'm sick and tired. I don't care anymore. I don't care. I just don't care," Wayne said.

It was the last few minutes of the workday. Joyce Halverson, a saleswoman, had a big problem. How was she going to move the furniture out of her bedroom at home to make way for a carpet man, who would arrive early the next morning? Her two sons were out of town. Her son-in-law and her husband both had back trouble. She needed a favor, and she thought all day about asking Wayne, whom she knew would be ready to help, but he had been so angry all day. She wasn't close enough to any of the other guys in the warehouse to ask such a favor of any of them, and she had to get that bedroom empty tonight. There was no one else. She hurried back to the warehouse, where she found Wayne punching out on the clock.

"Wayne, would you . . . I hate to ask you . . . if I can't find anybody else closer, would you mind coming over and helping me move this big heavy dresser? There's a dresser and a chest that I have to get out of my bedroom tonight."

"Well, yeah, I guess. Just let me know." He seemed noncommittal.

"Do you have something planned?"

"No," he answered, hesitant.

"Well, that's okay."

"Yes," he said, "just let me know."

"I'll let you know when I get home from work. I'll call you then," Joyce said.

"But you have to let me know before seven o'clock, because I don't answer the phone after seven."

"Fine, I'll call," Joyce said, turning back toward the showroom. Joyce noticed Wayne seemed to be in a hurry to punch out, but she thought nothing of it. Wayne was always in a hurry. He walked fast. He worked fast. She was used to his breakneck pace.

Shortly before seven o'clock, Joyce called him.

"Hi, Wayne. It's Joyce. Well, I don't seem to have anyone else who can do it."

"Okay, I'll be over," he said. "But I have to take a shower first."

When he arrived, Joyce thanked him for doing her this favor, and as soon as he was inside, she offered him pizza. It had just been delivered. She and her daughter, Jeanne, and her son-in-law were still eating.

"No, I already ate." Wayne thanked her. He had chowed down chicken and beer at the Reno Inn in East Missoula on the way home from work.

Wayne came into the living room and sat down on the sofa, visiting with Jeanne. Joyce remembered that once before when Wayne had been to her house for a Conlin's party, he had wandered into her bedroom and was looking at the pictures of her children on the wall.

"Oh, I know your kids," he said to her then. "I went to school with Jeanne and Heidi. Jeannie was a year older, and Heidi was a year younger." At the time, Joyce was taken aback by Wayne's awareness of her daughters' class rankings at Sentinel, where the big student population didn't lend itself to such familiarity.

Joyce offered Wayne a beer, a Budweiser, and he stayed in the living room visiting with Jeanne while Joyce and her son-in-law got the way cleared to move the heavy furniture from her bedroom into the den, where it would park until the bedroom was carpeted.

When she glanced in at Wayne and Jeanne, she could see that while Wayne was now hungrily chomping on a slice of pizza, her daughter seemed tense. All of a sudden, Jeanne looked nervous.

"Okay," Joyce intruded, "we're ready. First we have to go in the den and get the big sleeper out of the den."

Wayne knew that the flip-out bed frame of a sleeper sofa had to be tied down before moving the sofa, or it would spring open if it were inadvertently tilted too far forward.

"I'll go out and get my rope out of my truck," Wayne said.

"No, here, just use a belt," Joyce said.

"No, I'll get my rope. It'll work better," Wayne insisted.

"Wayne, just use this belt," Joyce said, getting a little bossy.

Wayne relented and took the belt. He secured the sleeper mechanism, still grumbling about his ropes, then moved the sofa out of the way.

"I don't know why," Jeanne whispered to her mother when Wayne was out of earshot, "but he makes me nervous."

When the den was free and clear, Wayne and Joyce's son-in-law each grabbed one end of her dresser. As they started to hoist it, Wayne clearly had the strength to manhandle its weight, and he tipped it ever so slightly forward.

"Oops, watch out for the drawer," he said whimsically. "Don't want any of those little panties to fall out."

Nobody reacted. It wasn't funny. It wasn't

appropriate. It didn't fit the moment. Just as Joyce well knew that Wayne, in the largest sense, didn't fit, even though she and everyone else day in and day out tolerated the juvenile moods of this full-grown man. Joyce was so inured to this kind of thing that she didn't even roll her eyes. Somehow that would have served as a payback for him.

The job got done in no time. And afterward, they all moved back into the living room, where they sat and visited for a while longer. At exactly nine-thirty, Wayne abruptly got up and announced that he had to leave. The manner of his announcement, lacking any transitory hemming and hawing about not really wanting to leave, made as it was without any hint at a reason why he had to leave at this exact time, seemed odd to Joyce. But she didn't pry. Wayne just seemed to be in a hurry again.

Chapter 28

"Oh, God
. . . I'm a Dead Man"

Doug examined the rifle once more. It was a Savage, a lever-action Model 99G Take-Down, and probably had been built in the 1920s. The bore was badly pitted, but the gun was worth saving. Someone had pawned it, and the owner at Missoula Pawnbrokers wanted to know if it fired well enough to be sold.

There was an interesting history behind this old hunting rifle. The Model 99 fired a Savage 250 round, which originally was called the Savage 250-3000, named so because it was the first cartridge to achieve a velocity of 3,000 feet per second, which was noteworthy in 1915 when it was introduced. This particular specimen had excessive head space, so Doug had to manufacture cartridges that would properly fit the bigger bore. After he set the rifle on its butt, leaning it against his workbench in the basement, he then stuffed his custom-made cartridges into an ammo box, wrapping tape over every three cartridges and labeling each load. So much powder. So much primer. Later, he would make entries in his logbook detailing how each load fired.

As he was close to finishing, he heard Kris come in the front door. He picked up the rifle and the box of cartridges, and with his one free hand, grabbed Kris's rifle, also a Savage Model 99. Hers was a newer model, which he had cut down to fit his wife's petite frame.

They were planning a night out with some friends. They had met John and Darla McKee through a wine-tasting group. But John and Darla and Doug and Kris weren't going to be sampling wines tonight. This was going to be a gun night. Darla, a novice shooter, wanted a chance to fire Kris's rifle before she borrowed it for antelope season, which was coming up. Doug wanted to give the old Savage a workout, too, and the McKee's place was perfect for this kind of thing. They lived in Frenchtown, a twenty-minute drive west of Missoula along the Clark Fork River.

It was a warm Wednesday night, and the prospect of taking the drive along the river and seeing their friends was something to look forward to. Doug was also eager to see how his cartridge loads worked out.

There was at least an hour's worth of light left by the time they arrived at the McKees'. John and Doug set up some targets, and Doug and Darla blasted away. The gun fit her well, and Doug, who was firing the pawnshop relic, was pleased to discover that with the right cartridge load, it could still be used. John joined in, shooting off a few rounds as Doug made some notes and packed up the six leftover cartridges. Darla headed inside with Kris to see to dinner, and soon the men quit. It was starting to get dark, but it was also getting a bit late to be making such a racket with gunfire.

The foursome ate barbecued chicken and drank a few beers. On previous occasions, when they got together like this, they would often let the party stretch on, and they would have a lot more to drink. But not on this night. John was beat. A foreman at Stone Container's pulp mill in Frenchtown, he had been working twelve-hour days because of a strike, and he was facing an early shift the next day. So at eleven-thirty, Doug loaded the guns into his Honda, and they all said their good-nights.

It was ten minutes to midnight by the time they neared their house on Parker Court. As they approached from the west, turning off Reserve onto River and then proceeding along Davis, which intersected their street, Doug noticed an orange and white Ford pickup parked obtrusively just off the road on the side lawn of their property. It was half on the street and half in the yard.

"Boy, that gets me," he said to Kris. "Look at that guy." It bothered him that somebody would occupy his turf that way, and after they both were inside the house, he wasn't going to let it go. He grabbed a flashlight, heading back out to investigate, and Kris, who had patted Sundance on her way through the living room, was making for the bedroom. She couldn't wait to get into bed. It had been a long day.

Doug kept a fourteen-foot fishing boat on a trailer under his backyard deck, and he often fretted about how simple it would be for someone to back up to it and drive away. As he headed out of the house, he first aimed the light under the deck. The boat was there, all right. Then he walked toward the pickup, hesitating as he got within ten feet of it, then coming up for a closer look. He could see someone slouched down on the front seat. The man moved slightly as the light was shone on him, but it appeared to Doug that the guy was sleeping one off.

"Somebody had too much," he called to Kris when he came back in. "That was as far as he could get so he came in for a landing and is gettin' a few ZZZs."

"Mmmm," Kris answered. She was already in bed, settling up against a pillow, flipping the pages of *People* magazine.

Doug went down to the basement where he soaked a cleaning patch in solvent, scrubbed the bore of the old Savage with a bristle brush, and then threaded the wet patch through the barrel. He left the gun leaned up against his reloading bench, right next to the six unshot rounds. Then, as he headed back upstairs, he started thinking about the strange truck outside.

"That's too weird," he called again to Kris from the kitchen. "I'm gonna go get a license number and call the cops."

This time, when he went back outside, the truck was gone.

Now, in the house again, he had turned out most of the lights and was getting a drink of water in the kitchen when he remembered it was garbage night. The next day, Thursday, was pickup day. Because Kris had the day off, they probably would sleep in some, so he decided he better take out the garbage now. He walked back down the short flight of steps to a landing and stepped down into the garage. He slid the two refuse containers across the floor to the overhead door and with one hand lifted it up. As he took about two steps onto the driveway he saw something out of the corner of his eye. Crouched down between an ornamental evergreen and the side of the house was the figure of a man, or part of a man. All he could see was someone's ass end. Doug's heart jumped into his throat.

"Who's there?" he blurted.

At that moment, the man behind the bush leaped out into the front yard.

"Wayne from Conlin's," the man announced himself.

Doug didn't recognize him, but his mind was putting it together. If he had said he was just "Wayne," Doug wouldn't have had any instant recognition. If he had said, "Wayne from work," Doug would have immediately thought of Wayne Lundberg, a taxidermist he knew.

"What the hell are you doing here?" Doug demanded, now seeing Wayne Nance's face in the little bit of light from the garage.

"Ah . . . ah," Wayne stammered, "I saw something out here. If you have a flashlight, you better get it."

The first thing Doug thought of was the orange and white truck. He didn't stop to think that it was even more strange that Wayne was standing in his front yard—at midnight—or that Wayne had been sneaking around in the bushes. Doug's millisecond-long rationalization was that maybe Wayne was out driving around and had seen the guy in the truck.

"Okay, I've got one in the house. I'll go get it."

Doug turned and reentered the garage, stepped up to the landing and was just about to take the last step into his living room when he felt a blow to the back of his head. The next thing he knew, he was lying on the floor in the living room, the back of his head was split wide open and bleeding, and Wayne was coming after him, brandishing a mean-looking black billy club with a lanyard that was looped on his wrist. Wayne was wild eyed.

Doug rolled up on his back, trying to kick Wayne with his right foot. Wayne turned to his right as he was coming up the steps, and Doug delivered a glancing blow that sent Wayne spinning into the wall. Wayne was down, and as he tried to get back up, Doug grabbed him, pulling him down again. Doug was all over him, and when he had Wayne tightly by the collar, he dragged him up the stairs where they both careened into Sundance's dog bed.

No one had said a word yet, but Kris heard a loud thud. It was the sound of something dropping. It was a noise she couldn't explain. Then there were thumps and thuds, the sound of bodies against the walls and the floor, and she came running into the living room. There she found her husband grappling with another man at the top of the stairs. She raced over to Doug, who she could see was bleeding profusely from the slice out of the back of his head.

They both watched as Wayne reached with his right hand across to his left side and pulled the gun, his father's quick-draw Ruger.

"Get back," he ordered. "I've got a gun."

Doug still had hold of him, but he let go, and then shimmied backwards on his butt farther into the room. When Kris saw the man's face, she didn't recognize it. It was fiercely distorted. The way the light struck the man's glasses didn't help either. It took a few seconds of looking at him and hearing him say "I've got a gun" for the picture to gel.

"Wayne!" she screamed. "What are you doing here? Why are you doing this? What's wrong? What's happening?" she yelled, cradling Doug's head.

"Get back! Get away from me. Get back a little ways."

Doug backed up some more, Kris holding him to her chest as he lay on his right side, up on one elbow, still woozy.

"Why are you doing this, Wayne?" Kris demanded, screaming at him.

It seemed Wayne would answer now. He dragged it out as he said, "I've done something really bad. I gotta get out of town. I know Conlin's got paid today. I know you probably have some money here. So I'm gonna get some money and I'm gonna get out of town."

No one talked for a couple of minutes as Wayne gestured for them to get farther back into the room, pacing back and forth. Kris rested Doug's head against an ottoman. Then Wayne produced a section of white clothesline rope he carried in a plastic breadsack he pulled from under his plaid, cotton-flannel shirt, which he wore tails out. Otherwise, Wayne was dressed just as he might be any other day, in blue jeans and a T-shirt. He took off his brown jersey gloves to cut a section of rope with a kitchen-type cutlery knife he pulled from a scabbard he wore on his belt, and told Kris to tie Doug's hands and feet.

"You don't have to tie us up," Kris said. "Don't worry about it."

"Do it."

Kris by now had figured that Wayne must have gotten into a fight with Rick Mace. That he probably had beaten the shit out of Rick, or maybe even killed him. That he needed to get out of town, and he needed money to do that. It all made sense to her. There was no point now in trying to sweet-talk Wayne, because Kris could see that he was seething, just the way he would be at work. He was cold, very matter-of-fact, with that familiar determined look on his face. He was set on what he was going to do. His voice wasn't especially loud, and it was not actually expressing anger. It was impersonal. Still, if she were going to bind Doug with this rope, she would tie a loose knot.

He told her to tie his hands behind him. After she did, Wayne leaned over to check.

"Tie it tighter," he said.

So she did, and then Wayne tied Doug's feet, and started moving around the house.

"Where's the money?" he asked.

"Well, it's in the little blue china cup in the bedroom. There's some money. I'll get it for you," Kris said.

"No. You stay on the floor."

Kris told him there was some money in her purse, which was looped over the back of a chair in the kitchen. She kept asking him questions, wanting to know why he was there and what it was he had done. Then she changed her tune, deciding she didn't want to know what Wayne had done.

"If you want some money? If you need the car? Take it. Just go. Go!"

Wayne didn't answer back. He just paced.

"Can I get something for Doug's head?"

Wayne picked up a white afghan from the back of a rocker and tossed in on Doug's head. When Kris complained that it was too scratchy, he got her a towel from the bathroom.

Wayne stuffed about $130 in his pocket, and continued to move back and forth throughout the house. In the kitchen, he tried to close the window blinds, but he was having trouble. He was pulling and pulling, but he couldn't get them to work.

"Wayne, let me do it," Kris called. "You're going to ruin those blinds!" Kris was remembering how expensive they were.

"Stay down and don't move."

Eventually he got them closed, and he headed back into the living room, where he pulled the shades down. Both Doug and Kris had commanded Sundance to lie down by the wall. The dog obeyed. They sensed that Wayne was getting antsy about the two of them being together. And when Wayne said he was going to tie Kris, Doug protested. He really didn't want Wayne to tie Kris, and he tried in vain to talk him out of it. After a while, when Kris also failed to convince Wayne that it wasn't necessary, Doug told her to forget it.

"You know, just don't say anything," he whispered to her. "It isn't working anyway."

Wayne tied Kris's hands together in front of

her and again started with his justification: "I've done something really bad and I gotta get out of town. Once I get out of town, I'll call somebody and they'll come and untie you. Then you'll be free. I'll be gone."

As Wayne talked, Kris studied the bloodstain on the carpet, thinking to herself, *Okay, how am I going to get all this blood off my carpet? There's just a little bit of blood on the carpet right now, and this is going to be over in no time.*

"Who should I call, who?" Wayne asked himself out loud. "You've got that friend," he said, looking at Kris, "that blond girl, your friend? Wanda?"

Everybody at Conlin's knew Wanda Smith. When Wanda came into the store, no one even bothered to wait on her, because they knew she was there to see Kris. Wayne had delivered to Wanda's house many times.

"What's her phone number?" Wayne asked, walking over to the edge of the table, reaching for an envelope that lay on the table.

"Well, Wanda's not home," Kris said. "She's in Spokane. But Bryan is."

"What's the number?" Wayne was stern.

As Kris gave him the number, Wayne scribbled it down on the flap of a paper he had ripped from the envelope. Both Doug and Kris were having different thoughts by now. Kris was thinking, *He's really going to do it. He is going to call them.* Doug, who through his daze was watching Wayne zoom from room to room, shutting the blinds, collecting the money, writing down phone numbers, zipping here, zipping there, was thinking, *For a guy who's done something really bad and needs to get out of town, he sure is dickin' around a lot*. It hadn't entered either of their thoughts that the situation could get any worse, that something really bad might happen to them. Instead, they followed Wayne's train of thought.

"I gotta separate you two. Or you'll untie each other too fast," Wayne said, reentering the living room again.

That made some sense, too. That he had to separate them. *Everything's going to be all right*, they said to themselves, *as soon as he leaves*.

It was now just after 12:30 A.M. Wayne had held his hostages for more than thirty minutes. Doug was down on his side, unable to see much of what was going on, but he saw Wayne lift his wife off the floor, heading for the bedroom. It was the first time Wayne physically touched Kris, and it was strange. She was in her nightshirt, and it occurred to her that she was in a pretty vulnerable position.

Kris felt almost weightless as Wayne carried her down the hall. He put her on the bed and proceeded to tie her hands and feet. She was still just thinking about when he was going to leave as Wayne fumbled with the ropes, trying for a good anchor to secure her hands.

The brass-plate headboard wobbled too much, so Wayne tied her hands to the frame. Wayne tied her right hand in a slip-type knot that closed tighter as it was pulled. He tied her feet together with one loop of rope secured by a square knot.

"You have any nylons?" he asked. It was the only thing he had said to her since bringing her into the bedroom.

"Yes," she answered, telling him which drawer.

Wayne opened it and removed a pair of pantyhose. He opened a second drawer, and removed a pair of Doug's white athletic socks, trimmed with a red band at the top. He stuffed a sock into Kris's mouth and tied the pantyhose around her head, securing the gag. Kris could feel that he hadn't tied it very tightly.

Then Wayne returned to Doug, who was still on his side, his hands tied behind him and his head resting on the ottoman. Doug was still bleeding, and not thinking straight, when Wayne stuffed a sock into his mouth. Wayne didn't say anything. *What's this?* Doug thought to himself. *No one has ever done this to me before. We're really playing games now.*

He realized he could spit it out, but he didn't, thinking, *I'll keep it in if that makes him happy. Let's just get him out of here.*

Wayne scampered back and forth between the bedroom and the living room a few more times, then came over to Doug.

"I'm gonna take you downstairs," he said, a little more frenzied than before. "I'm gonna tie you up down there, so that you'll be away from Kris."

Wayne appeared to be on an adrenaline rush now. He was getting more excited. As Wayne came closer to remove the sock from Doug's mouth, he sensed Wayne was a little unsure of himself. Doug didn't want to be taken to the basement, and he wanted to tell Wayne that there was no reason to do it, but his mind had decided not to argue, not to get Wayne any more agitated.

"I can't get down with my legs tied up," Doug said.

"Okay." Wayne untied his feet and helped him up.

"I can't walk down forwards. I'll go down backwards," Doug said.

Wayne stuffed the sock back into Doug's mouth, and stood above him on the stairs as he half-supported his prisoner and half-pushed him down the short flight of seven steps, all the time holding Doug's right arm. Wayne's revolver was back in the holster, where he had put it soon after he tied them both.

Wayne shut the door behind them, and that's all Kris heard—she knew it was the basement door because of the familiar sound made by its hollow core when it was closed. The basement was an unfinished space. There was a washer and a dryer, a framed-up bathroom wall, and Doug's reloading bench. Wayne pushed Doug right past the bench, right past the old Savage rifle and the stack of ammo to a structural support post.

"I'll tie ya to this. And then I'll call somebody and they'll come get ya," he said. Wayne then moved Doug up against the wood column support. Doug was facing the stairway and to his right—some fifteen feet away—was the reloading bench and the Savage. Hands still tied behind, Doug was weak. He started to slide down to the floor, leaning into the post. Wayne had let go of him, and just as Doug began his descent, he felt a blow to the head.

Wap! Wayne had hit him hard.

Doug fell to the floor. *Wap!* came the second hit. *Wap!* a third, and Doug was scrambling to get away, looking up at Wayne, who was chasing him with the club. Doug stopped when he got to the middle of the basement floor and reeled up on his rump, his feet in the air.

"Get out of here! Why don't you just get the money and get out of here? Why don't you leave us alone?"

Wayne moved the club to his left hand and pulled his gun again, pointing it at Doug.

"Get back against that post. Or I'll shoot you."

There was no doubt in Doug's mind then that Wayne would do it, and it was the first time that it had sunk in that they were in very bad trouble. But for now he obeyed, as Wayne produced another section of white cotton clothesline rope and looped it across Doug's neck and around the post. Doug feared Wayne was going to bear down and strangle him, but he didn't. He tied it tight and left it at that. Then he wrapped the rope around Doug's armpit, tucked it under his shoulder, looped it around the post, and then around the other armpit. As Wayne then tightened up the slack, Doug's shoulders were anchored to the post, just as his neck and head were securely fastened. Wayne then tied Doug's feet together, and just as soon as he had bound Doug's feet, Wayne was gone. The door slammed shut, alerting Kris, and Wayne was bounding back up the stairs.

The single bare bulb cast its harsh light on the rifle by the bench. Doug thought, *If I can get loose and get that rifle, I can stop this*. He started working his hands.

In the time Kris lay tied to her bed, all she could think about was getting loose so she could jump out the window and get next door or across the street for help. There was a phone on the nightstand, but her hands were tied, and even if she got free, she was going out the window, she told herself. It didn't occur to her that Doug's handgun was in the drawer. It was an AMT-Backup, an American-made, stainless steel .22-caliber, semiautomatic long-rifle job that he kept with the clip loaded but nothing in the chamber. The safety was kept off. Thus, to use the gun, all he would have to do is hand operate the slide that would feed a cartridge into the chamber. Kris was trying to work the knots with her fingernails, and she was making some progress when Wayne entered the room.

Wayne didn't say anything. He gave her a dispassionate look as he walked around the bed, checking the knots and inspecting the gag. Then he left, and she heard the basement door close again.

Doug had discovered that his rope bindings were tied unevenly. One hand was tied very tightly, but on the other the rope was fashioned in a loose loop. He got one loop undone and with his hands parted a little was starting to pull on the knots, trying to gain slack, when the door opened.

Doug pressed his hands together for appearance's sake. Wayne grabbed him by the arm and pulled him up off the floor, seeing if Doug was still affixed to the post. Then Wayne started to pace at Doug's feet.

"You gotta be smart. You gotta be smart," he said. "You're smarter than they are. You're gonna pull this off. You gotta think. Now think!

"What are you gonna do? How you gonna do it?" Wayne interrogated himself, giving no acknowledgement of Doug's presence as he got more agitated, more frenzied, betraying no apparent notice of the rifle that he walked past three times. Wayne was 100 percent into it, and Doug was fading. He could feel the blood trickling down his neck, and his head felt lighter now.

Wayne came around behind Doug and they both suddenly heard a noise upstairs. The bed, which was almost directly above them on the first floor, had moved. Wayne looked up, and in no time was shutting the basement door behind him. Doug worked harder on the ropes.

The racing back and forth—from the basement to the bedroom and back again—seemed to occupy hours. Doug and Kris had lost track of time. All Kris knew was that the basement door had shut again, and Wayne would be back in the bedroom, glaring but not staring directly at her, not saying a word, checking her ropes, and then leaving.

On one trip, she heard him close the overhead garage door. Kris had heard Doug's cries. She couldn't hear the words he was saying, but she could hear the voice, and it didn't sound right.

"Why are you hurting Doug?" she yelled at him when he came in again.

"He was lipping off to me. So I had to," he blared at her. The words were hard bitten. And Wayne was heading back downstairs.

Kris shuddered, and then began to shake. She realized that she was tied to her bed, wearing nothing more than a cotton nightshirt and her underpants. *What if he does something to me?* The thought occurred to her for the first time.

But just as quickly she blocked it. *You're not going to be any help if you don't stay calm*, she thought. *You've got to calm down. You've got to get out of here. You gotta work these knots, and that's it!*

Wayne was away from Kris for quite awhile, and she had managed to free her left hand. But she was still gripped by the panic that had just overtaken her since Wayne's last appearance. She didn't try to undo her right hand with the left, or use the phone. She was trying to untie her feet. With a strong jerk she pulled hard on the loop knot around her right wrist, and it cinched tighter. She also still hadn't remembered that there was a gun in the nightstand drawer. While not exceptionally handy with firearms, she would have known enough to work the hand slide to load a cartridge, but she didn't know where the trigger safety was, or whether it was on or off. Plus, she was right handed, and her right hand was still rigged to the bed.

When Wayne returned, after making sure the sound of the moving bed was no problem, Doug watched through a bleary haze as Wayne walked to the basement wall at Doug's left, standing there for a second, drawing a blank stare.

"I should just put this gun against my own head," Wayne said matter of factly.

The bed moved again, and Wayne was gone.

Doug didn't know what to make of the suicidal statement. In a flashing moment of levity, he mused to himself, *That's not a bad idea.*

The last time he came downstairs, Wayne hovered behind Doug more than before, and Doug was colliding with the sure knowledge that now they were in some real trouble. But

Doug didn't think Wayne would kill him, and neither did Kris believe that Wayne would go so far. When Wayne pulled the rope around Doug's throat, he wondered if he would be strangled. When Wayne lurked behind him, he wondered if he would be shot in the back of the head. But each time, Wayne would reappear, facing him, more and more frenzied, promising to call their friends.

"You're smarter than they are. You're smarter," Wayne rattled.

Doug knew that he was losing consciousness, that he was running out of time. He was worried about Kris more than anything. It was harder and harder to keep his eyes focused on Wayne. Then Doug couldn't see him at all. Wayne had gone around behind him, and that was when Doug felt it. It was like a punch to his chest. Doug looked up and Wayne was in his face, down low, with his hand on Doug's chest. Wayne was stooped oddly to Doug's right side, it seemed, and when he looked down he could see why.

The tip of the oak handle of a knife was sticking out of his chest, wrapped in Wayne's brown-gloved hand.

"*OUSHHHHH* . . ." came the escaping air, released in a croaky, rushing sound as Doug's diaphragm was severed. It was a sidearm thrust with a Chicago cutlery knife that came in just underneath Doug's heart.

Doug's life flipped over, and he looked up at Wayne.

Do you know what you have done? You have just killed me! his mind said to himself. Doug's mouth was open, but he couldn't talk. He couldn't make an noise. He had accepted his death, and it came in a simultaneous moment of total disbelief. In slow motion, Doug raised his eyes to Wayne's, and he looked him right in the eye. He saw nothing: no glee, no remorse, just a dead gaze.

Doug slumped, hanging limp in the ropes. He couldn't move. Wayne then removed the knife, with Doug watching as all eight inches of the smooth, narrow carbon blade glided out of his body. Wayne then put the bloodied knife next to Doug's pant cuff, which Wayne held between his thumb and forefinger, and wiped the blade clean.

Doug had never felt death before, and he also had never known the kind of rage that overtook his whole being—at the sight of Wayne cleaning the knife blade on his pant cuff. Having killed him, and now with this nonchalant, callous gesture, Wayne had conveyed how little it meant to him. As if punctuating his disinterest, Wayne just walked away. Doug's eyes were stuck wide open. He could see Wayne leave, and see that he was no longer in a hurry, and that he didn't even bother to close the basement door behind him.

Doug sat alone dying in the basement of the house they had worked so hard to get. His eyes stared outward. He had always believed that when someone died with their eyes wide open, like this, it meant that they had died in the wrong place. *Christ, I'm going to die with my eyes open! Look at this*, he thought. *And I'm hanging. And I have no control.* He felt a stirring in his bowels, and almost lost control, but didn't. Now he was seeing the room get smaller, as if he were looking through a peephole. The edges were fuzzy. *Here you go, you're dying*, he thought. The next thing that went through his mind was what a mess his shop was, that nobody was going to be able to figure out who belongs to which guns. Then he thought about Kris, and he hung for a few seconds as the room started turning to black, when he suddenly sat up. It was an immediate, jack-in-the-box move. Surprised, he felt a return of strength and coherence. *Okay, I ain't dead yet!*

Kris had untied her feet with her free left hand and was still tugging on the rope around her right hand when Wayne walked in.

"What are you doing! You called the cops, didn't ya?"

Frantic, Kris could see that it might have looked that way.

"No, I didn't call the cops," she said, thinking fast. "You'd have heard me."

"I can't leave you like this. I've got to tie you better," he said, moving around the bed to find a better place to secure her left hand.

Downstairs, Doug was getting free. When he turned his head to the side, he created new slack in the ropes around his torso and throat. He wiggled free of them and gave a giant pull to slip his hands out. *Okay, I'm gonna die. It happens. But this guy's going with me.*

Doug stood up and walked directly over to the bench and the rifle. He figured he had anywhere from ten to twenty seconds, and he based that on his hunting experience. He had shot many deer in the chest, and sometimes they'll run that long before dropping. He also figured there was only enough time to load one cartridge, not just because he was now that wounded deer, but also because Wayne might return any second. He drew the cleaning patch from the barrel, shoved a single round into the chamber, closed the lever, freed the safety, and closed the bolt.

Now. Now it's even, he said to himself as he went for the first set of stairs, silent as he could. He stopped at the bottom of the landing that led up to the living room. He knew he had to get Wayne to come to him. He couldn't risk confronting Wayne in the bedroom, where Kris was hostage.

Doug was too beaten to know whether he kicked the wall with his foot or knocked against it with his elbow, but he knew as soon as Wayne heard any noise, he would come running, and he did.

Doug was set. He knew Wayne was coming. The light from the kitchen would be momentarily eclipsed as he approached the top of the landing. The sound of his running footsteps would tell Doug, too. And he knew that Wayne wouldn't be able to see him until he turned around the half-wall partition at the top of the stairs. He would aim for the middle of the body.

Wayne came running, and when his wide-open eyes seized on the picture of a bloody, beaten Doug Wells, a dead man who was hunkered, aimed, ready to fire, he stopped in his fast-forward tracks. For only a second, there was fear in Wayne's face, but the face turned as the body began to pull away. Doug fired. The Savage 250 slug tore through Wayne's side, exited across the living room past the television, through the wall of the house into the night. Doug didn't hear the gunfire, or smell the discharge. But he could see that Wayne was gone again.

I missed! God, I missed him, is all he thought, but in the same split second he heard a wounded Wayne fall to the floor, behind the partition, beyond Doug's view.

"Oh, God . . . I'm a dead man!" was all Kris heard after the booming report of the rifle. It sounded like it came from the basement, and she assumed Doug had been shot. She knew it was Wayne's voice, but she also thought he was saying it to fool her, to let her think he, not Doug, had been shot, and the room went black. She passed out.

Doug clambered up the steps and encountered Wayne, who was on his hands and knees, trying to get up. Holding the Savage by its barrel, Doug slammed the stock down on the back of Wayne's head. Wayne was flattened. Doug hit him again and again, hammering Wayne about the head and neck. On all fours, Wayne moved in a bear crawl down the hallway toward the bedroom, with Doug right behind him, swinging away, pounding and pounding and pounding.

As Wayne got to the bedroom doorway, Doug licked him a good one, breaking the rifle's wooden stock. Splinters flew, and the lever action was thrust open, ejecting the single shell casing into the bedroom. Wayne rolled onto his back and covered his face with his right arm, and as Doug prepared to deliver the next thundering blow, Wayne yelled out.

"Doug stop! Don't do this! Please stop!"

Doug hit him again, and again until Wayne

was forced into a tight corner of the room next to the nightstand at the head of the bed, and then he hit him some more.

Kris came to. Her husband was raining blows on Wayne, who was cowered in the corner, and with her right hand still tied to the bed, she started to punch at Wayne, screaming, "You sonuvabitch! You sonuvabitch!"

Doug didn't have a clear target with Kris now flailing at Wayne's chest, and he could see that Wayne was moving his hands lower, toward his own gun.

"Get out of the way. I can't hit him," Doug said as he hurled Kris back onto the bed. When he looked back at Wayne, the revolver was pointed at him. Doug swung his rifle at the gun and ducked just as Wayne pulled the trigger. The slug went into the ceiling and through the roof and out into the sky. Doug's adrenaline-stoked brain made it clear to him that Wayne could finish them both off if he weren't stopped now, so he clubbed Wayne with all the fury he could muster. Wayne fired again, and Doug's foot went wild. The bullet entered above the knee and exited three inches below the crotch, and was stopped by his blue jeans. The sting woke him even more to battle. He started thinking about how to widen his attack strategy. His single-minded approach—just pounding away at Wayne—wasn't working, because Wayne wasn't dead yet. But there was no time. He hit him again, swinging wildly, catching the nightstand lamp and sending it flying. The bulb shattered.

The room was now pitch black, and Doug continued his feverish swinging in Wayne's direction. He felt something hit against the rifle. Then the darkness was marked by the muzzle flash of a third gunshot. Doug knew Wayne had to cock the single-action six every time, and he instinctively seized this interim moment to leap across the bed, reaching for the gun in the nightstand, the AMT-Backup. He chambered a round and moved the gun to his left hand, pointing it at where he thought Wayne was, and flipped on the overhead light.

As Doug watched Wayne, he moved the gun to his right hand. Wayne was slouched down, his eyes partly rolled up into his head. He was wheezing. His legs were quivering. Wayne had been shot in the head, just above and behind the ear, with his own gun. The Ruger's barrel had been jammed into the side of Wayne's head at the moment of fire in the split second after one of Doug's repeated swats with the rifle had hooked Wayne's hand and deflected the gun into a suicide lock. After a few seconds, Doug came around to the front of the bed and told Kris to get Wayne's gun off the floor.

"Throw it up onto the bed," he said, seeing that the hammer was down. It wasn't cocked and ready to fire again. Doug removed the clip from his semiautomatic, and removed the cartridge from the chamber, then placed it on the bed along with the Savage and Wayne's revolver.

"I don't know how long I've got," he said, lying down on his back across the bed. "Call 911."

Kris had to call twice. The first time she either held the phone upside down or had called the wrong number. She dialed again. It was 1:22 A.M.

"Someone's tried to kill my husband," she spit out the words, then hung up and moved back over to Doug, applying contact pressure on his chest to halt the bleeding.

The phone rang.

"Don't hang up," the police dispatcher told her. Apparently Kris had either given a name or address when she called. She couldn't recall. "How's the other guy?" the dispatcher quizzed.

"I don't know and I don't care. Just get someone here for Doug."

Wayne had been fatally wounded by the Savage slug that passed through his midsection. The slug severed the renal artery, hit the spleen, the pancreas, and the right lung and liver, clipping the ribs on its way in and out. The autopsy would conclude that Wayne would have had less than a minute to live after such a gunshot wound. As a result of Doug's seconds-long counterattack, Wayne's body from his knees to the top of his head had suffered some sixty bashes, cuts, scrapes, and abrasions, which had been meted out by Doug at a fierce rate of nearly one blow per second. The slug from the contact shot to the head traveled through Wayne's brain and lodged inside his skull on the other side.

Sheriff's Deputies Martin Spring and Gerald Crouch were having coffee at the Four B's Restaurant on the other side of town when they got the call of a shooting in progress at 100 Parker Court. Deputy Vincent Sparacino also responded.

Deputy Spring never drove as fast as he did that night. Deputy Crouch was in a second cruiser, and Deputy Sparacino in a third. An ambulance was dispatched at the same time, but was told to hold back from the house until it received an all-clear. All three police cars converged on the house at the same time. They went right to the front door and walked in. Sundance barked as the three men stepped up to the living room. The first thing they saw was the tipped-over couch and a blood splotch stretching across the living room. Down the hall in the bedroom, they found Kris hovering over her bloodied husband, who was splayed on the bed. In the corner, crouched, shaking and twitching, was Wayne. Guns lay on the bed.

First they checked on Doug, then Kris, then Wayne. Then the ambulance was summoned.

Deputy Spring was taken back when his eyes fell on the battered, bleeding, and dying body of his grade school and high school classmate, Wayne. Deputy Spring had, in fact, seen him only two weeks before, when Wayne had delivered furniture to his house. The oversized blade Wayne wore that day on his belt reminded Deputy Spring that Wayne always carried a knife in school, but still he thought it was unusual for him to be wearing such a big knife just to deliver his furniture.

Doug was carried out first. When they brought Wayne out, the paramedics lost their footing in a sight depression in the front yard and Wayne was dumped from the stretcher.

"Are you okay?" someone joked to Wayne as he was picked up, his legs still twitching and jerking, to be loaded in next to Doug. "Leave him for awhile," someone else said.

But they didn't. They loaded him in next to

Doug and headed for Missoula Community Hospital.

For the span of a semiconscious moment, as Doug lay on his back in a hallway just beyond an operating room in the emergency ward, his nightmare returned. The knife wound, which besides severing his diaphragm, had nipped one of his lungs. The doctors were waiting for the lung to collapse. He had been resting there for close to three hours now.

At one point he sat up and was shocked to discover he was all alone. He could see partway into one of the nearby operating rooms, where Wayne's feet were clearly visible on a table that was surrounded by doctors and nurses.

"His vitals aren't all that bad," the nurse was saying. "His respiration is there. His pulse is quick, but strong."

"He's okay," another one chimed in.

Doug could feel gravity pulling him back down, and he closed his eyes.

"I didn't even kill the sonuvabitch!"

Kris came over to him.

"Wayne's dead," she said.

Doug sat up again.

"Are you sure? Go check and make sure. They just said, 'He's fine.' "

"They were talking about you, hon." She patted him. "They're just finishing up on Wayne."

After the scene was secured, Deputy Spring started to search for Wayne's vehicle, looking for any sign that he may have had an accomplice. Deputies ran down the registrations on every vehicle within a block and a half of the

Wells house, and it was Deputy Spring who found the maroon Toyota four-by-four pickup—Wayne's truck. It was locked. Through the camper shell window he could see a large cardboard furniture box on a pallet. It struck him as a curious and morbid object to find in Wayne's truck, given what had just happened.

Deputies were dispatched to Rick Mace's home, because Kris had told them that Wayne may have done something to Rick. When a sleepy-eyed Rick answered the front door, all he was told was that somebody had been concerned about him. Rick pressed for more, but that's all he could be told, the deputies said. He would learn more in the morning. After the deputies left, Rick got a cold feeling about his younger brother, and he called 911. Again, he was told he would have to wait until morning to learn more.

A few hours later, when Wayne didn't show up for work, Rick didn't imagine any connection between the puzzling visit from the police in the middle of the night. It didn't even cross his mind. But by the time the rest of the Conlin's staff began to wander in to work, it became clear that something was up, since Kelly Bruce, the assistant manager, was being so secretive.

Though no one knew it yet, Kris had already called Kelly to tell her what had happened.

"Doug's in the hospital. Wayne attacked us," Kris told her, adding that Doug was going to be all right.

"How's Wayne?" Kelly inquired.

"He's dead."

Kelly, stunned by the news, wasn't sure what

she could tell the staff and what she shouldn't. So she kept it to herself, even when sheriff's deputies showed up to talk to Rick Mace. Next, a television news crew arrived, seeking information, but no one knew anything.

"Kelly," Joyce pleaded. "You've got to tell somebody something."

"Well I just don't know what I can tell you and what I can't," she quivered.

"Is it Kris and Doug? Could it be Wayne? How is Wayne involved in this?"

All anyone could figure was that whatever had happened must have involved Kris and Doug and Wayne. At noon, the radio was reporting that a Missoula couple had been attacked in their home by an intruder, who had been shot. Joyce ran out to the Heidelhaus, a restaurant on the strip, and picked up a copy of the Noon News, a free transcript of the radio newscast that was a popular read at lunch counters. They all studied the sparse account, which didn't identify the couple or the intruder. They all tried to put it together.

Sandy McManus, who was the only person at work who knew that Sheila was at Brad Flaherty's cabin on Flathead Lake, called her. Brad answered the phone.

"Who knows you're up here?" he said, handing Sheila the phone.

Sandy started to ask Sheila about some customers whom Sheila had waited on before. It seemed odd to Sheila. Was Sandy just making this up? Finally she interrupted.

"Sandy, why are you calling me up here?"

"Something really bad has happened. We don't know what it is. Listen to the news."

Chapter 29

The Knife and the Elk

That night, the TV news would carry the story of the Missoula couple who survived an ordeal with an intruder who didn't survive. The report would be seen on television screens across the state. Among the barest details of the story was the connection between the couple, their attacker, and Conlin's Furniture. But that was the single most important detail to Bob Shook, who sat in his living room fifty miles away in Hamilton, electrified by this information.

Christ, that's where the kids got the furniture, he thought, his mind leaping.

"Georgie," he called to his wife, "they said that this guy worked down at Conlin's."

Bob wasted no time getting on the phone. He called the sheriff's department, but was told that Sheriff Dye was gone for the day, and so was the deputy who was assigned to the Shook homicides. Bob told the deputy on the desk why he called.

"When they announced it on the TV, that this guy Nance, the guy that was working for that furniture company, tried to kill Wells and his wife, well right then, I says, 'You know that

324

sounds like the same thing that happened up here.' That's where the kids got the furniture," he said.

Bob was told the information would be passed on. It already grated on Bob Shook that the investigation into his son's and daughter-in-law's murders seemed to take so long. Over the past nine months, he had learned to live with the frustration. "How are things going?" he would occasionally ask Sheriff Dye's men. He really wanted to know why it was taking so long. Every time, the answer came back the same. He was not the only one who wondered why. Always he was told that these things take time. Bob's son, Steve, who was on the Hamilton force, finally told his father that the sheriff's department was at the end of the line, that they didn't know anything.

Bob knew he now had a red-hot lead, and he wasn't going to hesitate anymore. First thing in the morning, he would call the Missoula County Sheriff's Department.

Captain Weatherman was out when he called, but he was told he would be back soon. Bob stayed by the phone. When it rang, he was burning to tell Weatherman what he knew.

"When you go in, if you go in and check this guy Nance's house—" an excited Bob started to explain.

"We have been out there this morning. We're going back this afternoon," Captain Weatherman said.

"Be on the lookout for a statue of a bugling elk and a knife, a custom-made, bone-handled Kelgin hunting knife."

"I think I saw that knife this morning," Captain Weatherman answered.

Nine hours later, shortly after seven in the evening, Bob Shook got a call from the dispatcher at the Ravalli County Sheriff's Department. Sheriff Dye wanted to see him, and he could either come over to the office or Sheriff Dye would come to his home. An hour later, Bob and Karlene, Steve's wife, met with the sheriff in his office. Sheriff Dye handed him the knife, which he identified as the one he had given his son for Christmas two years before. Karlene, in turn, recognized the elk as the one she had made and given to Mike and Teresa.

When detectives went to Conlin's to ferret out the delivery receipt, to verify that Wayne had delivered to the Shooks, it was no longer in the file. Sometime in the last few months, after the insurance adjuster had called, the delivery receipt had disappeared. If Wayne had removed it himself, and no one else would have had any reason to take it, he failed to cover all his tracks that day. The record showed Wayne's initials on another delivery made that day in Stevensville, and his partner recalled that they had then gone on to Hamilton.

All day Friday, only a handful of law-enforcement officials and reporters knew that Wayne was on his way to receiving a posthumous designation as the serial killer who had preyed on his hometown for more than a decade, almost from the time he was old enough to act on his own. It was enough for those who knew him simply to digest what had happened, let alone discover too that he had been a prime suspect in the brutal, unsolved sex murder of Donna Pounds, a minister's wife, twelve years earlier.

Everyone at Conlin's who read the fifth paragraph of Larry Howell's banner front-page story in the Friday *Missoulian* was plowing new ground in their understanding of Wayne: "And in a bizarre twist to an already strange story, authorities said Thursday that Nance was one of two prime suspects in the brutal . . ." etc., etc., etc. They found out they had been working with somebody who turned out to be somebody else.

Those who knew Wayne from childhood, like Marge Frame, who couldn't understand the mean side of this little boy, learned what had become of the cute carrot-top who incinerated kittens. "Unbelieving at first, and that's when you start remembering all these things. And then you would hear other people say, 'I'm not surprised.' He was like the kid on the bus. Once you thought about it hard enough, it fit."

Bill Van Canagan had already had his aftershock on Thursday, when he learned the circumstances of Wayne's death, telescoping back to the still-fresh nightmare he had been unable to shake since senior year at Sentinel and then forward to the hot night only two weeks before when he flushed an intruder from the shadows outside his bedroom doorway. Had it been Wayne? Coming to get him? Shaken, he got on the phone. He had to talk to somebody about this.

Rick Davis was worked up, too, when he got a call from the sheriff's department.

"I think it would be a good idea if you came

downtown. We need to talk to you," the deputy said.

The investigation had focused on the old Ford pickup that had been parked in cockeyed fashion in the Wellses' sideyard, and led to the supposition that Wayne had an accomplice. Rick Davis fell into the dragnet because the Toyota pickup Wayne was driving was coleased by Rick. Was he the accomplice who had been slouched down on the seat of that old truck?

No, he had sold the Toyota to Wayne after he had left Conlin's employ.

"I cosigned for him. They said they would take my name off in six months, but I guess they didn't, or Wayne didn't."

The man in the old Ford pickup called the sheriff's department a few days after he learned that the police were running down all owners of older-model orange and white Ford trucks just like his. He was terrified that he would become entangled in a homicide investigation, when all he had been doing out there was surveiling his girlfriend, whom he suspected of two-timing.

The Saturday newspaper provided more bombshells. The barrage of connections between Wayne Nance and a series of sex-motivated murders emanated first from Sheriff Dye, who disclosed the link to the Shook homicides: the knife and the elk. Captain Weatherman noted that there were several other murders over the years that would be wrested from their dusty file holders and eyeballed for Wayne Nance signatures. Among them principally were the separate killings of three young women whose bodies had been found east of town.

A gigantic maw opened, swallowing the community's preconceptions about somebody who might have been a friend, a coworker, a joker, a drinking buddy, a son—or just the delivery-man off-loading a new stuffed chair for the den.

Captain Weatherman had been in Wayne's room in the spring of 1974, when he found the black bag containing the .22-caliber shells and casings and the bloodied but washed underpants. This time, when he led detectives on the search of the house at 715 Minnesota Avenue, concentrating on Wayne's room, they had to retrace a time continuum to comprehend what medieval tortures might have been contemplated or carried out in this unholy chamber. It was a sick eclecticism that they would record with their evidence camera, but what triggered their most intense interest was the sacral bed. What perversions were in mind here? The sheet was of green rubber. The bedposts were looped with rope ties. On the posts at the headboard, one side clearly was tied so as to permit escape from the ligatures, an indication to the detectives that Wayne had practiced on himself. Wayne's father told Captain Weatherman that his son had a skin condition that called for him to sleep on a rubber sheet. The detective inferred otherwise, and suspected that Wayne may have even used his bed as a sacrificial altar, removing his stabbed, bloody offering in the handy, leak-proof wrapper. Then out to the truck for disposal.

Among the items removed for evidence was a strip of coin-booth photographs that showed Wayne in three poses with a dark-haired woman exhibiting not much more than the trace of a smile. Her bangs were cut at the eyebrows. She wore oversized, gradient-tint glasses and a raglan-sleeved sweatshirt. In one pose, she and Wayne are kissing. Was she the 140-pound corpse he had pulled from the frozen earth at the Bonner Dam? Whom he had personified as Debbie Deer Creek?

George Nance identified her only as Robin, a drifter, and he took umbrage when Captain Weatherman solved at least part of the puzzle by positively identifying Robin as Debbie Deer Creek—one and the same.

A single hair recovered from the driver's-side door hinge of Wayne's truck was long enough and visually similar in color. Captain Weatherman immediately took it to the lab, where he was gratified to learn it was a forensic twin to Debbie Deer Creek's dark-auburn lock. Hair is not usually considered a final arbiter in forensic matchmaking, but in this case the layered series of hair dyes—natural light brown to deeper brown to the final dark auburn—matched without a doubt.

Wayne's father said his son's pickup was out of commission at the time Robin was around. Its clutch was out, he said. So they shouldn't have found one of her hairs in the door latch.

Captain Weatherman further certified to himself that Wayne Nance killed the mystery girl, Robin. He shipped her skull and the coin-booth photo to Dr. Charney, the forensic physical anthropologist at Colorado State University, where a photographic superimposition comparison was made. It produced a match.

"They do fit. I am certain that that's who

we're dealing with. I am certain that Wayne Nance killed her," Captain Weatherman said.

Sheriff Dye replayed the audiotape on which little Luke Shook was trying to say what the intruder's name was.

"I am certain now," Sheriff Dye said, "that when he came in the door, he said he was Conan the Barbarian." And on September 26, Sheriff Dye learned that the .22-caliber slug removed from Teresa's leg had been fired by the single-action six that belonged to George Nance.

While Doug was making his initial recovery in the hospital, Captain Weatherman came to visit, and he relayed a conversation he recently had with Wayne's father. At first George maintained that Wayne was set up by the Wellses, that he had warned Wayne about fooling around with a married woman. He claimed that Kris was, indeed, sweet on Wayne, and that when Doug found out about it, Wayne was invited to the house, where he was ambushed.

"Well, George has finally said, 'It looks like my boy did this,'" Weatherman told Doug. "'But he didn't do all these other things. So quit trying to pin all the crimes in Missoula on him.'"

There was another visitor, too, whom Doug will never forget. It was Mike Shook's brother-in-law, who had driven a couple of hundred miles, from the logging operation he worked at in the middle of nowhere, to thank Doug Wells.

"Sonovabitch," he said, spouting a friendly blasphemy. "I just came here to tell you you're a goddamn hero."

"Well, you just told me you're going to adopt three more kids, and you already have four of your own. I think *you're* the goddamn hero."

Epilogue

When Wayne returned to Kris in the bedroom for the last time, immediately accusing her of calling the police, he was signaling that his next move would be quick. The police might be on their way. He would have to kill her, and fast. There's no doubt Kris seemed to be facing the last few moments of her life.

Most victims of a serial killer don't survive more than two minutes once they come under the killer's control. But the Wellses, who had spent more than an hour and a half with Wayne, managed to kill their potential killer in return. Doug and Kris survived as living victims, witnesses to the fulminating rage that drove Wayne right down to the moment of the kill. They had no way of knowing what was going through Wayne's mind, but they can talk about what he did and what he said as well as how they reacted, all of which bears directly on the FBI's current research into the role victims play when they fall into the deadly clutches of a sociopath like Wayne Nance.

At the FBI's invitation, Doug and Kris have become regulars at the FBI Academy in Quantico, Virginia, where special agents of its Behavioral Science Unit profile killers by deduction: What they learn from the crime scene—and the victims—tells them something about the killer. How do they unwittingly abet these killers? As the killer manages to succeed again and again, how can he be caught? The Wellses make the trip four times a year, addressing seminars on the subject of their specialty: Wayne Nance, serial killer. Their courage and grit draw handclaps from the FBI agents who hear their story, at times spellbound, always fascinated to learn whatever they can about this most elusive kind of murderer.

"Did he take his gloves off when he tied the knots?" an agent asks Kris. "Yes," she answers, "when he cut up the ropes in lengths."

"Did the autopsy show that he was on anything?" another asks.

"There wasn't a trace of anything in him," Doug answers.

"Was your bedroom on the first floor so he could see in?"

"No. It's a split-level house."

"Was there ever any indication in the neighborhood of a Peeping Tom?" the question comes.

"No."

"When you got your gun from the nightstand, and turned the light on, why didn't you finish him off?"

"I was gonna empty the gun on him when I turned that light on," Doug answers, "but when I saw that he . . . I never saw a dead man before, but he sure looked like one."

No one knows exactly how many people Wayne killed.

Local law-enforcement authorities credit him with at least four murders: Donna Pounds, the girl named Robin, and Mike and Teresa Shook. He is the only suspect in the unsolved murders of Devonna Nelson and Chryssie Crystal Creek. Weatherman is certain, too, that Wayne was the masked intruder who ambushed Janet Wicker in her apartment.

There is no way to link Wayne to the Verna Kvale case, because as far as Weatherman could determine, Wayne was not on leave from the Navy at the time. But Dusty Deschamps regrets that the blob of semen recovered from her thigh is now lost, because it would have made for an interesting DNA comparison.

Nobody knows who killed Siobhan McGuinness. But the little girl's mother believes that it was Wayne, and she has profusely thanked Doug Wells for avenging her daughter's murder. "I don't know anything about you or how you have reconciled this within your soul, but I want you to know that I think of you often and with love and compassion. And if my hand could have been with you, I would have gladly struck and killed that motherfucking monster!" she wrote to him. "God surely must have acted through you."

Weatherman and Deschamps don't categorically exclude Wayne as Siobhan's killer, but they don't think he is responsible. The FBI's serial murder profilers, however, see the crime as a logical stepping-off point for a young killer like Wayne. It fits a typical pattern of graduation. An inexperienced killer starts off with an easy victim, hedging his risk. In time, he enhances the thrill of the kill by taking on more risk. In Wayne's case, as he became more self-confident, he ultimately challenged himself to conquer the protective male before vanquishing the female. Authorities now view that pillage-and-rape syndrome as an expression of Wayne's need to actually experience his own Viking fantasy.

Special Agent Hazelwood, an expert in serial sexual homicide, theorizes that one reason Wayne didn't tie Kris up as tightly as he did Doug was that, aside from the fact that Doug presented a genuine physical threat, perhaps Wayne was crossing over into his imaginary world.

"He was obsessed with Kris. He had built it up in his mind that she loved him. Not binding her tightly, and her not escaping, might have fit into his fantasy of her really being in love with him.

"The primary reason he's of such interest to us is because of the fact that he committed, to the best of our knowledge, all of his crimes within a very, very small area and was still able to evade apprehension or identification. Even though he was strange, even though he arose as a prominent suspect in what they think may have been one of his first murders, he was able to mislead the people, and that's what we're interested in.

"Law enforcement in general looks at M.O. much, much too heavily to link crimes," Hazelwood says. "We look at signatures. M.O. changes over time. It evolves with age and maturity. What doesn't change is the signature: stabbing and tying up.

"Wayne really got off on stabbing. You gotta look for the signature, and his signature was tying up and stabbing."

Siobhan McGuinness was stabbed.

Donna Pounds was tied up and shot.

Devonna Nelson was stabbed.

Verna Kvale was stabbed.

Debbie Deer Creek (a.k.a. Robin) and Chryssie Crystal Creek were shot and may well have been tied.

Mike and Teresa Shook were both tied and stabbed, and Teresa was shot.

The Wellses were both tied and Doug was stabbed and then shot.

After it was all over, the community breathed a sigh of relief. For months, the noonday commentaries on Missoula's street corners were peppered with testimonials of personal close encounters with Wayne Nance—"I went to Sentinel with him"; "He delivered a chair to me"; "I remember him from the Cabin, once . . ." Any mention of the Wellses drew an immediate salute. Doug Wells became a statewide legend. Those who might eventually forget his name would never forget the story.

The *Missoulian*, in its very first report on the incident, quoted an unidentified detective who said: "It's like Christmas for us. The good guys won." On its editorial page, under the headline, "A Killer Is Killed—and a Fear Is Lifted," the editors wrote: "Nance has been linked to the kinds of deliberate, meaningless, haunting crimes seldom seen in Montana . . . Horrible, tragic crimes now seem well on their way toward being solved, and western Montana may be a bit safer."

The Missoula Reward Fund, which had been started in 1974 to help solve the Siobhan McGuinness case, disbursed three thousand dollars to the Wellses. More than two hundred other financial donations were made to the couple, from individuals as well as through a benefit campaign that set up accounts at every bank in Missoula and at five savings institutions in the Bitterroot. The money defrayed mortgage payments and helped pay medical bills. Doctors signed over insurance checks. Hospital administrators told them not to worry about the bills they couldn't pay: Doug had performed a public service and the community owed him. It was not going to be the other way around.

It had taken twenty-two stitches to close up the gashes on Doug's head. Wayne had used a handmade club that the warehouse guys at Conlin's had watched him make. He had used Bonneville Power Administration lead wire, looping it up and back and up and back until it was the size he wanted. Then he wrapped it with black electrician's tape and fashioned a bolster to distinguish the handle from the club end.

The slug that brushed the sciatic nerve in Doug's right leg had given him a case of foot drop. He had almost no control over it for months. It hung limp at the ankle, and he was forced to wear a leg brace. Eventually his doctors extended his Achilles' tendon and reconstructed the ankle, and the nerve came back.

The stab wound to Doug's chest was a more serious matter. The knife had missed Doug's heart by a fraction of an inch, but it had severed his diaphragm and cut open the stomach lining.

Fluids escaping from his stomach migrated to his chest, irritating the pericardium, which wept in defense of the heart. As the pericardial sac filled, it put pressure on his heart. It was drained once, but in a week's time had hardened to the consistency of an orange peel. A quarter of an inch thick in places, it was crushing his heart and reducing blood flow to one-third normal. Because he could have suffered a heart attack at any moment, doctors performed emergency open-chest surgery and removed the protective membrane.

Even after Doug recovered from the physical trauma of the events on that warm September night, both Doug and Kris discovered their lives had been irrevocably changed. For months after the attack, Doug complained of a queer floating sensation and suffered from vertigo and bouts of disorientation, and he also had recurrent nightmares about Wayne. In one, he and Kris were driving down a one-way street, and when they came to a stop sign, there in a doorway of a building that was right at the curbside stood Wayne, glaring at him. In another, they were at a restaurant with some friends, and as Doug looked up, he saw Wayne. He was the busboy. "What the hell's he doing here?" Doug said, and one of his friends responded: "Why don't you leave him alone? Haven't you done enough to him?" Doug's last bad dream was set in a warehouse, where upon seeing a friend of his who was driving a forklift, Doug started to jump aboard, only to see the man turn at him, brandishing a knife. It was Wayne again.

"Every time we would go out and have our

nachos and beer, or sit down at lunch, pretty soon we'd be talking about it," Doug says. "I don't think there was ever a time when the final thing we would say wasn't: 'God, am I glad he's dead. That dumb ass, he fooled with the wrong people. He got it. He got what he deserved.' That was how we would pull ourselves out of it."

Before the attack, Doug used to sit out on the back deck in the evening, staring off beyond the city limits into the mysteries that lie beyond the mountaintops. There, in his hard-earned private reverie, he embodied an image akin to a Norman Rockwell ideal. But he no longer could be out there alone in the dark. And for a full year after Wayne's death, Kris would keep a gun with her at all times, even when she mopped the kitchen floor.

They also strategically placed loaded handguns around the house, and practiced like a SWAT team, ready for anything. One night, while they slept, the smoke alarm in the hallway just outside their bedroom woke them. In two flashes, Doug was at the front door, gun in hand, and Kris was at the patio door, gun up. When they pulled back from their positions to stop the ear-piercing beep, they discovered a large black spider inside. It had somehow shorted the alarm, electrocuting itself.

It was dead, all right.

COMPELLING READING